Plantations and Allegations

A small town Lowcountry mystery

Rachel Lynne

Seven Oaks Press

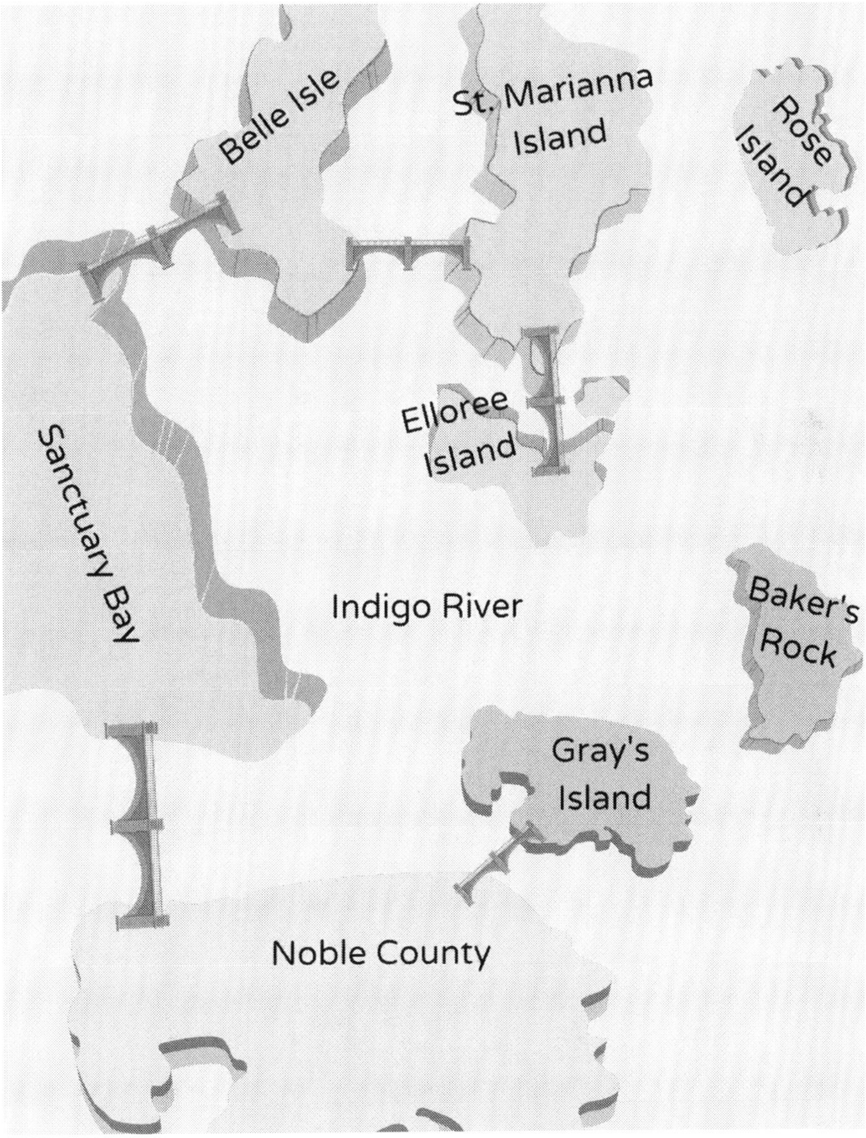
Belle Isle
St. Marianna Island
Rose Island
Elloree Island
Sanctuary Bay
Indigo River
Baker's Rock
Gray's Island
Noble County

Contents

Chapter One

The sun had barely crested the horizon when I turned into the entrance to Pennington Place, my friend Connie right behind me. After months of planning, it was time to bring our vision of a medieval wedding to life, and the bride couldn't have chosen a better venue.

Pennington Place Plantation was a stereotypical old Southern home, surrounded by giant live oaks draped with Spanish moss and naturalized areas of saw palmetto and southern maidenhair ferns. The landscaping made the grounds feel like an enchanted forest.

I turned off the main drive and guided the Scout into a parking spot next to the old barn we'd be using for the reception. After unloading my support dog, The Colonel, and commanding him to stay, I grabbed one of the many boxes of decorations as Connie pulled in beside my truck.

"Whew, it's going to be a scorcher!" My friend opened the side door of her van and removed the floral arrangements we'd designed. "I'm so glad you convinced Carrie to hold everything indoors. I couldn't imagine an outdoor wedding in this heat!"

"Me either." I wiped sweat from my forehead and signaled for The Colonel to follow me toward the barn. "August is always a bad time to hold an outdoor event in the Lowcountry, but with that hurricane churning offshore it's going to be even more humid than usual."

Connie trotted beside me, juggling a box of long-stemmed roses and another filled with candles. "Did you catch the weather report this morning?" When I shook my head, she continued. "Well, it's off the coast of Florida, just below Daytona I think, and they've changed the projected path."

My eyes widened. "Oh no, don't tell me..."

"Yep, some front or other is driving it toward the coast. They say it'll make landfall somewhere above Myrtle Beach, but they think it'll weaken to a Cat 1 by then."

Swallowing past a lump in my throat, I pulled the barn doors open and motioned for Connie to go ahead of me as I contemplated how the change in forecast might affect the wedding. Depending on how close it came to the sea islands, we could experience flooding and winds strong enough to cause structural damage.

Setting my box of sheet moss down, I turned to Connie. "When can we expect the storm to arrive?"

She shrugged and continued to unpack the roses. "It won't reach the Florida/Georgia line until tomorrow, so we'll feel the impact late Sunday, maybe? It's still up in the air." She raised her hands and made an air quotes motion. "We are in the dreaded 'cone of uncertainty'."

"Great." I sighed and headed back to the truck. "I'll have to get Dewey to secure Myrtlewood Plantation. Hopefully, I'll be able to help batten down the hatches at the town home." I rolled my eyes. "Add weather issues to my laundry list of problems."

Connie laughed. "Mayor Tomlin and her friends still giving you fits about the wedding?"

"Oh yes." I stooped and tossed a stick out of my path, smiling as The Colonel found a burst of energy and chased after it. "It's been one thing after another for weeks! But the main gripe is centered around Carrie's request that guests come in costume."

My friend bit her lip, but laughter escaped anyway. "I'm sorry, it's just ... I can hear Ms. Lou Lou fussing and your mama and Ms. Maybelle chiming in." Connie smirked. "What do you think they'll wear?"

I snorted. "Proper wedding attire, complete with hats and possibly gloves. They are all determined to bring a touch of decorum to what they see as a mockery of a sacred ceremony."

"Oooh, that sounds like a direct quote."

"Pretty close to one." Connie and I grabbed armfuls of supplies and started back to the reception hall. "I have talked until I'm blue in the face over this, but nothing I say makes any difference." I glanced at Connie. "That girl hasn't got the sense God gave a gnat and it just goes to show you can put lipstick on a pig but—"

"Oh, surely she didn't say that!"

"Not in those exact words but her meaning was the same." I unpacked the silver candelabras we were using for the centerpieces. "To be fair, Ms. Lou Lou likes Carrie, she just thinks she's spoiled and a bit of an airhead. According to Ms. Lou Lou, all this costume and medieval nonsense can be laid directly at *that woman's* door."

"I assume *that woman* is Mrs. Pope?" I nodded and Connie grinned. "Man, should we have hired some burly bouncers for this shindig? Sounds like the battle lines have been drawn."

"Don't think it'll come to blows, but then, I'm not taking any chances. The Tomlin family table is on the opposite side of the room from the Popes."

"Good thinking! There's enough drama around the plantation without adding a brawl."

I frowned. "What do you mean?"

Connie blinked. "You haven't heard?" I shook my head and she huffed. "How have you not heard about the return of the prodigal son? Everyone is talking about it!"

That would be the reason that I wasn't. "You know I leave the rumormongering to Mama."

My friend snorted. "Well yeah, but this is beyond a bit of so-and-so said or did you see what so-and-so wore to church." She looked around and then lowered her voice. "The heir to Pennington Place has mysteriously returned!"

"Mysteriously?" I snorted. "What, did he just appear in a puff of smoke?"

"You know what I mean." She rolled her eyes. "You have to admit it's a little curious that no one has heard from the man in ten years. Everyone assumed he was dead!"

"True, but it's no concern of mine." I turned my attention to decorating the banquet tables, but I'd fibbed a little. One would have to have been hiding under a rock not to have heard about the return of Christopher Pennington, or John Smith as he called himself now.

The Pennington family owned over a thousand acres as one of the last remaining intact plantations in the area. They also owned one of the largest shipping companies on the coast; the estate was estimated to be worth many millions.

A wealthy family always drew interest from the public, but the death of David Pennington and quick remarriage of his widow to Quinton Lyle was what started the gossip. The society matrons had considered it unseemly for Miriam Pennington to remarry within months of her husband's death, but it wasn't until her sixteen-year-old son and heir ran away that tongues really started to wag.

Along with a new husband, Miriam had acquired three stepchildren, all close in age to her own son. No one knew what happened to make Christopher run away, but rumor had it something had happened between him and his older stepbrother, Bradley. Speculation tossed up numerous theories, some form of physical abuse being an odds-on favorite, but no one ever knew the actual reason he left.

Several years went by with no word or sign of Christopher. That was when people assumed he'd met with an accident, and talk turned to who would inherit the estate after Miriam passed.

It should have been a rhetorical question considering she was only in her midfifties, but about seven months ago, the Grim Reaper came for Miriam.

The contents of her will set off another round of gossip. Despite having no contact with his family for over nine years and numerous private investigative firms having no luck in finding him, Miriam had not believed her son was dead.

She named a local law firm executors of the estate and left strict instructions on how the Pennington fortune was to be dispersed. Capital to keep the resort running was placed in a trust, and because there were no other living Penningtons, the executor was given six months to locate Christopher or confirm his demise.

If, after that time, he was not located, the entire estate would go to her husband, Quinton Lyle. Everyone, including the Lyle family, had assumed they were as good as owners of Pennington Place. In fact, all of Quinton Lyle's children were active in the management of the resort and were busy initiating improvements and generally acting as if they owned the place.

But about a week ago, Heather Franklin, the adopted daughter of Miriam's sister and cousin to Christopher, turned up at Pennington with a man she claimed was the heir. The cat had been among the pigeons ever since.

Sanctuary Bay citizens were taking bets on what would happen next, and since I'd made numerous trips to the plantation in preparation for the wedding, Mama and her friends pestered me for any tidbit they could share.

However, I'd kept my head down and did what I'd come to do, taking no interest in the Lyles or Christopher Pennington and his cousin Heather. I had the wedding of the year to pull off and who owned the venue did not factor into it.

I told Connie as much and got a huff for my troubles.

"That may be true, but can't you unbend a little bit? I mean, it's noble to say you're above all of the gossip, but it certainly isn't any fun!"

"Connie..." I sighed. "I appreciate how you and everyone else are fascinated by this turn of events, but I've enough on my plate with this wedding. Now grab the other end of this table runner, will ya?"

"Spoiled sport!" My friend stuck her tongue out at me but did as I'd requested, and the matter was dropped.

The bride had chosen a lilac and sage green color palette, but I'd opted for a deep, rich purple velvet edged with gold for the table runners. To recreate a medieval great hall, Connie and I had set up banquet tables in a U-shaped formation, with the open end facing a wall of recently installed Palladian windows that provided a breathtaking view of the river.

The old barn had also been upgraded with a catering kitchen, restrooms, and air conditioning, thank God. However, what they hadn't done was expand the size of the main room. I finished placing the runners and stared at the room.

"Connie? I know we measured and all, but I think once we place the head table in front of the windows it'll be too crowded for the dessert and gift tables. What do you think of putting them over by the dance floor?"

Instead of expanding the original barn, the Lyles had opted to add a sunroom as part of their campaign to make Pennington Place Plantation and Resort a five-star tourist destination. Connie and I had planned to use the extra space for the DJ and bar, but I didn't think adding two round tables would hinder that use.

"So long as they cut the cake before the booze starts flowing and the party heats up, I think it'll be okay. Just don't want any drunks knocking over the cake."

"God forbid! That was another bone of contention. Ms. Lou Lou was upset that Jeffrey hadn't planned on having a groom's cake."

Connie frowned. "Why would she be upset about that?"

"Because." I sighed. "It's one more tradition they aren't adhering to. I got tired of the grumbling and convinced Jeff to have one but, mark my words, his aunt will still have something to say."

She laughed. "Ms. Lou Lou is rarely at a loss for words but why would she get a bee in her bonnet over the cake? Wasn't that what she wanted?"

"Oh yes, she got her wish for a groom's cake, but I don't think she's expecting one like this." Connie's brow furrowed so I explained. "You know a groom's cake is usually decorated to reflect something important to the groom?" Connie nodded. "Well, around here that generally means a college football team, golfing, or maybe fishing. But Jeffrey is into role playing games, especially those set in medieval times, so..."

Connie grinned. "Don't tell me, the cake is in the shape of a dragon?"

"Close," I laughed. "He's asked for a cake shaped like a stone." She gave me a blank look. "The sword in the stone? The cake topper is a jeweled dagger. He'll pull it out to cut the cake! Clever, huh?"

Connie laughed. "That is very original, and you're right. Ms. Lou Lou is gonna have a meltdown!"

I shook out another table runner and we went to work on the next section of tables. "So long as I'm nowhere near at the time, I don't care." I smoothed the fabric across the table. "I think the desserts will be safe enough. They'll be done with the cake before the party kicks off, and I'll tell Marlena to place any leftovers on the bar that separates this room from the kitchen."

"Sounds like a plan. Did you want to put the moss on the table now?"

"Eh, let's place the candelabra first, it'll be easier."

Connie and I got to work setting the candles, using slabs of wood to vary the heights. Once that was finished, we added violet and white roses, seeded eucalyptus, and the final touch, dragon eggs.

I'd gone to the Gullah market and commissioned Ms. Ada to construct faux nests from seagrasses and Connie had found a vendor online that made glass eggs with scales painted in iridescent purples and greens. There were enough for each guest to have a party favor.

"Don't get me wrong, these look great, but what made you add imitation dragon's eggs?"

I giggled. "It's my little dig at Ms. Lou Lou for pushing me to take this job after I'd turned it down." At Connie's puzzled expression, I elaborated. "She got the wrong end of the stick about Carrie's theme." I shrugged. "She thought Carrie wanted a dragon wedding."

"Oh my goodness, and you just had to tweak her nose." Connie laughed and shook her head. "She is gonna pitch a fit!"

I grinned and placed the last basket of eggs on the table. "Nah, that wouldn't be ladylike. She'll just sigh and cluck her tongue and then jump on me later." I chuckled. "It'll be worth it."

Connie snorted and gathered up the empty boxes. "Okay, tables are done, except for the gold goblets and chargers, which the caterers will be bringing. What's next?"

The guests' tables were set; all that remained was to turn on the battery-operated candles just before they arrived. Workers were busy setting up the dance floor in the sunroom, but the tables for dessert and gifts would need to be added to that room.

Then there was the head table to set up, the guest book and seating cards table, and of course the chapel area still needed our touch. I listed the remaining projects and Connie grinned.

"Okay, I just saw the bakery van pull up so I'll get on the cake table first, then I can finish the reception hall if you want to start on the chapel?"

I wrinkled my nose. "You're just volunteering for all of that so you can avoid the heat!"

She laughed. "It wasn't my idea to decorate the path to the chapel!"

Rolling my eyes, I headed for the door, Connie's laughter trailing behind me. It was because of the heat that I was facing my current tasks. I'd convinced Carrie that it was far too hot and humid to ask guests to sit outside for any length of time, especially as the wedding was slated to begin at eleven.

The chapel on the property had been built for the plantation owners' use and was over a hundred years old. It was also very plain. The only redeeming feature was the fact that the tabby covered church was nestled amid a grove of live oaks, and to reach it one had to cross a weathered bridge that spanned a babbling brook.

Calling The Colonel to heel, I loaded him into the Scout and drove the short distance to the parking area closest to the chapel. Stifling a sigh, I gathered boxes of supplies and distributed them near each area I'd have to embellish.

Once everything was unloaded, I began. Connie and I had purchased dozens of lanterns in various sizes. The tree coverage was dense enough to warrant additional lighting, so I started by positioning tall, black, iron lanterns on either side of the winding path, then filling in with shorter versions, and finally placing potted ferns with floral picks of lilac and white roses between the lanterns.

One task down, many to go. A gust of wind set the live oaks creaking, making me look up. The overcast dawn had morphed into a typical summer blue sky, but fluffy white clouds tinged with gray were forming, and I'd need to check the storm forecast.

Depending on which way the hurricane moved, we'd catch some of the outer bands by late evening, and heavy rains always caused flooding issues on Belle Isle.

Hopefully, the wedding would go off without a hitch, and Connie and I would have everything packed up before any bad weather set in. The last thing I needed was to be stuck on a barrier island during a hurricane.

Chapter Two

O nce the path was decorated, I turned my attention to the wooden bridge. We'd ordered silk garlands of white wisteria, and I planned to weave them along the railing along with dozens of battery-operated fairy globes. I'd just placed the last globe and was sorting out the drape of the wisteria garlands when loud voices caught my attention.

The Colonel's ears twitched, and before I could stop him, he'd taken off in the direction of the argument. Rolling my eyes, I set the remaining flowers aside, grabbed my bag, and trouped after him.

"Colonel! Here boy!" Never the most obedient of pets, I was forced to trail after him all the way to the entrance of the chapel, only to find him flopped on the stone steps, tongue lolling.

The voices he'd went tearing after had quieted to an occasional word carried on the wind. I caught the words *air* and what might have been *fussy*, but frankly, so long as whatever they disagreed about didn't turn to violence, I was too busy to care.

"Boy, you are a menace I don't need today." He was pooped and clearly hot, so I stifled my scolds and went searching for a place to fill the collapsible water bowl I always carried.

Looking for an outside spigot, I rounded the corner of the building and almost tripped over Bradley Lyle and his wife, Olivia. He had a death grip on his wife's arm but dropped it like a hot poker as soon as we made eye contact.

"Oh! I'm so sorry. I didn't mean to interrupt." I tried to smile, but the heat was getting to me, and I was feeling more frazzled than I would have liked. "I was just looking for a hose pipe to fill up The Colonel's bowl."

"Ms. Daye, how are you? Is everything going to plan?"

I nodded at Bradley, but my gaze was on Olivia. She was a beautiful woman, with long blond hair, vivid green eyes, and a figure that turned heads. The few times I'd seen her, she was immaculately turned out and always gave me the feeling she was looking down her nose at the world. However, if her hard eyes and tightly clenched lips were anything to go by, she was struggling to hold on to her usual cool disdain.

Having no time for anyone's drama, I pasted on a smile and feigned obliviousness. If there was something brewing with the couple, no doubt my gossip-loving Mama would soon bring me up to speed, whether I wanted to know or not. In the meantime, I had a wedding to organize.

I met Bradley's gaze and nodded. "Yes, Connie is finishing up in the reception hall, the bakers are assembling the cake and dessert tables, and I'm about to add the final touches to the chapel. Did the nursery deliver all the trees?"

Struggling to smile, Olivia bobbed her head. "Yes, they arrived last night. I had them placed in the vestry." Her gaze flitted to her husband before she continued. "We, um, were just talking about the forecast for Hurricane Isabella."

Based on the palpable tension between the couple, as well as the few words I'd caught, it was highly doubtful the weather had been the subject of their heated conversation. But again, I let it pass. "Yes, Connie informed me that it's predicted to turn. Have there been any further updates?"

Bradley shook his head. "Next one is scheduled for eleven."

Great, I'd be up to my eyes in wedding details at that time. "Um, I'll be tied up with the wedding for the rest of the afternoon. Can you keep me posted if we need to change anything?"

"Absolutely." Bradley shot his wife another glare as he gave me a strained smile. "We're monitoring the weather closely and will apprise you of any threat to the event. For now, we are alerting staff and gathering supplies just in case."

Bradley Lyle was rumored to be a bit of a flake when it came to managing the resort. For the past week, I'd heard grumblings from the staff about being short of help and ill-equipped to do their jobs efficiently, but so long as his incompetence didn't interfere with the wedding, I was content to stay well out of it. I smiled and started to slide past them when Bradley reached out and touched my arm.

"A moment, Ms. Daye." From the corner of my eye, I saw Olivia give a slight shake of her head. Her husband gritted his teeth and then dawned a fake smile. "We've had some, uh, *disturbing* incidents occur around the resort lately."

My eyebrows shot upward. Disturbing? What did that entail and how might it affect me and my clients? I began to question Bradley when Olivia rushed to explain.

"Nothing for you and our guests to worry about, but we've added additional security patrols and will be locking the main gates at eight. Should anyone need access after that time, they'll need to alert the front desk clerk."

Far from putting me at ease, her statement set my stomach churning. I was about to press for more details when Bradley's phone rang. "Excuse me, Ms. Daye, I must take this call." He gave his wife a pointed look as he answered his phone. "Olivia? Shouldn't you be at the spa? I seem to recall a shipment of products were arriving today."

With another nod to me, he walked away while issuing orders to whomever was on the phone.

Olivia bit her lip and watched as her husband faded from sight. It was obvious something was troubling her, but I was conscious of the clock ticking, and even if I weren't under time constraints, I wasn't inclined to get mired in her problems. Lord knew I had enough on my plate.

Raising the dog's bowl, I gave it a little shake by way of an excuse not to linger. "I need to fill this and then I'll get out of your hair."

She jumped and turned toward me, a puzzled look in her eyes. "What? Oh, yes there's a faucet around back." She waved in the general direction of the main resort. "I should be getting back ... um, remember what I said about the entrance."

I nodded. "I will. The reception ends at four and we should have everything cleaned up long before you close the gates, but if something comes up, I'll do as you said."

With that, she walked away, leaving me to fill The Colonel's bowl and ponder what the couple had said and not said. Had there been theft at the resort? A problem with a guest or employee? Was there a danger to me and the wedding guests?

None of my questions could be answered without deviating from my time schedule, so I buried my concerns and got to work on placing the trees we'd rented from It's About Thyme nursery.

Once the trees were in place as a backdrop for the ceremony, I attached bouquets of roses and ferns to the pews and stood back to admire my handiwork. Fingers crossed that all went according to plan, I left the Scout and walked back to the reception hall.

The ceremony wasn't slated to start for another two hours. Connie should have completed the reception hall and I'd need to check in with the bride, but aside from that, I was twiddling my thumbs.

Intending to grab a bite from the restaurant located in the main house, the questions that had plagued me as I decorated the church returned and I decided to have a friendly chat with the reception clerk.

Pennington Place was an interesting setup for a resort. There were ten bedrooms in the main house, along with the restaurant and conversation areas set up in the former living room and library. I hadn't toured the entire home, but I seemed to recall hearing the Lyles had also done some remodeling, turning one of the downstairs rooms into a cocktail bar.

The plantation had been slowly converted to a hotel and tourist destination while Miriam was alive. They'd started with a small bed-and-breakfast in the main house and then expanded. Former slave quarters had been turned into one- and two-bedroom rental cottages, the barn was a banquet facility, and two years ago they'd put in a golf course and were planning to build a fifty-room hotel overlooking it.

An Olympic sized pool and spa were added last year, and I'd heard there were plans to nestle more cottages among the woodlands on the property, if they could get cooperation from the Gullah families living on parts of the plantation.

The Gullahs were families descended from the African slaves brought to South Carolina to work the indigo, rice, and cotton plantations. Once freed, they settled on the Sea Islands and built communities. Their culture and language were unique and blended African traditions with those of the Europeans.

Many owned restaurants and other small businesses on the islands and surrounding Pennington Place.

There were Gullah families living on the plantation in a small town comprising several acres on the north end of the island. Their village was standing in the way of further development of the resort, and while driving to the property, I'd seen several signs urging people to protest the Lyles' plans, making me wonder if that was the reason the expansion plans had been tabled.

Despite the potential conflict, many Gullahs were employed at the resort. As I crossed the lobby, an elderly man known locally as Gator, because in his youth, he'd made a living trapping and selling alligators, was manning the front desk.

"Hey there, Gator, life treatin' ya well?"

"Oh can't complain, Ms. Holly, can't complain. Though if'n it blows up a storm these ol' bones will be a' achin'."

"Yeah, I'm right there with ya, Gator." I rubbed at my thigh and winced. The shooting that ended my career as a sheriff's deputy had also left me with an injured leg, and I could relate; rainy weather always made my leg throb. "Just hope it holds off until I get through this wedding."

He bobbed his head. "I hear ya. What with everythin' goin' on 'round here, be lucky if only thing messin' with them folks' nuptials is some rain." The old man's eyes were wide, and his

Adam's apple bobbed as he swallowed hard and crossed himself, drawing attention to his neck.

My eyes narrowed as I studied the small, flannel mojo bag hanging there. Having lived on the islands all of my life, I was familiar with the hoodoo beliefs practiced by many of the Gullahs and older people in general. However, it was rare these days to see outward signs of the practice.

A mojo bag meant for protection usually contained High John the Conqueror, cedar, cinnamon, and other herbs, along with rocks or some other talisman blessed by the root doctor that prepared it. I was aware of only one root doctor in Noble County, and to my knowledge she hadn't officially practiced in years.

"Auntie Pearl been around lately?" I asked, with a casualness I was far from feeling.

The question had barely left my mouth before Gator's eyes bulged. He drew a harsh breath and swallowed convulsively before he managed to speak.

"Why you askin'?"

His reaction sent chills down my spine. It was obvious he was afraid of something. "Because"—I nodded toward his mojo hand—"it's been a long time since I've seen someone wearing one of those. Everything all right with you?"

He swallowed again and looked around before leaning forward and whispering, "Yes ma'am, thanks to 'dis protection from Auntie Pearl, but there's some bad juju floatin' around 'dis place, Ms. Holly. Best get that weddin' o'er with and hightail it out of here."

My heart raced as Gator's words sank in. Bad juju? What did he mean by that? And why did he seem so scared? Could it have something to do with the *incidents* Olivia and Bradley had mentioned?

I couldn't deny that the whole situation was beginning to make me uneasy. "Gator, Olivia mentioned they've heightened security on the resort after some trouble. Your needing a protection spell have anything to do with that?"

He licked his lips and looked everywhere but at me. His chest rose and fell in short bursts and for a minute, I thought he'd ignore my question. I was about to change the subject when Gator swallowed hard and leaned forward, looking around and then lowering his voice to just above a whisper. "Anyone asks, you didn't hear this from me."

I nodded and he gulped before continuing. "Near as I can tell, it all started a few weeks ago, just afore that boy turned up claimin' to be Christopher Pennington, you know?"

"Mmm, I've heard he showed up with his cousin, right?"

"Yes ma'am. Right after, one of da maids was cleaning out a closet and found one of Mr. Quinton's old shoes." He gulped. "Was filled with red pepper, Ms. Holly."

I wasn't sure of the significance in finding pepper in a shoe, but from Gator's body language I assumed it was nothing good. "Um, I take it that's bad?"

He snorted. "Means someone's puttin' the hoodoo on Mr. Quinton."

"I see." Though I really didn't. But Gator obviously believed it. "Gator, why would someone want to put a curse on Quinton Lyle?"

He shrugged. "Could be lots of reasons, only I don't think the curse is meant just for him."

I frowned. "Why do you say that?"

He licked his lips. "Cuz of the other stuff."

Geez, getting information from Gator was like pulling teeth! Refraining from rolling my eyes, I gave him a soft smile of encouragement. "What else has you worried?"

"Friend of mine was passin' the old graveyard and saw someone taking dirt from atop o' a grave and 'den a letter come, and Ms. Felicia opened it and the goofer dirt poured out all over 'dis counter!" He threw his arms wide and looked down at the polished wood. "Not long after, Ms. Felicia takes sick. She says it's just a cold but…"

His eyes were huge as he motioned toward the mojo bag he wore. "I made me a wash of basil and eggshells and scrubbed the whole desk down, but when 'dat jar broke, well I knew it was fixin' to get bad 'round here so's I went to Auntie Pearl for a protection spell."

Trying to figure out how basil and eggs fixed a dirty counter, it was a few minutes before I mustered a reply. "That, uh, is disturbing." I frowned as something Gator said came back to me. "Gator, what were you saying about a broken jar?"

His hands shook as he once again crossed himself. "It were a war jar, Ms. Holly. Someone is declarin' war on dis place and I want no part of it. Handed in my notice jus' this mornin'!"

My eyes widened. Gator had worked at Pennington Place for over a decade. "Wow, I'm sorry to hear you're leaving, Gator. Pennington won't be the same without you."

"Thank ya. I'll miss d' place that's for sure, but I ain't gonna stick around and get caught in no war."

The hair on the back of my neck rose at another mention of war. "Gator, what do you mean by war? What was in that jar?"

He sniffed and shook his head. "Don't rightly know, as I ain't a conjurer, but my old gran knew 'bout such things and I heard tales about them war jars. The conjurer uses water dey gathered from a storm, even better if they gets it from rain during a hurricane, then they add rusty nails, some roots, needles, broken glass…" He shrugged. "Least ways that was some of what I seen in the one busted on the front porch."

"Okay." I nodded. "Doesn't sound like good intentions were meant, but by war, what do you think is coming to this plantation?"

He lowered his head and stared at the heart pine floors for several minutes before shivering and meeting my gaze. "Death, Ms. Holly. Death be comin' to Pennington."

Chapter Three

The wedding started on time and went off without a hitch, though I'd known a moment of unease when I'd made a last-minute inspection of the church and found a cross pattern made of stones near the altar.

My knowledge of hoodoo was limited but I had no doubt the cross was tied to the bad juju Gator had mentioned, and if the metal button comprising the middle of the cross was anything to go by, whatever curse or message was being sent was directed at Quinton Lyle; I could think of no one else on the property with the initials Q.A.L.

I'd quickly cleared the debris away before guests saw it, but my stomach had been in knots throughout the ceremony. It was only after we were halfway through the reception that I finally started to relax.

Connie and I were guests as well as coordinators and once the banquet started, we were free to join our families and simply enjoy the event. My friend was off socializing, but I'd opted to put my feet up and spend time people watching. My bulldog was happy with my choice as he'd used his dopey looks to beg for food from all and sundry and was now snoring under the table.

Surveying the reception hall, I had to admit we'd given the bride and groom their fantasy wedding. The old barn glowed in the soft light of hundreds of candles while a string quartet softly serenaded the guests as they finished their meals.

Many of the guests, mostly young and clearly friends of the happy couple, had come in medieval regalia, adding to the feeling of being transported back in time. My gaze moved from a group dressed like Henry VIII and his wives to Ms. Lou Lou and her crowd.

True to form, Madam Mayor and her cronies were decked out in what they deemed appropriate wedding finery complete with hats, and as I'd predicted, a few wearing gloves. The contrast was startling and tickled my funny bone. Tate glanced up from a conversation with Congressman Reid and met my gaze. With a grin, he nodded at the table of King Henry impersonators and wagged his eyebrows.

Stifling a snort, I rolled my eyes and returned to observing the crowd. Everyone that was anyone in Noble County had been invited, a fact I attributed to Mr. and Mrs. Pope's desire to belong to the "country club set." Several politicians were present, as was local business mogul J.T. Minton.

Minton was deep in conversation with Quinton Lyle, and judging by Mr. Lyle's face, it wasn't a pleasant one. Since it was common knowledge that J.T. was looking for a large tract to develop an upscale golf community on Belle Isle, I couldn't help but wonder if he was angling to purchase Pennington Place.

Thinking the rightful heir would have something to say about such a proposition, I looked around for the prodigal son, but it appeared he'd skipped the festivities or had been smart enough to find a quiet corner away from prying eyes.

The Colonel snorted and got to his feet, telling me he was ready for a walk. We were almost out the door when I heard my name called. I turned and stifled a sigh as Ms. Lou Lou, Mama, and Ms. Maybelle plowed through the crowd, the looks on their faces telling me they had bees in their bonnets.

Sighing, I pasted a smile to my face and turned to greet the blue-haired brigade. "Evenin' Ms. Lou Lou." I nodded at Mama and Ms. Maybelle and then turned my attention to the mayor as she proceeded to dissect every aspect of the event.

"Holly Marie, everything looks lovely!" As she paused for breath, I braced for the *but* I was sure was coming. "However, what on earth possessed you to put those trees in the church? What was wrong with some simple flowers on the altar? And I wish someone would tell me why we were subjected to that ridiculous trumpeting as the bride arrived! Why, in my day Mendelssohn was sufficient and—"

"Ms. Lou Lou, the couple wanted to hold an outdoor ceremony, but I convinced them that it is far too hot to ask guests to sit outside. The trees were my way of giving them the feeling of still being in nature."

I struggled to keep my tone civil as I defended my choices. Really, how was it any of her business? She may have raised Jeffrey as her own, but to my knowledge, the Popes paid for the entire wedding, so I didn't see where the mayor's opinion entered into the equation. Not that I was gonna tell her that!

Ms. Lou Lou continued to harp about the guests in costumes and the lack of a traditional wedding march when I reached my tolerance for busybodies. "Ma'am, I realize this wedding wasn't to your taste, but Carrie and Jeffrey love the medieval stuff. The costumed guests and a herald were appropriate for their theme." She started to argue but I held up my hand. "I'm sorry. We'll be cutting the cake soon and I need to take The Colonel out first. Come on, boy, walkies!"

Leaving the hens to cackle, I rushed outside and drew a breath of fresh air. The sun was lower in the sky but the humidity was cloying. Still, I'd found a bit of peace—for the moment anyway.

Guiding The Colonel around the barn, I choose a path that ran along the riverbank and set off on our walk. While it was still stiflingly hot and humid, the approaching storm's outer bands provided an occasional respite. I hadn't seen any updated forecast, but according to Bradley Lyle, the current course for Hurricane Isabella meant we'd see significant wind, rain, and storm surge as early as tomorrow evening.

My mind focused on devising a plan to secure both our family's plantation and our main home in Sanctuary Bay before the storm hit, and I failed to notice a couple standing in the path just ahead.

The sun was in my eyes, but I could clearly see that it was Olivia Lyle and Christopher Pennington. I was about to call out a greeting when someone else beat me to it. I squinted and could just make out a woman with flame-red hair; I was pretty sure it was Heather Franklin making a beeline for her cousin.

As she drew closer, I heard her say something like leave him alone, and then Olivia smirked and reached out, drawing her hand down Chris's chest. With another glance at Heather, she pressed her bright red lips to his cheek, gave him a come-hither look, and then pressed something into his hand.

With a seductive smile, Olivia strutted away, her hips swaying in a suggestive rhythm as old as time. Heather scowled as Olivia passed, but continued on to where Chris waited with a bemused look on his face. The Colonel tugged at his leash, drawing my attention, but when I looked back, Heather had her arms around Christopher and was nuzzling his neck.

Poor guy looked just as uncomfortable with his cousin's attention as he had with Olivia's. Eyes wide, I backed away, intending to return to the reception via another route. No way did I want to be involved in whatever I'd just witnessed. I was saved a longer walk when Christopher Pennington stepped away from Heather, tossed something into the river, and stomped off toward the hotel, leaving her trailing in his wake.

Now what had that been about? Olivia, a married woman, had been making a not-very-subtle pass at the Pennington heir and it seemed as if Heather was also vying for his attention.

As I walked back to the reception, I recalled the bits of conversation I'd overheard between Olivia and Bradley. I'd caught the words *air* and *fussy*.

At the time, the words made little sense and I had been too busy to ponder them, but in light of what I saw, I had to wonder if Bradley had meant *heir* and if he was aware of his wife's pursuit of Chris Pennington, perhaps the word I'd heard was not *fussy*, but *hussy*.

I snorted and followed The Colonel into the barn. Olivia's behavior a few moments ago made the latter a distinct possibility. Shaking my head, I guided The Colonel into the barn. The Lyles' marriage was none of my concern. My focus needed to be on keeping my family and community safe during the impending storm, but I couldn't help but wonder what other storms were brewing just out of sight.

Entering the reception to find the best man giving a toast, I slipped into my seat and handed The Colonel a snack. With the toasts concluded, guests began to mill about while they waited for the cake cutting and dancing to begin.

I was about to check on the catering staff when my friend Jessica leaned closer and began to update me about the shooting that had left me injured and Shawn Dupree dead.

"So, I'm working through the list your contact at the DMV provided, but—"

"Does anything look promising?"

We both turned as Roland Dupree, the father of the young man that had lost his life the night I was shot, scooted his chair closer.

Jessica shrugged. "Maybe? It's difficult to say at the moment. The images of the truck were grainy and the angle only provided a partial tag number. The girl Holly put me in touch with at the DMV set search parameters for several models and colors of vehicles along with the partial number. The system generated a list of ninety possible matches in Noble County."

"Ninety! How are we going to find our truck? It's like a needle in a haystack."

I patted Roland's arm. "We'll get there, Roland, but it's gonna take some time."

His defeated expression broke my heart. His only child was dead. The official report claimed I'd shot him after he shot me, only my memories said Shawn was laying dead on the ground when I rolled onto the scene.

The conflict with the report and my recollection of events had set us on the current course of investigating what really happened while trying to remain under the radar of local law enforcement; in no way did I think our sheriff's department was corrupt and getting on their bad side was the last thing I needed.

Thus, we had to bide our time and let ace reporter Jessica beat the bushes under the cover of working on a story. However, I understood his pain and frustration. Had it been my son, I'd be climbing the walls and screaming from the rafters that something was fishy.

"I just don't understand why we can't confront the sheriff! At the very least, that report is false due to incompetence. Do we really want that for our community?"

Biting back a sigh, I tried to explain yet again. "Roland, we discussed this. By letting Jess look into the images, we have a layer of anonymity. Anyone looking at what she's investigating will assume it is for a story. If you and I go in with proverbial guns blazing, it'll start a firestorm. If there is corruption, they'll destroy evidence and go to ground. Yes, we want the truth, but don't we also want justice?"

"Yeah. Yeah, I want whoever is responsible for Shawn's death prosecuted—"

"Well then, we have to stick to our plan." Thinking to change the subject and lighten the mood, I waggled my eyebrows at Jessica. "What do you make of this reappearing heir business?"

We'd been conversing in a quiet tone but I posed my question at a normal volume and it reached Connie's ears. "Yes! What have you learned, Jessica?"

Jessica rolled her eyes and directed a mock scowl at me. "You just had to bring it up ..."

I grinned at her aggrieved tone. "Eh, inquiring minds want to know!"

She huffed. "You, along with everyone else in Noble County!" She turned to Connie. "To answer your question, I've learned precious little. I've tried speaking to the executors and they are sticking to the no comment routine."

Connie started to speak and Jess interrupted her. "Before you ask, yes, I've also tried interviewing the Lyles, the man claiming to be Christopher Pennington, and the cousin that swears he is."

Connie slumped in her seat. "No dice? Not even one juicy tidbit?"

My former boss and best friend since grade school laughed as he picked up on our topic. "Poor Connie, no new gossip for you today."

Connie wrinkled her nose at Craig. "Not looking for gossip," she replied primly. "Merely curious about the fate of Pennington Place. It's a popular venue for events, so it's only prudent I take an interest if it might affect my business."

Craig snorted. "A likely story. Face it"—he glanced at his girlfriend, Marla—"you ladies are only interested because the guy is good looking and possibly rich."

Marla smirked. "Well darling, a girl can never have too much of a good thing and Chris Pennington, or whoever he is, is most definitely eye candy."

Connie laughed and started to add her two cents when Mama bore down on us. "There you are, I've been looking all over for you!"

"I've been right here." Mama looked both worried and perturbed. Never a good sign. "Is something wrong?"

She huffed. "They are about to cut the cake."

And? I'd done my job. Of course, that response would only earn me a scold from my mother, so I forced a smile onto my face and tried to be helpful. "That's great." I glanced at the kitchen. "After the bride and groom make the first cut and get their pictures, Marlena can assign someone to cut and plate the rest."

Mama huffed. "That's just it, they can't cut it."

I frowned and started to inquire further when Mama motioned for me to follow and sailed off toward the sunroom. Rolling my eyes, I asked Craig to watch The Colonel and demanded Connie accompany me. If I had to suffer, so did she.

We arrived to find controlled chaos. Connie had set the cake tables in the far corner, just in front of the door leading to a patio. Carrie and her new husband were standing to one side looking nervous, while Mrs. Pope and Mayor Tomlin scurried around, looking under the table skirting and arguing behind their fake smiles.

"What's going on?"

Ms. Lou Lou rounded on me, hands on her hips and a scowl on her face. "It's that ridiculous groom's cake. The topper is missing."

My brows rose. "Someone pulled the knife out of the top?"

She rolled her eyes. "Apparently." She huffed and started muttering about grown men acting like children. I tuned the familiar refrain out and turned to Connie.

"Did they forget to insert the sword?"

Connie shook her head. "No, it was there earlier. I watched the baker insert it into the top layer."

I shrugged. "Well, it's gone now. Just grab a knife from the kitchen."

"But what about the pictures? Jeff wanted to enact the whole drawing the sword thing."

I sighed. If it wasn't one thing it was another. I was beyond ready for the whole shebang to be over with. Thinking quickly, I headed to the kitchen. "Give me a second."

I borrowed a knife from the caterers and hurried back to the sunroom. Nudging everyone aside, I walked behind the table and carefully inserted the substitute. "Sorry it's not a fancy jeweled dagger, but..."

Jeff grinned. "That's okay. Only, what happened to the dagger?"

I shrugged. "No idea. Maybe someone thought the jewels in the hilt were real?"

He laughed and turned back to his bride; the incident forgotten in his eagerness to role play King Arthur. Connie and I stepped back to allow the photographer a better shot and in minutes the guests were clapping as the *sword* was freed and the cake was dished up.

Crisis averted, Connie and I returned to our table. We'd just settled when the sound of drums rang out. I frowned and glanced back at the sunroom.

The band had set up in the corner opposite the cake table but they hadn't taken the stage yet. So where was the noise coming from?

I leaned over to talk to Connie when a collective gasp filled the hall. I frowned as everyone started crowding around the windows behind the head table.

Tate returned to our table after talking to a colleague "What's going on?"

"No idea, thought it was the band."

I shook my head. "Nope, they haven't started playing yet. I think that racket is coming from outside."

"Gotta be. Come on, let's go see."

Deciding it was too much trouble to push through the other guests, Tate, Connie, and I walked outside and followed the sound. The solitary drumbeat was now accompanied by indistinct chanting. I couldn't decipher what was being said, but something about the sound sent shivers down my spine.

We rounded the corner and I gasped. Clustered on the lawn were about a dozen people dressed in traditional Gullah robes. One man was beating a steady rhythm while the others formed a semicircle around a wizened old woman who was muttering and sprinkling something on the ground.

"Tate!" I clenched his hand and swallowed hard. "Is that..."

"Looks like it."

We watched as the old woman, known locally as Auntie Pearl, the Gullah root doctor, continued to enact a strange sort of ritual involving candles, a goblet, and bundles of herbs.

"What is she doing?"

I glanced at Connie and then continued to watch the Gullah conjurer as the incidents Gator had relayed ran through my mind. Drawing a shaky breath, I gulped and said what we were all thinking. "Pretty sure she's cursing Pennington Place."

Chapter Four

Massaging the small of my back, I bent and lifted the last box of candelabras, depositing it by the door with the others. The appearance of a Gullah root doctor, combined with the first rain bands from Hurricane Isabella, had dampened the partying mood and the reception had broken up an hour earlier than planned.

While I felt sorry for Carrie and Jeffrey, I couldn't deny feeling relieved. The sooner Connie and I cleared the mess and went home, the better.

"Do you really think she cursed this place?" Connie asked, her voice barely above a whisper.

I stifled a sigh. It was the third time she'd posited the question and my patience was wearing thin. "I don't know what to think," I replied honestly. "But something's definitely off with this whole situation."

Connie started to comment but I walked to the sunroom, leaving her to finish folding the table runners while I dismantled the dessert table decorations. Staring at the gold cloth, with remnants of frosting and cake crumbs, I pondered how the ceremonial dagger disappeared.

The *how* was actually pretty easy to answer. During dinner, the sunroom hadn't been occupied, though it was in view of the other room. But someone could have slipped into the room, removed the dagger, and then walked right out the side door located behind the dessert tables.

Running with that theory, I stepped onto the patio and glanced around, thinking perhaps someone had taken it as a joke and then, after the furor the missing dagger caused, been too embarrassed to confess. There were several potted palms and other tropical flowers scattered around the flagstone patio, but the soil was undisturbed in all of them. Checking behind and beneath the furniture cushions with no luck, I gave it up as a lost cause and returned to my packing. It wasn't as if the dagger had been expensive, but still, who would want to take what had obviously been intended as part of the event?

Ms. Lou Lou had said it was a result of letting people come in costume. I snorted. As if that alone welcomed ill-mannered behavior. Shaking my head at the absurdity, I began clearing my decorations from the table.

One box was full, and I'd started on another when an almighty crash disturbed the silence. Connie screeched and came running.

"What was that?" Eyes wide, she glanced around the room and then focused on the windows that provided a view of the river. "Is it the curse?"

"Oh, don't be ridiculous!" I huffed and shoved the patio door open. "It came from outside."

"Don't! Don't go out there—"

"Connie, it's the storm." Nothing on the patio was disturbed, though the taller plants were swaying in the wind. Connie hesitantly followed me, still rambling about curses and begging me to come back inside.

The patio was sheltered on two sides by the building and landscaping. I stepped off the paving and looked around. "Probably something upended by the ... there, you see?" I pointed to a plastic trash can rolling across the lawn. "As I said, it's just the wind blowing things around, which reminds me…"

Pulling out my phone, I dialed my brother's number as I grabbed a box with one hand and headed toward my truck. I'd just opened the back door when Dewey answered.

"Yeah, whatcha want?"

Rolling my eyes at his rudeness, I shoved the box inside and called The Colonel to heel; no way did I want to chase him halfway across the plantation in the dark. "Come on, boy, let's find Connie." We started back to the barn. "Dewey, I think we're going to see more of this storm before morning. Start securing anything lose around the house and I'll help you put the storm shutters up when I get—"

"No can do."

"What?" I came to a stop on the path as my blood began to boil. "Dewey, I don't care what you're doing, we've got to—"

"Yeah, I heard ya, but I'm not home."

Gritting my teeth, I forced myself to keep a civil tone, otherwise I wouldn't put it past my brother to make things difficult out of spite. "Well, where are you?"

"Right behind you."

I spun around to find Dewey grinning like a fool. "What the—Dewey, this is no time to be messing around! They are saying Isabella will roll by us as a Cat 1! Just because it isn't making landfall here doesn't mean we won't catch bad weather! The eyewall will probably skirt the Sea Islands and you know what happened the last time one did that. Now get going and I'll be home as soon as I—why are you shaking your head?"

"Because I'm here working security."

I closed my eyes as his words sank in; Olivia Lyle's statement ran through my mind. The heightened security measures included hiring Sentinel Security personnel ... wonderful.

The buildup to the wedding and then the actual event had taken its toll on me. I could sleep for a week but thanks to Isabella ... I drew a deep breath and accepted the situation; no sense in whining about what couldn't be helped.

Mentally composing a list of what could be done tonight, I turned to my brother. "Are the shutters in the garage loft? Oh, and where are the ratchet straps to secure the trashcans?" Not waiting for a reply, I snapped my fingers for The Colonel and continued walking toward the barn. The sooner I finished loading the decorations, the sooner I could move on to my next task.

Dewey fell into step beside me. "I put them shutters in the loft, all labeled like you told me and there's a plastic bin in the garage with all the tools to tie stuff down but Holly, you can't—"

"I know I can't put the shutters up by myself. I'll call Tate and see if he can help—no!" I glanced at Dewey. "Call Whopper and see if he's sober and ready to make some money."

Dewey rolled his eyes. "Course he's sober, well probably cuz it ain't much past seven and he can always use some dough but"—Dewey came to a halt and glared at me—"Dang it Holly, will you stop and listen for a second?"

Scowling, I slowed and looked over my shoulder. "What is it? I've got to hurry home and—"

"That's just it! You can't get home."

"What? Why can't I—"

"Cuz the bridge is out!"

That stopped me in my tracks. I slowly turned and looked at my brother. "What did you say?"

Dewey huffed. "It's what I been tryin' to tell ya! We're stuck out here cuz there was a wreck just afore you get on the swing bridge. Traffic backed up both ways."

Hands on my hips, I demanded to know how he'd managed to get onto the island.

"I'd just crossed and was sittin' at the light when I heard the crash. It was on the other end so's nothin' I could do but drive on. When I rounded the bend I looked back at the bridge and..."

He shrugged. "It's a mess. Cops all over, ambulance, thought I saw the coroner's van, too, so you know what that means."

Closing my eyes and tipping my head back I prayed for the day to end. If Dewey was correct and there'd been a fatality, the bridge would be closed for hours while they investigated. With a weary sigh, I motioned for Dewey to follow. "Come on, let's go tell Connie we're havin' a slumber party."

"I still don't see why we couldn't go to Myrtlewood. I mean, it's nice of the Lyles to give us a room, but if we'd stayed at your plantation we could have started preparing for the storm, and we wouldn't have to worry about that curse!"

"Oh, would you stop? There is no curse!" Opening the complimentary toothbrush, I started cleaning my teeth as Connie rattled on about the Gullah root doctor.

While I wasn't concerned with the alleged curse, I had to admit that staying at Myrtlewood would have been ideal. But, as I'd explained to Connie, we didn't keep Myrtlewood supplied with food and took the bedding back to the town house to launder after we used it for the Fourth of July weekend. I'd forgotten to take it back, so we'd have been well and truly roughing it if I'd given in and spent the night there.

Frankly, I was too tired for that. Hopefully, the worst of Isabella would stay offshore until tomorrow evening and I could start securing things after a decent night's rest.

"Bathroom is all yours; which side of the bed do you want?" The only room available had been a king suite. L-shaped, the room contained a small parlor complete with a working fireplace; not that we'd be using it at this time of year.

Harkening back to the antebellum era of its birth, Pennington Place's main house was furnished in a late Victorian style. The sofa and high-backed chairs looked the part but were far from comfortable, though The Colonel had made himself at home.

Patting his head, I strode to the sleeping area, hoping the antique four poster canopied bed was equipped with a modern mattress.

Connie pointed toward the right side and then made her way into the bathroom. I set my phone on the nightstand and hooked it up to the charger before crossing to the French doors that provided access to a covered porch that ran along the upper story of the house.

Royal blue and gold draperies framed a beautiful view of the river, though the cloud coverage from the approaching storm made it impossible to see now that the sun had fully set. Checking that the doors were locked, I made my way back to the bed, stifling a moan as my tired body connected with the feather-soft mattress.

As tired as I was, I had too much on my mind to sleep. Frustrated, I blew out my breath and propped myself against the headboard. I was reaching for my phone as Connie got into bed.

"Did you get ahold of Tate?"

"Mmm, he had just left the scene when I called. It was a fatality— God rest his soul—and the passenger was flown to Charleston."

"Oh no, what happened?"

"It was a county dump truck hauling sand over to Goodwin Park to fill bags. Tate wasn't sure what caused the accident, but the bridge will be closed until the engineers can assess the damage."

"Woah, how long will that take?"

I shrugged. "Normally? A few hours for them to check it and, then if it's structurally sound ... but with this storm moving, who knows?"

Connie winced. "So, we're stuck out here? Can someone come over in a boat tomorrow?"

I shook my head. "Thought of that. We'll have to wait and see what the river looks like. Dewey said there were whitecaps as he was driving over. Anything more than three- to five-feet waves and it wouldn't be safe."

"Oh man, is that likely?"

"Unfortunately, yes. Thankfully, they're washing our clothes so we won't be walking around dirty. I spoke to Elijah, the chef, and he's cooking some chicken and sweet potato for The Colonel's breakfast." Thank God, because on top of everything else, I did not need a petulant bulldog.

"Did you get someone to check on your place?"

Connie nodded. "Yep, my neighbor is putting my trash cans in his garage and strapped my patio furniture to the fence. What about you? Who's gonna look after Ms. Effie?"

I snorted. "Well, I asked Tate, but with this wreck and the weather, it's all hands on deck for emergency services. I did get Whopper to go over and get the shutters on and stuff."

Connie chuckled. "Oh boy, how much did that cost you?"

I wrinkled my nose. "More than he's worth, but beggars can't be choosers."

"True, but is Ms. Effie gonna ride out the storm alone then?"

"I wish." Connie's eyes widened so I explained. "I talked to Mama and tried to convince her to go to Ms. Lou Lou's or even

Maybelle's, but she's stubborn and doesn't want to leave the house unprotected." I snorted. "Not that she could do much if something happens. But get this, Tate called me back to say that his dad is going over."

Connie's brows rose toward her hairline. "Dr. Sawyer is gonna stay with Ms. Effie?" At my nod, she laughed. "Man, we'll hear the explosion from here!"

I prayed she was wrong, but I didn't have high hopes. Mama and the senior Dr. Sawyer had spent a lot of time together while I was staying at Sandpoint Abbey a few months ago. I'd been surprised but pleased that she had a good friend, but that all changed when the couple, who Mama insisted weren't a couple, attended Ms. Lou Lou's garden party.

Tate and I had been delayed, but when we arrived his father was covered in iced tea and Mama had demanded Maybelle take her home. We'd learned from Ms. Lou Lou that Tate's father had allegedly made a date with the infamous Ruby Gilroy, Noble County's answer to a femme fatale, and then canceled in favor of Mama.

Ruby accused Dr. Sawyer of two-timing her, made a big scene, and then dumped tea over his head. Mama had been horrified, embarrassed, and hurt. I hadn't heard the end of it for over a week.

Dr. Sawyer had been trying to apologize for the past month or more, the house was full of floral gifts and assorted gourmet food baskets, but Mama wouldn't give him the time of day. Lord only knew what would happen when he showed up at The Oaks. The thought of that confrontation made me glad I was stuck on Belle Isle, hurricane or not.

The rustling of paper drew my gaze toward Connie. She grinned and waved a teal wrapper at me. "I couldn't resist. Did you try these?"

"No, I already brushed my teeth."

Connie shrugged. "So did I but I couldn't resist." She extended her hand. "Try one. They're from Girard's in Savannah! He makes the best candy!" I refused and she shrugged, unwrapping another.

"Where did you get them?"

"From the maid. They have nightly turn down service, complete with gourmet chocolates left on the pillow. She said they do it every night at 8:00 p.m. You were on the porch talking to Tate when she came by."

"Huh, fancy. If you leave me any, I'll have them for breakfast."

She laughed and headed back to the bathroom. "There are two more on the nightstand. I've had my limit." She patted her hip. "Swimsuit season."

Snorting at her nonsense and sliding the chocolate back far enough that my inquisitive dog wouldn't help himself, I opened a weather app on my phone and studied the radar. Hurricane Isabella was a monster. The eye was just above the Bahamas, but its bands stretched all the way to the mouth of the Savannah River.

We've had a few showers and gusty winds, but the full power of the storm wouldn't reach us until Sunday afternoon or early evening. Connie returned and I turned off the light. I'd get a good night's rest and head to Myrtlewood early in the morning. With any luck, I'd manage to secure the property before heavy weather arrived. However, with the way my day was going, I wasn't holding my breath.

Chapter Five

A scream, followed by The Colonel barking his head off, brought Connie and me out of a dead sleep a little past eleven. I flipped on the light as Connie scrambled from the bed and ran to the French doors.

"What was that? Do you think it was the curse?"

Gritting my teeth, I flipped the covers off and reached for the robe I'd borrowed from the spa. "For the last time, there is no such thing as a curse! Come on, it sounded like it came from one of the rooms."

Commanding The Colonel to stay, I flipped the old-fashioned door latch over and glanced at Connie. "You coming?"

She rolled her eyes but trailed after me as I crept into the hall. The scream had awakened the other guests, and as I rounded the bend in the hall, I found several people clustered around. They spotted me and all started talking at once.

"Did you hear it, too?"

"What was that sound?"

"I think it was that voodoo stuff. I've read about it turning people into zombies!"

That nonsensical statement made Connie gasp. I gave the older woman who'd uttered the inane comment my stern "cop" frown. "There are no zombies roaming around Pennington Place." I looked at the assembled crowd.

The older woman appeared to be one part of a couple, if the way she clung to a gray-haired man in pinstriped pajamas was any indication. Standing to the left of the couple was a young man bundled in a robe similar to mine, though a bit of denim showed just above his ankle. If he'd pulled on his jeans, why bother with the robe?

I gave myself a mental shake. It was an inane thing to ponder under the circumstances. As we stood around looking confused, Christopher Pennington stuck his head out of his door.

He met my gaze and frowned. "What's going on?"

"Didn't you hear that scream?"

His brows rose as he shook his head. "No, I was in the shower." He dragged a hand through his hair, drawing my gaze. He'd claimed to be in the shower, yet his hair was perfectly dry.

I was about to comment on that fact when Pennington distracted me.

"Where's Heather?"

A quick look showed she wasn't part of the group and my inner alarm bells started clanging. The scream had woken everyone staying on our floor except Christopher, or so he claimed.

It was doubtful anyone with a room on the second floor wouldn't have heard the scream. Perhaps she was in another part of the hotel. Fingers crossed, I asked. "Do you know which room is hers?"

Christopher pointed at the door behind me and my stomach churned. Seemed my internal warning system had been right; it was time to be concerned.

We all turned toward the door as everyone started chattering again.

"Did the scream come from in there?"

"Oh Walter, I knew we should have checked out today!"

The guy in the robe chuckled and hummed the Twilight zone theme. "Maybe the curse got her."

Unamused at his levity, I scowled at him and then knocked on the closed door. "Ms. Franklin? Are you all right?" I tried the knob but the door was locked.

"Holly? Do you think…"

Ignoring Connie because I was sure she was firmly on the Gullah curse train, I knocked again and loudly called Heather's name. "Someone go down to the desk and ask the clerk for the pass key."

The older man, Walter if I'd heard right, nodded and started for the stairs but Christopher stopped him. "There's no master key. The doors lock with that weird latch thing."

Rats! He was right. I pounded on the door again before remembering the porch that ran along the backside of the house. Without bothering to explain, I went back to my room and stepped onto the porch.

The Colonel trailed after me as I walked along the veranda until I came to the doors I estimated led to Heather's room. I knocked again and then tried the handle when I got no response. The doors were locked, but a gap in the curtains allowed a glimpse inside.

Cupping my hands around my eyes, I peered into the room. Heather's was smaller than mine, but included a fireplace and two wing backed chairs clustered in front of it. Though the room was cloaked in darkness, a slight glow from embers in the fireplace provided enough light to make out basic shapes.

Puzzling over why anyone would light a fire in August, I let my gaze roam around the small seating area and then moved on to the adjacent double bed, stopping as I detected something laying on the rug at the foot of the bed.

My stomach dropped. I fished in the pocket of my robe and pulled out my phone. Odds were good it was Heather on the floor, but it remained to be seen if she was having a medical emergency or was long past needing that kind of intervention.

The touch of a button and the flashlight feature provided enough illumination to know I wouldn't be returning to bed.

"Come on, boy. Let's go find some strong men."

The Colonel and I returned to the hall long enough to requisition the brute strength of Chris and the guy in the bathrobe. A couple of strong shoulders thrust against the French doors, and we stepped far enough into the room to confirm my suspicions.

Not that it mattered, but I'd also solved the mystery of the missing groom's cake dagger; it had found its way into the chest of Heather Franklin.

F inding Heather's body had upset Chris to the extent I'd asked my other helper, a guest named Dylan Carter, to help him to his room and give him a stiff shot of liquor. That done, I'd closed the French doors and informed the other guests that there'd been a death and I'd appreciate them all returning to their rooms and remain there until the police arrived.

Lots of grumbling about who put me in charge occurred, but in the end they'd done as I asked, and I turned my attention to the obvious murder of Heather Franklin. Connie, The Colonel, and I made our way down to the front desk as I placed a quick call to Dewey.

"What? How'd that happen?"

I rolled my eyes. "Take a guess." He huffed at my snarky reply but I rushed on before he could start an argument. "Look, just be on alert for anyone or anything suspicious and be careful; there's a killer on the loose."

Beside me, Connie gasped and directed a wide-eyed look at me. I hung up and ignored her obvious fear but my friend grabbed my arm, drawing us both to a halt.

"No." I suppressed a sigh and continued down the stairs.

"But Holly..." Connie quickly caught up with me. "What if—"

"Connie, this had nothing to do with any curse!"

Connie and I had been friends since we were fourteen, but I'd never have guessed she was so gullible. She'd been harping about the Gullah curse since the reception and I was tired of it all.

I couldn't say who murdered Heather, but I *could* say they were a flesh-and-blood mortal soul. Convincing Connie, however, was a challenge I wasn't up for.

She continued to prattle about supernatural nonsense until we reached the desk. Seeing who was on night duty made me want to scream. Gator was the last person my friend needed to interact with.

Suggesting Connie take The Colonel out to do his business took all my powers of persuasion, ending with a call to my brother. Only when I assured her that Dewey would meet her behind the house did Connie agree.

Not that I blamed her for being nervous; while I didn't for a minute believe Auntie Pearl's root work had killed Heather, I wasn't ashamed to admit the murder scared me. The gates were locked, and Dewey and one of the Pennington staff had been patrolling the grounds. It was not impossible someone from outside the resort had killed her, but it was unlikely.

My dog, my brother, my best friend, and I were stuck at a resort on an island we couldn't leave, and one of the other occupants was probably a murderer. Drawing on my law enforcement training, I pushed aside my concerns and approached the desk.

"Evenin' Gator, don't you ever go home?"

He laughed. "Hey Ms. Holly, could say the same for you! I's supposed to be gone hours ago but that Tameka done called off and Ms. Felicia's so sweet ... I couldn't leave her hangin'. What you up so late for?"

Gator's mention of Felicia Lyle made me smile. She was the only one of the Lyle clan about whom I had nothing but good things to say. She was also, despite her oldest brother's title, the real workhorse at Pennington.

Thinking of the mess about to fall on her made me frown. She'd get no help from her father or brothers, to say nothing of her sister-in-law. Hopefully, the police would make a quick arrest. All I could do for her was make the call, which wouldn't happen until I'd dealt with Gator and his superstitions.

"Gator, there's been an incident with one of the guests, could you—"

"Incident? I knew it! I knew sometin' bad was gonna happen." Eyes wide, he clutched his mojo bag. "It's the curse! Ms. Holly, I told ya—"

"Gator!" This was why I'd sent Connie outside. With Gator's fears, hers would have only multiplied and I didn't have time for any more nonsense. "This has nothing to do with any curse!" His lower lip jutted out, putting me in mind of a four-year-old denied a treat.

I closed my eyes for a moment and prayed for patience. "Just call the Lyles please, I'll take care of the rest."

With a mulish look, Gator did as I requested, leaving me to call the police. Not wishing to be overheard, I headed onto the front porch and dialed the non-emergency number. Something told me not to call 911. They'd dispatch to the nearest available officer, but it'd be broadcast to anyone with a police scanner, and lots of people in Noble County monitored those for entertainment and gossip material.

"Sergeant Milroy, how can I help ya?"

Ah, my luck was changing. I'd went through the academy with Gene Milroy. "Hey Gene, it's Holly Daye."

"Well, hey stranger! You doin' all right?"

Under the circumstances... "Yeah, doing good. But, uh, got a bit of a situation out here at Pennington Place."

"Oh yeah? The Lyles finally do in that guy claimin' to be the heir?"

He laughed at his own joke until I burst his bubble, then he was all business. "Murder. Huh. Okay, I'm gonna call Joe Brannon. Give me your call back number. Is the scene secure?"

I rattled off my cell number, assured him I'd contained the crime scene, and then waited on a call from Detective Brannon. I didn't wait long.

"Hello, Detective."

"Ms. Daye, hear you've found a body ... again."

His tone suggested I was always finding bodies and I bristled until I considered how many deaths I'd been involved in recently. "Yes sir, the deceased is Heather Franklin."

He made some noncommittal noises before asking, "You're sure she's dead?"

I almost snorted. "Oh yes, she's definitely dead. Dagger through the chest from what I could see. As soon as I saw the body, I backed out of the room and locked the door."

"Good job and certainly sounds like murder..." He trailed off and I could hear voices in the background and snippets of his conversation. He was explaining the situation to someone. "Daye, we've got a bit of a problem here. I'm gonna put the sheriff on the line."

My brows rose. I'd only worked under Sheriff Tanner Felton for six months before my injury sent me into early retirement. In that time, I'd come to the conclusion his motivations for seeking the position had more to do with politics than a zeal for law enforcement.

I wouldn't have said he was incompetent, but I also wouldn't have said he expressed much enthusiasm for the job. What could have brought him into the office after hours? I didn't wait long for an answer.

"Holly Daye? Sheriff Felton. Hear ya got yourself a murder victim."

"Um, yes sir. Appears to have happened shortly after eleven."

"Oh? Are there witnesses then?"

"No, but the victim's room is next to mine and I, as well as the other guests on this floor, were awakened by a scream around that time."

He was quiet for a few seconds and then cleared his throat. "I see. And you're sure this is murder?"

"Very sure, sir."

He mumbled something and then came back on the line. "Look, Daye, the bridge is out, and small craft warnings mean we can't take a boat out—"

I tensed. "So, you're not sending anyone—"

He again cleared his throat. "'Fraid not. Is there an immediate threat? Anyone else in danger?"

Were we at risk? Someone had driven a dagger into Heather's chest, but before I'd cleared everyone from the room, I'd noticed a crude doll was between her body and the hilt of the knife. I hadn't examined it closely, but at a glance I'd have said it was meant to be a stereotypical voodoo doll.

Connie would claim it was the result of the curse, but I didn't believe that for a minute. It was more likely the killer was trying to cast suspicion on the Gullah root doctor or one of her followers. My gut said the motive for murder had been personal and not the work of a homicidal maniac. I relayed my beliefs to Sheriff Felton.

"Good, good. Well not good but you know what I mean."

My lips twitched at his bluster. The man was floundering and clearly out of his element. No wonder he'd hired Joe Brannon as Noble County's only detective; they were birds of a feather.

"Yes sir, I get what you're trying to say." Figuring he wasn't sure how to proceed, I took pity on him. "The hurricane should reach us by tomorrow evening, correct?"

"What? Oh, yes that's what emergency management is telling me, though it's slowed so it might hit us Monday. We're under evacuation orders for Zone A, though they've left it a bit late.

Between this storm and the bridge accident, I've got every available officer working."

"I understand, sir. Would it be all right if I just secured the scene and maybe took witness statements? Then, once Detective Brannon can get here..."

"Yes! Splendid idea, Daye. Takin' the bull by the horns as they say. Sheriff Goodwin always spoke highly of you and I can see why." His voice faded as he addressed someone in the room then he cleared his throat again and gave me my marching orders.

"It's settled then. Brannon will be out there just as soon as it's safe to travel. We've every confidence you can handle the situation until then. Any questions?"

Plenty, but since I had little confidence he or his detective could answer them I didn't bother. "No sir, I'll do what I can to preserve evidence and wait for Detective Brannon's arrival."

"Excellent. Ya'll batten down the hatches and stay safe; this Isabella looks to be a humdinger. One more thing, Daye. Are you armed?"

My eyes widened. I was a trained and licensed firearms holder, but since the shooting, I hadn't touched a weapon. Him asking me if I was carrying made my stomach cramp. Was he anticipating my needing a gun?

"Um, no sir, I no longer carry..."

"Perfectly understandable under the circumstances, but I don't like the idea of y'all being out there without protection. You feel this murder was personal and I think your reasons are sound, but I'd sleep better knowing you weren't out there defenseless. But it can't be helped. Don't worry, Daye. You've got a good head on your shoulders and I'm sure everything will be fine."

"Yes sir, thank you. I'm not carrying, but I'd assume at least one of the Lyles is a firearms owner. We'll be okay."

"Sounds like you have the situation under control. I'd say call if you need us but..."

I chuckled. "Yes sir, we'll probably lose service. I'll do my best and then leave it in God's hands."

"Very good. Sometimes, that's all we can do. Stay safe, and we'll see you on the other side of this thing."

I hung up and leaned my head back against the chair. Wow. Stuck on an island with a murder victim, a Cat 1 barreling toward us, and no law enforcement in sight for the foreseeable future.

If it weren't for bad luck, I'd have none at all.

Chapter Six

After a short pity party, I gave myself a mental shake and got down to business. I'd just hung up from conferring with Tate when Connie and Dewey joined me. The Colonel flopped at my feet as Connie dropped into the chair beside me and wrung her hands.

"Well? When will the police get here?"

Debating the gentlest delivery of the truth, I gave up and figured it was better to rip the Band-Aid off quickly and dropped the bomb. "They aren't coming, Connie."

Her reaction was predictable. "What do you mean, they aren't coming?" She jumped from her chair and started pacing. "There's a dead body upstairs!"

"A fact they are aware of." She started to speak but I held up my hand. "However, the bridge is out and a small craft warning means they can't come by boat. Same reason we're stuck here."

Her shoulders slumped as she dropped back into the chair. "But... but they're the police! It's their job..." she trailed off and stared at the wooden planks of the porch floor.

I opted not to reiterate the problems we, and by extension the police, were facing. There was no sense in beating a dead horse and Connie wasn't stupid, just scared. We needed to devise a plan. Better to give her a purpose than let her dwell on what couldn't be changed.

"I talked with Detective Brannon and then with Sheriff Felton..."

Dewey sat on the top step and scratched The Colonel behind his ears. "What's their plan?"

"On their end? Wait for the storm to pass."

"But what about her body? It could be days before they make it across the river. Won't she, um, you know, start to, uh..." Connie closed her eyes and shuddered.

Stink. Yes, in this heat, a body would begin decomp fast. Air conditioning wasn't enough to preserve a body, never mind we'd likely lose electric service when Hurricane Isabella arrived.

I hadn't checked, but a place like Pennington should have a generator capable of keeping basic utilities going, but even then, we couldn't leave Heather laying on the floor of her bedroom.

"I spoke to Tate just before y'all came back."

"And? What'd he say?"

Poor Connie, the eagerness in her eyes suggested she was waiting on a miracle. I hated to tell her otherwise. "Um, pretty much confirmed what I already knew." I glanced at Dewey.

My brother's behavior was often my cross to bear, but when the chips were down, I knew I could count on him. In fact, I couldn't think of too many other people I'd prefer to be stuck with. Connie was also resourceful and brave; she'd remember that once she shook off her fear.

"Sheriff Felton has unofficially put me in charge of the crime scene."

"What, he deputized you?"

I shook my head. "No Dewey, he can't actually do that—at least I don't think he can—but, no matter, I've been through the police academy. I'm still qualified to be a deputy. He's tasked me with securing the crime scene, taking witness statements, and anything else that arises while official law enforcement is unable to respond."

"So, you're the police."

I smirked at Connie. "Between us three? No, I'm just a citizen same as y'all. But, under the circumstances, we're going to stretch the truth a bit."

"Why?"

"Because Dewey, we've got a killer on this island and something tells me it's one of the people staying at this resort. Better if everyone believes I have the full weight of the law behind me."

He nodded. "That makes sense. Keep everyone in line and stop anyone from trying to take charge."

"Exactly." I smiled at Connie. "Deep down, you know this murder had nothing to do with any curse, right?"

Her nod was hesitant, but I'd take what I could get. I smiled at her. "Good, then we need to put our heads together and figure out who killed Heather."

Connie frowned. "So we're going to investigate? I thought Sheriff Felton just wanted you to preserve evidence."

"He did, but won't we all feel better if we can find the killer? I mean, regardless of where Isabella makes landfall, we're gonna catch a whale of a storm and I sure as heck don't want to be stuck in that mansion with a murderer."

Connie shivered. "No way." She straightened her spine and nodded. "Okay, let's find a killer."

Dewey bobbed his head. "Where do we start?"

With my brother and friend on board, I began to formulate a plan. "Great, I don't think I can do this without y'all. The first thing we need to do is inform the Lyles." I glanced at Connie. She wasn't going to like what had to happen after speaking to management.

"Um, once I've spoken to the Lyles, I'll need to examine the crime scene and, uh ... we're gonna have to find a place to store the body."

As I'd expected, Connie's face turned puce and she was swallowing rapidly. "Hey." She met my gaze and I smiled. "Dewey can help me with that."

Her lips tightened. "No, I can do it. Gotta man up, as they say."

Dewey and I laughed and then I gave my friend a reprieve. "I appreciate your willingness to help, Connie, but you'd be doing me a great favor by getting the names of everyone who is staying at Pennington."

I considered who was working the front desk and figured I'd better keep Gator and Connie far apart. She'd decided to push aside her fears of hoodoo and hexes but I wasn't going to test her resolve. "Get with Felicia Lyle. From what I hear, she is the actual brains of this outfit. Bradley just likes to look important."

Dewey snorted. "Your source is right. Man's full of himself."

I nodded. "Better to keep his involvement to a minimum then, huh?"

"Yep." Dewey got to his feet as a gust of wind bent the live oaks and a flash of lightening lit the sky. We all looked up to see the clouds, backlit by the moon, swirling in a counterclockwise formation.

"Outer bands are moving in." He clapped his hands and tipped his head toward the sidewalk. "Let's get this show on the road, girls. It's do-or-die time." He started toward the path that led to the Lyle family home.

Connie had paled at Dewey's poor choice of words. I gave her a reassuring smile, but I privately thought his words were apt; if we didn't find the murderer soon, it might well be *do or die*.

H olding my tongue, especially amid fools, had never been my strong suit. But, with Connie's warning looks, I was managing—barely.

"Look, all I'm saying is, let's not be hasty. The last thing we want is panicked guests, not to mention how bad a murder on the premises will be for future business!" Quinton Lyle sneered at me. "Are we going to take a decorator's word for it? Perhaps the woman died of natural causes. It's not like she's a doctor."

Felicia Lyle cast an apologetic look my way before gently reprimanding her father. "Daddy, a woman has lost her life. I think it's grotesque to be worried about business at a time like this."

"Oh spare me, Felicia. Dad's right, this is a PR nightmare! I've worked too hard to build this resort's reputation to have it marred by the death of what amounts to a careless victim!" Bradley threw back his shoulders and sniffed. "Now, this is my resort and I'm making the decisions around here. We'll simply keep the room closed and wait for the police." He met everyone's eyes and ordered. "And no one is telling the guests anything more than that the retched woman died!"

"Is that really the best way—"

"Son, maybe it'd be better to—"

All of the Lyles started talking at once, arguing for their method of handling the situation and I reached my limit of patience. Putting my fingers in my mouth, I let loose a piercing whistle that turned all gazes toward me and elicited a snort from my brother.

"Listen up. Heather Franklin did not die of natural causes, unless you can tell me how it's natural for a dagger to find its way into a person's chest?" Felicia gasped and Bradley directed a venomous look my way. With no more comments from the peanut gallery, I continued. "We are dealing with murder. As I stated before, I've spoken to the police, specifically Sheriff Felton and Detective Brannon." I turned and held Bradley's gaze as I continued.

"Contrary to what has been stated, *I* am in charge, per the Sheriff of Noble County. The first order of business will be to examine the body, take forensic samples, and then relocate the deceased to a place suitable to slow decomposition."

Bradley started to object. "Mr. Lyle, the only thing I require of you is the latter. Where can we store Ms. Franklin's body that will maintain a temperature lower than thirty-nine degrees?"

Red faced and sputtering, it took Bradley a few seconds to respond. "Now see here, I'm not letting a *decorator* turn my business into a—"

"Mr. Lyle? As you are aware, I'm a former Noble County sheriff's deputy and the sheriff has given me full authority until emergency services are able to access this island. If you interfere in an active investigation..." I trailed off, letting his imagination fill in the blanks.

I really didn't have the authority to arrest him, but I doubted he'd call my bluff. A pregnant silence settled over the room until Bradley cleared his throat.

"Well of course, ha-ha, no one wishes to obstruct our county's finest doing their job!" His tone was forcibly cheerful.

My smile was tight. "Good. We'll need a cooler to store the body."

Olivia gulped. "Well, there's the restaurant, but our food is stored in there!"

"That will work, but you'll have to find alternate storage for food—"

"But we just received an order yesterday! There's too much to store it all in any regular sized refrigerators. Can't we just leave her in..." Olivia shuddered.

I started to shake my head and insist the body be moved into the restaurant cooler when Felicia hesitantly spoke. "What about the cooler in the barn?"

My eyes widened. I'd never made it into the catering kitchen built into the barn but assumed it would have a smaller fridge. "The barn has a walk-in cooler?"

Felicia nodded. "Yes, and it should be empty now that the reception is over. I can go check if you like."

"Please." I addressed the rest of the Lyle clan. "If the barn's cooler fits the requirements, we'll move Ms. Franklin there when I'm ready."

Quinton Lyle started to speak but I held up my hand. "I'm going back to examine the room and get things ready for the removal process. In the meantime, I'd like someone to accompany Connie to the front desk, or wherever you keep guest records. She's going to make a list of everyone staying at the resort."

I turned to Bradley Lyle. "While we're doing those things, I need someone to make a list of everyone else that is on the property."

He pursed his lips, but grudgingly nodded. "Olivia can handle that. I've got to get hurricane preparations started." He glanced at Dewey. "Since you failed in providing security, perhaps you'll be more useful hanging storm shutters."

Dewey's face flushed. "Look here, ain't none of this my fault! Maybe if ya hadn't tried to rip off the Gullahs you wouldn't a been cursed!"

Oh, not Dewey too! If one more person spouted that crud about curses, I'd scream. Annoyed as I was, the Lyles' reactions were interesting. While Bradley was busy muttering about gullible fools, he flashed a warning look toward his wife.

Olivia flushed scarlet and chewed on a fingernail while the patriarch of the Lyle clan donned a clueless expression and avoided eye contact. Felicia looked bewildered and the baby of the family, Chas, was alert.

While preparing for the wedding, I'd observed the youngest son doing nothing more than lounging by the pool and hitting on pretty women, so I'd dismissed Chas Lyle from the moment I gathered the family. He reeked of liquor and had sat in the corner in a stupor.

Dewey's mention of the Gullahs had brought his head up, and while his expression remained sullen, he was looking at his brother through narrowed eyes. What were the Lyles up to? There was a secret there but unless I found it had bearing on Heather's murder, I'd file it away as merely curious. I had a murder to solve.

"Dewey will be assisting me, Mr. Lyle. I suggest you ask some of your guests to help in the hurricane preparations. Connie, if you'll get that list together?" My friend nodded and I tilted my head toward the door. "Come on, Dewey. Grab some plastic bags and gloves from the kitchen and meet me back at the room."

Calling The Colonel to heel, I left the Lyle family house and took the path back to the hotel. The wind gusts were bending the live oaks and a glance at the river showed white caps of at least three feet.

So far, we'd only gotten wind and a few sprinkles as the outer bands blew in, but a glance at the horizon showed ominous clouds building. I licked my lips and drew a steadying breath as an old saying came to mind—something about ill winds blowing nothing good.

Chapter Seven

I'd had to detour to take The Colonel back to my room and make sure he had enough to occupy himself so I didn't end up with a charge for damages. Dewey was waiting outside the French doors, looking impatient.

He waved a cardboard box at me as I walked across the porch. "'Bout time. These work? Couldn't find nothin' else." He handed the box to me along with a black magic marker. "Grabbed that, too. Figured you'd want to label everything."

"I'm impressed! We'll make a real cop out of you yet."

My brother snorted and pulled on a pair of food service gloves. "No thanks, happy as a rent-a-cop." At my puzzled look he shrugged. "One person in the family with a bullet wound is enough."

He had a point. "Okay, stay out here while I clear a path—oh, and slide these socks over your shoes." I handed him a shrink-wrapped package of herbal infused socks I'd swiped from the spa.

Dewey frowned but did as I'd requested. "What are these for?"

"Keep us from contaminating the scene by bringing something in on our shoes. Ideally, we'd have paper suits, booties, hats..." I finished donning my makeshift forensics suit and shrugged. "This will have to do. You ready?"

"Yeah, what do you want me to do?"

"Bag and tag any evidence I find and keep your eyes peeled for anything suspicious or out of place." Motioning for him to wait, I nudged the French doors open and gingerly stepped over the threshold.

The heart pine floors were worn and scuffed, but scrupulously clean, making anything laying on them stand out like a sore thumb. A cursory inspection yielded nothing suspicious, so I motioned for Dewey to enter and crossed the room to begin documenting the crime scene.

"Tate gave me a brief tutorial in crime scene forensics. First we take pictures, then we bag her hands." I held out my hand. "Give me a few of those bags, will ya?" I tucked two bags into the waistband of my jeans and then pulled out my phone. "I'll photograph the sleeping area; you do the living room side."

We worked in silence. Stifling a sigh at the senseless death, I snapped pictures of the body in situ. Heather had been a beautiful woman; her creamy skin and lush red hair had stopped men in their tracks. Such a shame her future had been cut short.

Shaking off my dreary musings, I got down to business taking pictures of the bed, the nightstand, and dresser. After that, I zoomed in on the body, making sure I showed the wound, the weapon, and the body in relation to the bed and other furniture.

I was just about done when Dewey moved toward the door that led to the hall. I heard his phone click a few times and then he sniffed. "Hey, what's that smell?"

Frowning, I turned. "I don't smell anything." I looked at his feet. "Maybe it's those socks?"

He shook his head. "No, I didn't smell it until I come o'er here."

Stepping closer to him, I sniffed. My nose twitched as I detected a sickly, slightly sweet smell. "What is that?" Dewey shrugged and we both looked around, trying to determine the source. Seeing nothing unusual, I walked around the room, doing a sniff test.

"I only smell it when I'm standing here."

Dewey nodded. "Yeah, me too. It's really strong near this door."

We both frowned and looked closer at the heavy oak door.

"Reckon it's some kind of polish?"

I shook my head and got down on my knees. Starting at the bottom, I sniffed my way up the door. "Huh, the smell gets stronger closer to the doorknob, and it's overpowering right around here." I pointed to the wood surrounding a brass plate that mounted the lock to the door.

When Connie and I had been shown to our room, I'd noticed the odd locking mechanism. Instead of a deadbolt or even a push button handle, the only lock on the main door was a simple latch mounted on a brass plate. To secure the door, you dropped the latch into a bracket mounted on the opposite door frame.

A few good kicks would break such a lock, and I'd been mildly alarmed to find such lax security. I'd contemplated putting a chair beneath the knob, but Connie had teased me for being paranoid, and since we weren't staying in a huge hotel filled with hundreds of random people, I let the matter drop.

Now, I was again concerned for everyone's safety. Heather's murder showed I was right to be. However, her room had been locked. We'd had to gain access via the French doors, which had also been locked, and those doors did have a dead-bolt. So how had the killer gained entry?

I peered at the old brass latch, trying to figure out how someone could have gotten in. "There is only one way someone got into this room that I can see." Dewey quirked an eyebrow. "She had to have known her killer and let them in."

He nodded. "Probably." He looked around the room. "Or maybe there's a secret passageway…"

If the house hadn't been built in the late 1700s, I would have laughed at Dewey's suggestion. But, in those days, natives were still attacking settlements. Pirates also made use of the many barrier islands, and importing and enslaving unwilling people were also risks.

It was entirely possible the original owners had provided an alternate means of escape or just a place to hide. I followed Dewey's gaze, noting the outside wall that held the French doors.

"Well, can't be a secret passageway on that wall..." My gaze moved to the fireplace. "And this is an interior wall. The other side is the hallway. Can't be there."

I tipped my head toward the wall on the other side of the bed. "And that wall backs up against my room. It's possible the builder left a gap between the two rooms and made a passageway."

Dewey walked over and started tapping on the wall. "It's just plaster from what I can tell. Doesn't sound hollow, either."

"Yeah, and the only other wall divides the room from the bathroom. You can check it, but I don't think there's a secret passage in here."

He tapped on the other wall and then shrugged. "Well then, the killer had to have come in through one of these doors. No signs of damage to the doors so, you're right. She must have known whoever it was and let them in."

"Yep, but that leaves the question of how they exited this room and managed to lock the doors from the outside. It's not possible to do that with a deadbolt, so they had to have left via the hallway."

We both focused on the thick oak door with the odd smell.

"It's like you said. They had to have left this way, only how could they lock this thing from the outside? A coat hanger maybe?"

It was a decent theory. Maybe the killer had slid a wire hanger between the door and jamb, hooking the latch and dropping it into place as they pulled the door shut.

I examined the door jamb. "If they'd used a wire hanger, the wood would have scarring. Look how tight the seal of this door is."

"Yeah, it's solid as a rock and tight as a tick." He stood back and shook his head. "I don't think that's how they did it."

"I don't either." Puzzled, I stared at the lock. "There are no scratches on the brass plate, and it stands to reason there would be if they propped it with something."

Dewey walked closer and scratched his head. "What do you mean. Prop the latch with what?"

Continuing to stare at the lock, I shrugged. "That's just it, I don't know what they could have used, but somehow the killer must have lifted the latch, held it in place, and then closed the door, removing whatever the prop was, and making it look like the door was locked from the inside."

"Well, if that's true, there'd be something lying on the floor."

My brother had a point and both of us knelt to search the wooden planks. "I don't see anything—wait, what's this?" I pointed at a scattering of gray particles.

"Ah, that's just dirt." He stood and, with his hands on his hips, surveying the room. "Shouldn't we get her out of here?"

"Yeah, but I don't think this is dirt." I touched the little pile of what looked like dirt and rubbed it between my fingers. It dissolved immediately, leaving a powdery residue on the tips of my gloves. "Dirt would be gritty and it wouldn't crumble into powder."

Dewey huffed. "Then what is it?" He glanced at the door and wrinkled his nose. "Think it has something to do with that weird smell?"

I got to my feet and shrugged. "No idea, but I haven't got time to worry about it." I tipped my head toward the body. "For now, we'll just assume the killer exited through this door and somehow locked it behind them."

I removed the plastic bags from my waistband.

"What are you gonna do with those?"

Squatting next to the body, I carefully lifted her arm and slipped a bag over her hand, pinching the top seal closed around her wrist. "Hopefully, this will preserve anything she might have under her nails."

I quickly did the other hand and then struggled to my feet. "Though I have to wonder if anything we collect will be admissible in court."

Dewey snorted. "Well, why are we doin' it then? Let's just move her out and be done with it."

I rolled my eyes. "Because Dewey, there's a chance a good prosecutor will get it into evidence, and even if it isn't, we might find something that lets *us* solve this murder."

He grudgingly agreed with my reasoning. "Fine, let's just do it then."

No longer concerned about contamination, I began to examine the body, starting with the plastic enclosed hands. Her fingernails were intact and there were no noticeable scratches that might indicate a struggle. I was about to move on when I turned her hand over and noticed a mark. "Hmm, look at this."

Dewey sighed. "Do I have to? This is creepin' me out."

"Oh, get a grip." My brother stepped closer and peered down at the hand I was holding.

"What am I supposed to be looking at?"

"That." I pointed to a pale band running around the third finger of the left hand. "Looks like she was in the habit of wearing a ring." I glanced at Dewey. "Wedding ring, perhaps?"

He frowned. "Maybe ... nah, she wasn't married."

"How do you know that?"

"Well, I guess I ain't sure, but when I was patrollin' I come across her and that guy claimin' to be Christopher Pennington."

"And? What did you see that makes you say she wasn't married?"

He snorted. "They were layin' on a lounge chair by the pool. Well, he was." He tipped his head toward the body. "She was on top of him, kissin' his neck or so it seemed. Gotta say, he didn't look like he was into it." He grimaced. "Not that I blame him. She was pretty and all, but makin' out with your cousin? Nasty."

"Ha, yes it is, but from what I gather, she was adopted by Miriam Pennington's sister and she didn't grow up around here, so they didn't see each other that often."

Dewey's observation was interesting. I'd seen a similar scene with Olivia and Chris. She'd been flirting and Heather had run her off. She'd then done some flirting of her own and just as Dewey said, I hadn't gotten the feeling Heather's advances were welcomed.

Had the two women been competing for Pennington's affections? If so, Olivia had a reason to want Heather out of the way.

Making a mental note to find out where Olivia had been around 11:00 p.m., I turned to my brother. "Dewey, pull the covers off the bed and spread them on the floor. We'll use them to move her when I'm through."

While he prepared a sling to move the body, I set Heather's hands down and continued a cursory inspection of her body. Finding nothing else of note, it was time to do what I'd been dreading.

Dewey returned to the sleeping area and peered down at the body. "Okay, got the blanket laid out, what's next?"

A sour taste filled my mouth as I considered my next move. "Need to remove that dagger and bag it for evidence—"

"Oh, heck no! That's just—"

"I know!" I bent over and reached for the handle of the dagger. "You think I want to pull this thing out? Get another bag and write the date and contents on the front."

While Dewey did as I'd instructed, I sucked in a breath and forced myself to pull the weapon from Heather's chest. It took considerable force to get it free, and by the time I slipped it into the waiting bag my stomach was rolling.

"That was..." I shuddered. "Unpleasant."

Dewey snorted. "Down right gross!" He glanced at the body and frowned. "What's that?"

A glance to where he was pointing made my eyes widen. I'd forgotten about the doll. "Not sure, I noticed it when we broke the door down."

I was pretty sure the object was meant to be an effigy of the deceased but I'd have to clean it off to be sure.

Gulping, I picked it up and groaned. As I'd suspected, the item that had been skewered to Heather was a voodoo doll.

Above me, Dewey gasped. I glanced up to see he'd gone a bit green around the gills and was staring at the body with wide eyes.

"Is that what I think it is?"

"If you're thinking voodoo doll, it is. Hand me another bag." Slipping the sodden doll into the plastic casing. "It's crude, but I think they always are. They've used twine to shape the doll's body. Look, it's coming apart at the shoulder. Doesn't that stuffing look like Spanish Moss?"

"Yeah. Who'd make one of those things and why is it dressed like a bride?"

I blinked and looked at the doll again. What I'd assumed was meant to resemble hair did in fact look like a wedding veil. "This makes no sense; Heather wasn't the bride yesterday."

"You think they killed the wrong person?"

My eyes widened. "Oh Lord, Jeff and Carrie stayed in one of the cottages last night." I shooed Dewey toward the French doors. "We've got to check on them!"

Wide-eyed, Dewey tossed me the box of storage bags and ran. I followed, but with my bum leg I couldn't keep up. Moving as fast as I dared, I contemplated what we'd found.

Not for a minute did I believe the Gullah curse had caused Heather's death. More likely, someone was taking advantage of it to frame the Gullahs. But why a doll dressed like a bride? Was it a message? A warning?

I still needed to look for evidence in the victim's belongings and I hadn't done more than photograph the other side of the room, but at the moment, Jeff and Carrie's safety was all I could think about.

Gray clouds were building again as another band of the storm closed in, adding to my concerns. Our situation was getting worse, and I was at a loss on how to turn the tide so I did the only thing I could. I prayed.

Chapter Eight

I'd arrived to find the happy couple in a mild state of shock. Naturally, they'd been unaware of what was happening in the wider world so Dewey and I brought them up to date and I tried to assure them we were in no immediate danger, from the killer anyway.

Privately, I was in no way confident of that fact, but the storm had already postponed their honeymoon trip; no need to add to their misery.

Dewey and I were passing the barn when he stopped and scratched his head. "Ya know, it's at least another 150 yards to the house. Can we carry her that far?"

My brows rose. I hadn't thought about it. "I can't." I thought a minute and suggested. "Why don't you see if you can borrow an ATV from the resort?"

"Good idea. I'll meet ya back at the house."

Dewey ran off to rustle up some mechanical assistance and I continued to make my way back to the room. Connie intercepted me as I was navigating the stairs to the porch.

"Hey, are you finished in the room?"

"No, had to check on Jeff and Carrie. I'm heading back now." I briefed her on what we'd found so far, hesitating a beat before telling her about the voodoo doll.

"Oh my God! See? I told you there was something to that! "

"Connie, a curse didn't kill Heather." I didn't roll my eyes, but it took effort.

Connie huffed and came to a stop, resting her hands on her hips as she demanded, "Then why the doll? You have to think there's something to that curse now that you've found it!"

I quirked a brow. "Do I?" I snorted and motioned for her to follow me. "Connie, while I do think there can be a psychological effect with this curse mumbo jumbo and some of the herbal mixtures have limited efficacy, that doll was probably planted by the killer to cast suspicion on the Gullahs. It's the only rational explanation."

I gave her a measured stare and waited. Wild-eyed, Connie opened her mouth, floundered for words for a few minutes, and then the fear drained from her eyes and she sighed. "Fine. It was probably like you said. But why frame the Gullahs?"

I shrugged. "Because they made themselves an easy target by pulling that stunt during the reception?" I opened the French doors. "Come on, I'm pretty much done, nothing to contaminate now."

Averting her eyes from the area where Heather lay, Connie perched on the edge of a chair near the fireplace and set a sheaf of papers on the coffee table. "I printed the guest registry. Figured we could use all the other information listed." She shrugged. "Not much here, really. Just names, addresses, and date of their stay."

"It's a start. Thanks for doing that. It'll save time." My gaze settled on the fireplace and I recalled seeing a glow when I'd peered through the doors earlier. I grabbed a poker and rooted around in the small pile of ashes beneath the grate.

"What are you looking for?"

"Not sure." I told her what I'd observed and continued sifting. I saw no signs of charred wood, only bits of paper. Most of whatever had been burned was reduced to ash, but there were a few fragments partially intact. "Hand me one of those plastic bags, will ya? They're on the dresser."

"Sure, but why would someone light a fire in August? It's crazy hot outside." She handed me the bag and watched as I placed the fragments in the evidence bag. "You think the killer did it? Or Heather?"

Hmmm, that was a good question. "You know, I was assuming the killer did it, but could just as easily have been Heather." I turned the bag in several directions. "Guess it depends on what was written on it."

Most of the fragments were plain white paper, but after shaking the bag I noticed writing and some sort of impression on one piece. "Why don't you take this. See if you can figure out what was on it."

She frowned but accepted the bag from me. "I'll have to take them out of here to do that; it'll be like a puzzle." She met my gaze. "Won't that be tampering with evidence?"

The short answer was yes it would be tampering, however, if we were gonna find the killer the paper needed to be examined. It was either a clue to the motive or something irrelevant. We'd never know which category it fell into unless we pieced it together.

She peered into the bag, but I noticed her gaze kept shifting to the other side of the room. I took pity on her. "Why don't you take that back to our room? I'll join you after Dewey and I move ... well you know."

She grimaced and stood. "Okay, thanks. That's just..." she shuddered and walked to the door. "So, you're okay with me touching these?"

I turned from my search of the dresser drawers and considered her question. "Well, I'm guessing any fingerprints would have been burned off by the fire, but I'm no expert. Grab a pair of gloves. Dewey brought some from the kitchen."

She did as instructed and left me to do my task. I'd just located Heather's pocketbook and cell phone when Dewey returned. "You ready to move her?"

I nodded. "Yeah, let me drop this bag off in my room and we'll do it." I crossed the porch, left the purse with Connie, and hurried back. I was dreading the job ahead and the sooner it was over, the better.

A flash of lightening drew my attention to the sky. The outer bands had been coming in waves. Mostly we'd seen brief showers and gusty winds. The sky was darkening quickly, telling me we wouldn't get off so lucky with the next round.

I entered the room and clapped my hands. "Okay, Dewey." I blew out a breath and glanced at the body of Heather Franklin. "You ready?"

My brother gulped. "No, but what choice do I have?"

I grinned and set the evidence bags outside the French doors. "None, but I appreciate you helping me all the same. I've been thinkin' about how we should do this."

I walked over to the bed. "Let's kind of roll her onto the sheet I laid out, then we'll use that to move her to the comforter. Figured the sheet would transfer less fibers and we'll need the strength of the heavier blanket to carry her down the stairs."

"Makes sense." He reached for her legs to help me roll her onto the sheet. I drew a deep breath and bent over. "Okay, on three. One, two…" Rolling a body that neither of us wanted to touch was no easy feat, but with a little elbow grease, Dewey and I managed to get her onto the comforter.

"Gross. I didn't sign up for this."

I rolled my eyes. "She didn't either, Dewey." I studied the next step and realized I'd never be able to tote her down the stairs. "I hate to ask anyone else to do this, but I'm gonna need a strong helper. Let me go ask that Dylan guy if he'll help."

Crossing to the door that led to the hall, I was again brought up short by the strange, sweet smell. Still unsure where it was coming from, I lifted the latch and the brass lever stuck to my gloves.

Frowning, I looked at my fingertips. They were stained light brown and whatever had been on the latch had made my gloved fingers tacky. I pondered what might have caused it for a second but a huff from Dewey sent me scurrying into the hall. I didn't blame him; I was more than ready to be finished.

My worries that Dylan would be hesitant to help us were unfounded. He readily agreed and in short order he and Dewey had Heather's body loaded onto the back of the ATV.

"Thanks so much, we can take it from here."

He smiled. "Hey, no problem. Always happy to help."

A crack of thunder made us all jump. A glance upward showed we'd be getting wet very soon. "Well, we'd best get a move on. Better get back inside. From the looks of those clouds the next round is gonna be a gully washer."

Dylan laughed and pulled a brown and white box from his shirt pocket. It was small and rectangular in shape with strange looking words on the front. I frowned, unable to figure out what it was until he grinned and said, "Yeah, gonna grab a smoke first."

He tucked the box back into his pocket. "This place doesn't allow smoking, but I found a spot over there next to the HVAC to grab a quick one. I call it the leper colony. Talk to you guys later. Let me know if you need any more help!"

"Will do. Can't think of anything I need right now, but with this storm bearing down, Bradley could probably use some help installing the storm shutters."

He lit his cigarette, exhaled a cloud of blue smoke, and nodded. "Sure, I'm in construction so that should be a piece of cake." He looked up and laughed. "Might as well do something besides watch it rain. Came down to play golf but every hole would be a water hazard today!"

"Ah, sorry your vacation is being ruined. Check with the front desk, I'm sure they can tell you where to find Bradley." I waved and hurried to join Dewey in the vehicle. "Those clouds look ready to burst. Let's hurry and get this over with."

Much as I found it distasteful to manhandle her body, Dewey couldn't drive fast enough to suit me. Former cop or not, I'd handled my first dead body. Hopefully, it would be my last.

Chapter Nine

The downpour I'd predicted ended just as Dewey and I finished in the barn. Fortunately as the band of showers swirled off shore, the sun came out, and with it, cloying humidity.

My fondest desire was to shower and then hole up in my air-conditioned room, but The Colonel needed a walk and food, in that order. True to his word, Chef Elijah had prepared a veritable feast for my dog; he'd also set up a buffet for us humans.

Settling The Colonel on the porch with his sweet potato and chicken, I made my way back to the dining room and joined Connie at a communal table.

"Mornin', y'all." I took a seat next to Connie and loaded my fork full of eggs. It was halfway to my mouth when the older gentlemen I'd seen in the hall just before we found Heather started talking.

"Morning! You're the lady that took charge last night, aren't you?" I nodded and he continued. "Appreciate you doing that, but don't suppose you could tell me what all that ruckus was about?"

I deposited my food and chewed while I considered how much to tell him.

The Lyles hadn't wanted to alarm the guests. If we were dealing with hundreds of people I might have agreed, but there were probably less than twenty-five people on the property, and with the police unable to respond to the murder, I figured it was best if everyone was on their guard.

I swallowed my bite and smiled. "As you know, a guest has died."

He nodded. "Yes, I'm sorry to hear that, but what's being done? I haven't seen an ambulance or the police arrive."

Ah ... here was the part where things got tricky. "Um, I'm not sure if you heard but there was a wreck at the base of Goodwin bridge early last evening."

"No, I hadn't heard, but what's that got to do with the death?"

"Nothing, aside from the fact that there is suspected damage to the bridge making it unsafe to use. It's been shut down until engineers can inspect it, and with the storm coming, that is going to be a while."

He nodded, but I could see his wheels turning so I rushed on to forestall further questions. "With the storm approaching, there are marine warnings, making it impossible for the police to respond at this time."

His eyes widened, while his wife gasped. "What? You mean there's a dead body across from my room? How did they die? Is it contagious? What's being done?"

I shook my head. "No, nothing like that and we've moved the body to a secure and cool environment. Ms. Franklin um..." The man and his wife were looking more alarmed by the minute, and I was seriously reconsidering my belief that the guests deserved to know about the murder.

But, as soon as I started questioning them, they'd realize something was amiss and it'd be better to approach potential witnesses without a history of animosity. Which wouldn't happen if I lied to them now.

"Uh, it is my opinion that Ms. Franklin was the victim of foul play—"

"Foul ... murdered! Is that what you're saying? Some woman was murdered across the hall from us?" He grabbed his wife's hand and started to rise. "Come on, Maude, we're leaving."

"Sir..." I motioned for him to resume his seat. "While I understand your desire to leave, there isn't anywhere for you to go. You can't leave the island, and there are no other accommodations out here."

The man's wife looked ready to jump out of her skin. She was clinging to his arm and gnawing at her lower lip. He was pale but sank back onto his seat and patted her hand absently before swallowing a few times and finding his voice.

"Well that's, that's ... you mean to tell me we're stuck out here with a killer?" His voice got louder as he continued. "Where's the manager? What are they doing to protect us?" He again started to get to his feet. "Come on, Maude. I want a word with someone in charge!"

I cleared my throat and stood, reaching across the table to extend my hand. "Hello, I'm former Deputy Sheriff Holly Daye."

I'd deliberately mentioned my former occupation and it had the intended effect. The man shook my hand and then sat down. "Walter Randall, this is my wife Maude. You said you're law enforcement?"

"Yes, I was a Noble County sheriff's deputy for over two decades." He started to interject but I beat him to any further questions. "I'm retired, but I've spoken to Sheriff Felton and the county's detective. They've asked me to take charge of the scene and gather witness statements. Everything is under control, Mr. Randall, and I'll let you know if it's time to start worrying, okay?"

He stared at me for several seconds before relaxing. "Yes, yes, I can see that you're a capable sort, but do you think we're in any danger?"

Oh, how to answer that? "Well, yes and no. I don't think this killing was random, which means the threat to everyone else is low. However, I advise being on your guard. My brother Dewey is an employee of Sentinel Security. He's patrolling the grounds, and my best friend and business partner here is Connie Rogers." I tipped my head toward Connie, who gave a little wave. "I'm not going to tell you we are the only ones at the resort you can trust, but…"

Walter nodded. "Understood. Nice to meet you, Miss Rogers."

Connie grinned. "Oh, call me Connie!" Her gaze roamed over him for a second. "For so early in the morning you look hot and tired. Can I get you a cold drink?"

He chuckled. "No thanks, that tea you'ins drink is too sweet for me! The manager asked for volunteers so I've been out putting up storm shutters." He chuckled. "This heat is brutal! I don't know how you stand it!

I smiled. "We locals are used to it. Appreciate y'all helping out. From what I'm seeing on the radar, the eye is going to stay offshore, but we're on the right side of the storm so it's gonna get rough, but we're prepared. What brought y'all down? Did you get to enjoy any of our beautiful area before this mess blew in?"

He laughed. "Ha, stupid me thought I'd bring my blushing bride of fifty years down here to celebrate our anniversary." He laughed again and shook his head. "I'm never gonna hear the end of that decision!"

We all laughed and Connie smiled. "Congratulations! Sorry your plans have been scuttled. Where are y'all from?"

The change in conversational topics seemed to have relaxed Maude a bit. She found her voice and managed to put on a shaky smile. "We're from Mars."

Connie blinked. "Um, where?"

Walter laughed and squeezed his wife's hand. "Good to see you getting your sense of humor back, sweetheart." He turned to Connie. "Maude's way of a joke. Always makes people wonder if they're talking to a mental patient." He chuckled. "We're from Mars, PA. Just north of Pittsburgh."

Connie laughed. "Ah, had me wonderin' for a second! Welcome to the Lowcountry, we're glad to have you and sorry for Isabella. We didn't invite her!"

Maude's smile was weak. "It can't be helped, but, um..." She glanced at me. "What did you mean about the eye and something about being on the right?"

I swallowed another mouthful of eggs before replying. "You know there's an eye to a hurricane, right?" Maude nodded. "Well, hurricanes are circular storms, they rotate counterclockwise, in this hemisphere anyway. The eye is the calm center around which the winds swirl. Since they move in a leftward rotation, the section with the most strength is the upper right quadrant. That's going to at least brush by us as it moves north and that's problematic, especially for us."

I'd tried to temper my explanation so as not to raise fears, but judging by Maude's wide eyes I wasn't successful. She swallowed a few times and gulped tea before asking. "Um, problematic? What does that entail and why is it worse for us?"

Oh, more tricky questions. I needed to be careful in how I answered. Maude seemed the nervous sort. "Um, Isabella is clocking winds of seventy-three miles per hour last I checked. It's off the coast of Georgia and will reach us by tonight or early Monday. We've already seen some of the outer bands."

Maude nodded. "Yes, I was watching the television earlier. They were saying it's expected to increase?"

I flashed a tight smile. "Yes, there's a front that is expected to feed the storm a bit. Whether it does or not, we'll probably see sustained winds over seventy when that eye wall rolls past."

She gasped. "Are we safe? Will the house collapse?"

And that was why I hadn't wanted to explain. I sighed. "This house has survived much stronger storms over the past couple of hundred years. It'll likely be just fine. The resort keeps the trees limbed and there are none close enough to hit us should they fall. The winds will be fierce, but the danger is less from direct damage than it is storm surge."

"Wh-what's that?" She stuttered and her hands shook slightly as she took another sip of tea.

"It's when the wind pushes water toward the shore. We've seen storm surges up to twelve feet before, especially when there is also a high tide. Storms like this are worse for us. We're called the Lowcountry for a reason. We flood when it's just heavy rainfall. Isabella will dump a lot of water, and added to the storm surge..."

Maude went pale and looked ready to faint. Her husband wrapped her in a hug. "Maudie, we'll be fine. It's like she said, this place has been around for hundreds of years. It'll be okay, right Holly?"

Judging by Maude's reaction to my explanation of hurricanes and their impact, I should have agreed with her husband. However, my conscience wouldn't allow me to lie. I did try to soften the impact of the truth though.

"We'll probably weather the storm just fine, yes." Maude visibly relaxed and I almost stopped there. But there was that pesky inner voice again demanding I tell the truth. "But we will almost certainly see flooding, trees down, and power outages."

"There, you see Maude? Nothing to worry about, it'll be just like a bad thunderstorm at home."

I'd kept my tone light and matter of fact, delivering the truth without varnish, but Walter Randall chose to interpret my statements in such a way that he downplayed what was heading our way. In good conscience, I should have contradicted him, but I fought the urge. I'd relayed the information, what they did with it was on them.

The front door slammed, bringing me out of my musings. Dylan strolled into the dining room, looking carefree if a little wilted. "Morning everyone." He tipped his head toward me. "You get everything sorted?"

"Yes, thanks again for your help. I know it wasn't pleasant."

"No problem, happy to help." He glanced at Walter. "Speaking of help. You ready to get back to it? I watched an update on the storm. Seems to have slowed down a little and we might be worrying for nothing, but still best to have those storm shutters up."

Walter nodded. "Absolutely! I'll be along in just a minute."

Dylan nodded, grabbed a bottle of water, and left. Walter waited until the front door slammed before turning to me. "Appreciate you setting my wife's mind at ease, Holly." He winced. "You said we'll lose power. What will we do for food? And this heat, God I'm not relishing the thought of being stuck in here with no air conditioning and unable to open a window!"

"Power lines will almost certainly come down, but I checked with Bradley Lyle. The rest of the resort will lose power, but the main house is wired to a generator. We'll have water, lights, and blessed air conditioning."

His eyes lit up and a smile stretched across his face. "Well, thank a benevolent Lord. Guess we'll just sit back and have ourselves one of those hurricane parties!"

I smiled at his bluster. I was about to tell him that generator or no, riding out Isabella would be no party, but he patted his wife's back and headed for the door. "Whelp, best hightail it out there." He shook his head and chuckled. "That Dylan kid, nice and all, but he doesn't know one end of a screwdriver from another!"

I shared a laugh with Walter, but as he left my brow furrowed. Something he'd said was bugging me ... I was trying to figure it out when Connie cleared her throat and raised her eyebrows.

"What is it?"

She glanced in Maude's direction, then tipped her head toward the hall and rose. What was up with her? Puzzled, I trailed behind and got my answer.

"Are you ready to look at the registration list? We don't have much time before Isabella blows in."

I sighed. I'd had less than four hours of sleep. Coupled with the stress of dealing with a dead body, I was exhausted both mentally and physically, but Connie was right.

Being stuck in the house with a murderer on the loose made my skin crawl. We needed to find the killer before the storm hit, and even if Isabella had slowed, time was running out.

Chapter Ten

Ushering him into the library, I settled The Colonel by the air conditioning vent and plopped onto the sofa to wait for Connie to retrieve her list from our room. The cool leather and soft cushions had lulled me and I jerked to attention when she closed the door.

"Ha, caught you catnapping!"

Yawning, I pulled myself upright and motioned for her to join me. "Yeah, I'm beat. But let's get this show on the road. Who knows? Maybe we can solve this thing quickly and I can get some sleep before the storm hits."

Connie snorted and set the registration list on the coffee table. "Nothing like blind optimism." She pointed to a short stack. "Okay, this is the list of guests registered at the resort and those are the people that live on the grounds permanently."

Leaning over, I scanned the list. "I'd forgotten about Pennington village. Currently, there are five cottages occupied there?"

Connie nodded. "Yes, Chef Elijah Jones and his sister Daphne share a house. She is an aesthetician employed at the spa. Then there's Gator's place, up until yesterday he worked in the main house. Then there's Peter Kent, he's Felicia Lyle's fiancée and the golf pro. Another is shared by three maids, Charise Acton, Joanie Manson, and um, I can't remember the other woman's name..."

"Says Tameka Harris. I've only seen one housekeeper. Are all three ladies here now?"

Connie shook her head. "They're supposed to be, but Tameka was off Saturday and went into Sanctuary Bay. She can't get back, obviously. Charise works in the main house, and Joanie floats but usually is in the laundry and spa."

"Okay, who lives in the other cottage?"

Connie gulped. "Auntie Pearl, the Gullah root doctor."

My brows rose. That was something I hadn't known. Pennington Village had originally been the slave quarters for the plantation. After emancipation, many of the Gullahs had moved to nearby Saint Marianna Island and developed a thriving community, but a few families had stayed with the Penningtons.

Those families had passed their cottages down for generations, so I wondered why Auntie Pearl was living in one. To my knowledge, she'd never worked for the Penningtons. So how had she come to have a home there?

Auntie Pearl residing in Pennington Village did explain why she was seldom seen in Sanctuary Bay anymore; the village was remote. Bordered by marsh on one side and acres of agricultural fields on the others. It was curious, but since I didn't think the root doctor and her curse had anything to do with the murder, it was not worth my time. I also didn't need Connie dwelling on her superstitious fears.

"Good work. Grab a pen and paper and let's make a list."

Connie dug in her purse for something to write with, reminding me I still needed to look in Heather's handbag. I'd do it after we compiled our suspect list.

"Ready." Connie scribbled across the top of the paper. "Do you want to make a T-list with all the names and then we can figure out motives and stuff?"

"Sounds like a plan. Start with Christopher Pennington."

Connie's eyes widened. "Are you thinking he's suspect number one or are you just throwing names out?"

I cocked my head to the side and considered her question. Until she'd asked, I was just listing the people that had been on our floor the night of the murder but now... "It's a bit of both." She frowned and I explained. "The guests staying on our floor would be the most logical suspects because their presence could be explained, should anyone had seen them near Heather's room. But, Christopher, or the man claiming to be him, has a strong motive."

"For killing the woman who was going to vouch for his identity?" She shook her head. "I don't follow."

"Well, let's say he *isn't* the rightful heir, and that Heather and he had conspired to lie so that he could inherit and presumably share the wealth. So, if that was their plan, and then for some reason Heather backed out..." I shrugged. "I don't know, ignore me. I'm tired."

Connie shook her head. "No, no. It's definitely possible. I mean, she was the one who claimed he *was* Chris Pennington. He doesn't remember, or so he claims. Is there any other way of proving he is the heir?"

There were several ways, all would take varying degrees of time, and, in the case of one option, expense. "Yeah, DNA testing would be the most obvious method. In fact with Heather dead, that will likely be the executor's next step." The Colonel snuffled in his sleep and moved so his head was resting on my foot. I patted his head as I worked through my theory.

"But both of Christopher's parents are dead. Miriam was cremated. His father has been gone for over a decade. He's buried in the family plot I believe. With Miriam nothing but ashes, I'm guessing they'll have to exhume the body, and that takes a court order. So, like I said, it'll take time."

Connie nodded. "Well, is there a rush to prove he's Chris Pennington?"

"Maybe? Lots of money went into renovations here, and there are a lot of expansions in development stages. Then there is the shipping company. Millions of dollars at stake and the Lyles want control of it. Not sure what Christopher thinks, but if I were him, I'd want this settled quickly, before the Lyles can run through any more of his money. The clock is also ticking in regard to Miriam's will."

"What about it?"

"Mama told me, and I have no idea how she knows this but you know Mama and her grapevine, she's probably right!" Connie laughingly agreed. "Anyway, Mama said the will gave the executor six months from the date of her death to find her son.

After that, it all goes to Quinton Lyle and, through him, his kids. Miriam died in late April. It's August now, so you do the math."

"Ah, I see what you mean." We both fell silent for a few seconds, then Connie frowned. "You know, based on what you said about that will, the Lyles have a big, as in millions of dollars, reason to want Heather out of the picture."

She was right, and I had thought of that. "Yes, number two on the list has to be Bradley Lyle."

Connie scribbled his name. "If you're listing them in order of suspicion, shouldn't Quinton be next? He's the one that will actually inherit if the heir isn't confirmed."

I nodded. "True, but Quinton is an aging playboy. He likes the good life that marrying money provided, but he wasn't poor before hooking up with Miriam. Granted, owning a couple of strip malls isn't in the same league as the Pennington fortune, but he could furnish his lifestyle off the rental income. Probably wouldn't leave much for his kids, but he doesn't strike me as the type to care."

"Ah, I didn't realize he had money of his own." She glanced at her list. "So, Chris then Bradley." She cocked her head to one side. "Why him over the other Lyles?"

"Simple, he thinks of himself as a hotelier extraordinaire. It's not just the money with Bradley, it's his identity."

"Good point. The man is, how did Dewey say it? Full of himself."

"Exactly. Now, just below Bradley, I'd say his wife has a strong motive." I waited until Connie had added Olivia's name before elaborating. "Just like her husband, Olivia struts around here playing lady of the manor. From what I noticed during the week leading up to the wedding, she walked around looking busy, but never actually did much. She likes to feel important, but she's also a high maintenance woman. Designer clothes, fancy sport car ... I don't think Olivia is planning to lose her place at Pennington, regardless of the outcome with the heir."

Connie's brows rose. "What do you mean? You think Chris is in danger, too?"

"What?" I cottoned on to her meaning and shook my head. "No, I didn't mean she'd kill him, though she might have killed Heather. I saw her putting the moves on Chris yesterday and Heather ran her off, that's where I got the notion Heather was also after Chris in more than a cousinly way. I also interrupted an argument between Bradley and Olivia while decorating the church. From what I overheard, I think Olivia is after Chris. If Bradley remains the owner of Pennington, she'll stay with him but, if not..."

Connie chuckled. "Man, she's a real piece of work. I'll put a star by her name. Who's next?"

I shrugged. "Felicia and Chas have the same motive as all of the Lyles, but they aren't high on my list."

"Chas is almost always drunk. I don't think he'd put that much energy into keeping the gravy train rolling."

"Ha, very true. I've thought the same, and Felicia? I don't know. She's sweet, efficient ... the opposite of her family. She could be fooling me, but instinct says she's genuine."

"Yes, she's really nice. We worked together on that fundraiser for the animal shelter. I can't see her killing anyone, especially in such a brutal way."

"Agreed but keep her on the list. The Lyles have the most motive, at least they do if this is about the inheritance of Pennington."

Connie quirked a brow. "You don't think it is?"

Did I? It was the million-dollar question. "Honestly? It's the most likely reason, but then there's the doll."

Connie's brows shot up. "But you said..."

I sighed. "Yes, I know what I said and I stand by that. A curse didn't kill Heather."

"Then why—"

"However," I interrupted. "Someone wants us to think this is about a curse. Question is, who and why?"

Connie shrugged. "To get attention off the real reason."

"Exactly. Trouble is, we haven't figured out what that is. When we do, we'll have our killer."

"So we need to figure out the motive. How are we gonna do that?"

It was a good question—a very good question. Using the approaching storm as a deadline meant the clock was ticking. If we didn't uncover the truth in a few hours, we'd be stuck inside a house with a killer. "Let's finish compiling the list of suspects, assign working motives for each, and then we'll start interviewing them. If we divvy up the list, we'll make better time."

Her brows rose. "You want me to help you talk to suspects?"

Her shocked tone made me blink. "Yeah, I thought you wanted to help. Are you not comfortable with that?"

She rushed to explain her hesitation. "No, it's not ... I'm just surprised you want me to do that. I'm not law enforcement, where would I start?"

"No need for training. You'll just talk to them, start a conversation. You're good at that."

Her expression showed her skepticism but she nodded anyway. "Okay, if you think I can do it…" Connie looked down at her list. "So we have the Lyle family and Christopher Pennington. Anyone else?"

"Go ahead and write down the names of staff. I don't see any motive for one of them to be the killer, but we have to eliminate them. Besides, staff notice things others miss. They might be unaware that they know something relevant."

"Sounds good. Ready to get started?"

She started to rise but I shook my head. "Not yet, we need to add the guests, especially the ones staying on that floor."

She frowned but started to write. "Surely you don't think that nice old couple had anything to do with this?"

"Nothing suggests they have any reason to, but we have to cover all bases." She finished jotting down the guest names and I reached for the paper.

As I'd asked, Connie had listed Pennington and the Lyles first, then the staff, followed by the guests. I grabbed her pen and marked off Jeff and Carrie Pope. The newlyweds hadn't been in the main house and Dewey and I had already talked to them. It didn't mean they hadn't seen or heard something pertinent to the case, but with time running out, I'd leave them until last.

If the Pennington inheritance was at the heart of Heather's murder, Chris and his stepfamily were the prime suspects, and Connie's writing had conveniently kept their names at the top of the page. I folded it in half and used the edge of the table to tear it in two.

"Here's your half, ready to get to work?"

She accepted her sheet and drew a deep breath. "Ready as I'll ever be, I guess." She scanned the names and then met my gaze. "How do I start? I mean, what should I say?"

"Be friendly, keep your tone light and casual. Just tell them you're helping me take witness statements and need to ask them a few questions."

She frowned and nibbled at her bottom lip. "Okay, but what are the questions?"

Snapping my fingers for The Colonel to get up, I made my way to the door. "Start by asking them where they were around 11:00 p.m. last night, then, depending on how they answer, just play it by ear."

"*Just play it by ear.*" She snorted. "Easy for you to say." She slid past me and headed for the kitchen. "Here goes nothing. Wish me luck!"

I waved and stepped onto the porch. The whirring sound of an electric drill merged with the men's voices as they rushed to complete the installation of the storm protection before we were faced with Isabella's wrath.

Hooking The Colonel's leash onto his harness, I set off down the path that led to the Lyle family home. Gusts of wind bent the live oaks, and the river was choppy. The bands of the storm were increasing as the hurricane drew closer.

Looking south, I could see charcoal clouds hovering oppressively over the distant point of Hilton Head Island; we'd see another heavy rain shower within the hour, and soon the rain would become constant. Connie's request for good wishes rightfully extended to all of us stranded on the tip of Belle Isle; very soon, we were gonna need all the luck we could get.

Chapter Eleven

Pennington Place Plantation had been the home of the Pennington family since the 1700s and at one time, the family had many members. Some illustrious ancestor must have needed more space or didn't like some of their relations because some time in the 1920s, another home had been constructed on the north end of the property.

When Miriam Pennington decided to turn the original manor house into a hotel, her family had been relocated to the massive art deco style house. A white monolith with oddly placed windows and minimal decorative trim, the locals called it the white elephant; I just thought of it as an eyesore.

Knocking on the door, I waited for several minutes before Chas opened the door. He muttered a halfhearted greeting and swept his arm for me to enter. I was about to explain the reason for my visit when he walked across the glaringly white foyer, calling over his shoulder.

"Dad's in the lounge."

I snorted. Apparently, I was expected. I followed him to find Quinton Lyle nursing what looked like whiskey. He glanced up when I entered the room and rolled his eyes.

"What is it now? Can't a man drink in peace?"

My lip curled in disgust. It was barely ten o'clock and the man was slurring his words. He had a resort full of guests facing a Cat 1 hurricane and his answer to securing the property and ensuring the safety of his guests was to get drunk.

Based on what I knew of Quinton, I couldn't say I was surprised. Feeling nothing but disgust and eager to escape his presence, I decided to get straight to the point.

"Mr. Lyle. Where were you, between ten and eleven Saturday night?"

His only reply was a grunt into his half-empty glass. Gritting my teeth, I asked again. "Quinton! Can you verify your whereabouts at the time of Ms. Franklin's death?"

Bleary eyed, he met my gaze. "I'm a suspect then?" A sneer marred his handsome, if dissipated, face. "Do you know who I am?"

Pompous little man. I gritted my teeth and managed to maintain a professional demeanor I was far from feeling. "Yes, you're a man who stands to inherit millions if the rightful heir to the Pennington fortune isn't found by the end of this month. Heather testifying on behalf of her cousin threatened your bank account. I'll ask you again, where were you?"

He snorted and drained his glass, before slamming it onto the coffee table. "Interfering busybody, just like that mother of yours. I ought to—"

"Dad! That's enough. He was with me, Ms. Daye."

Surprised, I turned to see Chas rising from a wing backed chair set before the fireplace. I thought he'd left after showing me into the room. Sleep deprivation was getting to me. I gave myself a mental shake for being so careless. Under the circumstances, my lack of situational awareness could be dangerous.

"I see, and where would that be, Mr. Lyle?"

He smirked and saluted me with his martini glass. "In the bar, of course."

"I see." There were a million things I wanted to say to Chas, all of them pertaining to the path leading to alcoholism and a wasted life he seemed determined to follow. However, I wasn't the young man's parent and I had more pressing concerns. "Can anyone verify that you and your father were in the bar?"

He shrugged and rose to top off his glass. "Doubt it. Bradley sent all of the nonresident staff home after the four o'clock storm update. Dad and I had to serve ourselves."

He made it sound like such a chore. I was sure I'd be forgiven for my lack of sympathy to their plight. Quinton's behavior irritated me, his reputation for being an arrogant jerk preceded him.

His son, however, hadn't been alive long enough to earn a similar one. I recalled the look he'd given his older brother when Dewey had accused him of ripping off the Gullahs.

I wasn't sure if that accusation had any bearing on my case, but the mere fact that mentioning it had brought Chas out of his stupor suggested there was hope for him. I decided to take a different tack. My mother was not only the queen of gossip. She was also a master at shaming people into compliance. I was not her daughter for nothing.

"Mr. Lyle, you don't seem to be taking this situation seriously. A woman, not much older than you, has lost her life. The least you could do is take my questions seriously."

He glared at me for a moment, his lower lip thrust out. When I didn't respond he sighed and dropped his gaze to the floor. "Fine, Dad and I were drinking in the hotel bar. We started around eight and I poured him into bed a little after ten-thirty, happy?"

I quirked a brow. "And what did you do once your father was safely tucked in?"

He snorted and shook his head. "You don't give up, do you." It was a rhetorical question, but the answer was no, I didn't concede ground, especially when a life was taken and people were at risk from an unknown perpetrator.

A slight uplift of his lips told me he'd received my silent answer. "If you must know, I went to the pool house."

"You went swimming?"

He shook his head. "Nah, it was raining. The pool house is set up as a game room." He shrugged. "I shot a few rounds of pool, drank enough to keep the nightmares away, and fell asleep on the couch."

His answer had the ring of truth to it, but I had to confirm. "So you slept in the pool house?" He nodded. "Any idea what time that was? Can anyone confirm that you were there all night?"

"The news was just going off so, about eleven-thirty?" He shrugged. "I was alone, so the answer to your second question is no—wait." He frowned and stared at the wall behind me. "I remember hearing something outside just before I passed out."

"You heard something. The wind? We had some powerful gusts as outer bands rolled through..."

Chas shook his head. "I know, that's why I got up. Thought maybe some of the pool furniture was blowing around, you know?"

I nodded. "So you went outside and checked?"

He snorted. "Nah, I could barely stand. I managed to make it to the window, though." His brow furrowed. "I remember looking at the lounge chairs. One was tipped over and I was about to go back to the couch when something moved by the dock."

My eyes widened. Finally, we were getting somewhere. "What was it? A person?"

He closed his eyes, a look of deep concentration on his face. "I saw something arc through the air and land in the water but..." Chas opened his eyes and dragged a hand through his hair. "Sorry, it's all a blur. I was pretty wasted at the time."

I nodded. "That's all right, we'll check it out. What can you tell me about Heather?"

He snorted. "That I didn't kill her."

In no mood for his sarcasm, I pursed my lips. "That remains to be seen, but did you have any contact with the victim? Know anything about her?"

Chas snorted. "Apart from her liking men you mean?"

I frowned. "What?" I frowned, trying to follow his train of thought. Coming up empty, I demanded. "Mr. Lyle, I've had less than four hours of sleep and no patience for games. Explain that remark, please."

A smirk twisted his lips and he shrugged. "Nothing, except she seemed to be loose with her favors, if you know what I mean." At my pointed look he held up his hands in a defensive gesture. "Okay, okay. I never talked to her, but I saw her making a play for Chris—"

"We don't know for sure he's that rotten kid!"

Chas glanced at his father and rolled his eyes. "Whatever Dad. The chick was all over the guy that *claims* to be Chris Pennington, happy now?" Chas looked at me and shrugged. "I saw her in the clubhouse having drinks with Peter Kent, too." He waggled his eyebrows. "They were pretty friendly, you know?"

Interesting insinuations and I could verify his statements as to Heather and Chris. Making a mental note to tell Connie, I thanked Chas and walked toward the door. "By the way, you wouldn't happen to know where I can find your sister, do you?

"Felicia? Probably still at the spa. She tried to get me to help her do storm prep on the place this morning."

Making no comment on his lack of courtesy toward his sister, I focused on my next destination. It was fortuitous. Daphne Jones also worked at the spa, perhaps I could kill two birds with one stone and save Connie a trip. "Thanks for your help, Chas. If you remember anything else—"

"I'll let you know." He glanced at his father, now slumped in his chair with his chin resting on his chest. "Come on Dad, let's get some coffee and sober up. There's a hurricane coming, time to make ourselves useful."

From the sounds of it, Chas was planning to become a contributing member of society, if only for a moment. A fact that left me feeling a bit lighter, despite the gravity of the situation we were facing.

Placing a call to Dewey, The Colonel and I set off on the path that led to the spa and fitness center. The phone rang several times and I was just about to end the call when my brother came on the line.

"Yeah? What is it?"

I rolled my eyes but refrained from scolding him on his manners. "Where are you?"

He snorted. "Hiding from Bradley."

I laughed. "What's he done now?"

"Ah, nothing, just trying to get me to help with the storm prep. I keep tellin' him I was brought in for security, but the man thinks hiring me gives him the right to work me to death. I'm making my rounds and trying to stay out of his sight. Did you need somethin'?"

"Yes." I relayed what Chas had told me. "So, it may have been the hallucinations of a drunk, but if you could look around by the dock while you're patrolling, I'd appreciate it."

"No problem. I'm by the storage sheds, but I can go along the river next. Any idea what I'm looking for?"

"Nope, not a clue. If someone *was* down there though, and they *did* throw something in the river ... it's possible it didn't get hauled off by the current."

"Gotcha. I'll call if I find anything."

Dewey ended the call but his mentioning hurricane preparations reminded me that the clock was ticking in more ways than one. I coaxed The Colonel into a trot and arrived at the spa to find the shutters in place and no lights on inside. I was about to go back to the main house when I heard a crash followed by a curse. The sound had definitely come from inside the spa.

Housed in a Lowcountry style home with a wide front porch and double front doors, the spa was situated in a glade surrounded by towering live oaks. It's isolation from the main resort made it a perfect place to unwind and find inner peace.

Mounting the steps, I crossed the porch and knocked on the front door. When no one answered, I turned to the windows. The shutters were designed to allow minimal light to come through, but they stopped flying debris. It also stopped prying eyes.

After peering through a front window and being unable to see more than indistinct shapes and shadows, I gave up and pounded on the front door. I did this several times and finally, Daphne appeared.

Covered in something greasy and holding pieces of broken glass, she opened the door and frowned. "I'm sorry, we're closed until the storm passes. You can call and leave a message if you want to make an appointment. Daphne started to shut the door and I put my foot between the door and the jamb.

"Hold on, please. I'm Holly Daye and I need to speak to you and Felicia, if she's still around."

Daphne pursed her lips. "I know who you are. You're trying to figure out who killed that woman. What do you want with me?"

Hostility was rolling off her in waves, and for the life of me, I couldn't think why. I'd never formally met her and hadn't accused her of anything. What reason did she have for being rude?

Irritated but falling back on the old adage about flies and honey, I pasted a bright smile on my face. "That's right, Sheriff Felton has asked me to take witness statements and hold the fort until the police can reach us. Can I come in? I promise it won't take a minute."

"I didn't see anything." Her tone was still surly, but she stepped back and held the door wider. I counted it a small victory. Ignoring me, Daphne opened a treatment room door and dropped whatever she'd broken into the trash can. She took her time, and I was tapping my foot when she finally returned, wiping her hands on a towel.

"Get on with it, then."

My brows rose. Could she be any ruder? Suppressing the urge to call her on her lack of civility, I forced myself to smile. "I just need to find out where everyone was around 11:00 p.m. last night." My smile never wavered but I watched her closely. Daphne scowled and looked at a point over my shoulder. "Told you, I didn't see anything. Felicia's in her office." She pointed toward the back of the house and started back to the treatment room.

"Ms. Jones? I wasn't finished talking with you."

With a huff, she jerked to a stop and turned to look at me, well at something behind me, because she still wouldn't meet my gaze. "But I was." When I continued to stare at her, she rolled her eyes and finally looked directly at me. "What do you want to know? I told you I didn't—"

"Yes ma'am, I heard that. However, I understand you live on the Pennington property, so I need to know where you were last night around 11:00 p.m."

If possible, the scowl on her otherwise pretty face deepened. She added a curl of her lip and I received the unspoken message loud and clear. She held me in contempt. That was her prerogative, but I wasn't backing down.

Our gazes locked and we stood for several seconds in a silent battle of wills until finally, Daphne sighed. "I got tings to do."

She'd lapsed into the singsong dialect of her Gullah roots. I was getting to her. "As do I. Simple question, Daphne. Where were you last night?"

What was it they said about looks killing? If there were any truth to that adage, I'd be meeting my maker. As it was, Daphne nearly snarled her answer. "Ain't none of your business, but I was visitin' a friend in the village."

The village was located on the edge of the plantation. If she was truly visiting, it could only be one of a few people, and judging by her hostility, I strongly suspected the identity of her friend. Still, I had to confirm my hunch.

"Then that friend can verify your whereabouts. Who were you with?"

Once again, Daphne avoided my gaze and for a moment I thought she'd refuse to answer. I was about to press her when she rolled her eyes and huffed. "I was with Auntie Pearl, okay?" She snorted. "Question her. If you dare..."

With that, Daphne walked into the treatment room, slamming the door behind her.

I shook my head at her implied threat. Did the woman really think I'd be cowed? She obviously didn't know me well.

Chapter Twelve

Shaking off my irritation with Daphne's behavior, I stomped through the spa until I located Felicia's office—a cramped space tucked beside the laundry room. She was hunched over a pile of papers when I knocked on the half-open door.

Seeing me, she set her pencil down and rose to greet me. "Holly! What brings you here? I'm afraid we aren't offering any treatments until the storm passes."

Smiling, I entered the room and perched on the edge of a chair. The Colonel trotted over to Felicia and threw up his paw, demanding to be pet. If I hadn't already thought Felicia was the good Lyle, The Colonel confirmed it—no better judge of character than a dog.

"While I'd dearly love a day of pampering, that's not why I'm here." Felicia cocked her head to the side, a puzzled look in her eyes. "I'm taking witness statements."

Her eyes widened. "Oh, that's right! I'd forgotten you were going to do that." She laughed. "Sounds silly to say you've forgotten when a woman is dead. But I've been so busy with the spa and now Olivia's ignoring her responsibilities." She sighed. "Sorry, I don't mean to whine." She pasted a bright smile on her lips and straightened in her chair. "Don't mind me. How can I help?"

"No problem, I've seen how hard you work around here. I won't take more of your time than necessary; I just need to know where you were around 11:00 p.m. last night."

She frowned. "Um, Saturday night around eleven? Let's see. Joanie laid out, so I was stuck doing the laundry. I also had to finish inventorying the delivery because Olivia claimed a migraine and went to bed ... it was after midnight before I left here."

I nodded. "Okay, so you were working in the spa until midnight?" Felicia nodded. "Did anyone see you? Where did you go when you left?"

Her eyes widened. "Um, I was alone, but I did take a break when Peter called. That was around ten? I went home after I finished."

"Thanks. That's Peter Kent, your fiancée?"

Her lips twisted into a mockery of a smile. "Yes and no." At my puzzled look, she laughed. "Yes, I sat on the porch and chatted with Peter for about twenty minutes and no, he isn't my fiancée."

I blinked. "Oh, someone said you were engaged."

Felicia snorted. "They probably heard it from Peter. He's been rather free with that information." She must have noticed my confusion because she added. "He's asked, I've not replied."

"Ah ... playing hard to get?"

"Hardly," She chuckled. "He's nice enough, certainly handsome and he can be fun, but I'm not sure he's marriage material, if you know what I mean?"

I could infer any number of reasons for her statement but I was looking for background on every suspect so I shook my head. "Not really. Weren't you dating?"

She grinned. "Oh yes, we've dated for over six months. Like I said, he's charming and knows how to show a girl a good time."

"Then what's the problem?"

"I've grown up with a father who over imbibes, and my baby brother is a terrible womanizer." Felicia shrugged. "I have no desire to marry someone with those qualities."

I tipped my head in salute. "Smart lady."

Felicia chuckled. "I try."

I laughed and then redirected the conversation. "So you were on the porch talking to Peter around 10:30?" She nodded. "And you said he called you. Was he at home?"

Felicia's brow furrowed. "Um, I think so. He said he was watching golf and I heard clapping in the background."

I'd have to check with Connie to see if their stories lined up but as of now, neither was a strong suspect. Felicia had mentioned sitting on the porch during her phone call. The path from the main house to the Lyles' home ran right past the spa. Felicia and Peter might not be high on my suspect list, but her father was.

"You said you took the call on the front porch of the spa. Did you happen to see your father and Chas walk by?"

Eyes wide, Felicia stared at me. "You're asking—I thought you were just taking statements. Holly, are my family suspects?"

I blew out a breath and considered the best way to answer. I could beat around the bush, but time was running out. I wanted to find the killer before the storm hit and the direct approach would save time.

"Technically? Everyone on the property is a suspect. But there's no denying the Lyles have the most to gain by Heather's death."

Instead of taking offense, Felicia merely looked puzzled. "I don't understand. Why would any of us want her dead?"

Her response confused me. I'd just gotten through saying she was smart. "Felicia, Heather brought the heir back to Pennington and she was prepared to give sworn testimony that he is Chris Pennington. Your family stood to lose millions."

She laughed, causing me further confusion. "Um, what's funny about that?"

"Nothing," she chuckled again and shook her head. "Nothing. Only it's all so ridiculous and based on what you're thinking, I can only imagine what the gossip mills are churning out."

"Ridiculous how? Are you saying the inheritance issue isn't a motive?"

She nodded. "I can't speak for the others because I don't know what they are planning to do about Chris's reappearance, but I'm not fighting his claim."

"So, you believe Heather? Believe that rather fantastic tale of amnesia?" I'd thought her nice, I'd thought her smart, but naïve? That hadn't crossed my mind.

"No, that story has a bunch of holes. But as to believing Heather"—she shrugged—"I don't have to; I know he's Chris Pennington."

My brows shot upward. "How can you be sure? According to people who knew him as a teen, he bears a resemblance but they won't swear to it."

A soft smile lit her face and she got a faraway look in her eyes. "I just know."

There was a hint of something in her tone and expression. If I had to sum it up in one word, I'd have said it was affection. "Felicia, why did Chris run away all those years ago?"

She quirked a brow and turned her secret smile on me. "You'll have to ask Chris. That's his story to tell."

Oh, I intended to! I'd always planned on speaking to the alleged heir, but prying into why he'd left hadn't been on my radar. It was now. Felicia had made it clear she wasn't spilling the goods, but I had to try.

"Did it have something to do with what's happening with the Gullahs? Does their cursing the plantation have anything to do with Chris?"

She blinked and sat up straighter. "What? Where's that coming from?" She shook her head. "I don't know why Auntie Pearl put a curse on Pennington, but I'm positive it has nothing to do with why Chris ran away." She glanced at the papers spread out on her desk. "Was there anything else you needed? I've got to finish checking these invoices and then get a bag packed. Apparently, Bradley has decided we are all staying in the main house tonight."

"Good decision."

Felicia laughed. "Well, even a broken clock is right twice a day."

"Ha, very true." I snapped my fingers and The Colonel heaved his way to his feet. "I won't keep you but, there is one thing I'd like to ask."

"Sure, anything I can do."

"Before I came to your office, I spoke with Daphne. She was not cooperative, and after I pressed her to answer my questions, she claimed to be visiting with Auntie Pearl last night. Felicia, when did Pearl move into Pennington Village? Last I'd heard, she was living on Saint Marianna Island."

"Oh, she moved here about six months ago. Elijah asked us to rent the cottage to her." Felicia frowned. "You say Daphne had to be forced to answer your questions?"

"Yes. In a word, she was openly hostile."

Felicia's brow furrowed. "That's ... I don't understand. Daphne is always professional. She's not as chatty as her brother, but why would she be rude to you?" Her eyes widened. "Oh Holly, you don't think she had something to do with Heather's death?"

Nothing I'd found suggested Daphne's involvement, but it was a fair question based upon her refusal to answer my questions. I told Felicia as much and she sighed.

"I hate to think that, but what other reason could she have?"

There was another. "Felicia, I thought the Pennington Village cottages belonged to descendants of the slaves that worked the plantation back in the day. I understand you've used the empty cottages for staff, but why did you allow Auntie Pearl to move in?"

"Well, the family that owned it did not have descendants, so it sat empty for years. Then Elijah requested we let Pearl have it; she's his great-aunt. I didn't think it right to say no."

Now that was news to me. "The Gullah root doctor is related to Elijah and Daphne?"

"Yes, why?"

"Let me get this straight. You did Elijah's great-aunt a favor and now she's cursing you? What's that all about?

Felicia sighed. "I wish I knew..."

If I hadn't seen Chas's reaction to the topic earlier, I'd have thought Felicia was lying. However, I didn't put it past Bradley to exclude his siblings from business dealings. The man strutted his stuff around the resort and treated his sister like a general dog's body.

"Felicia, when I was telling your family about the murder, Bradley and my brother got into it, and Dewey said something about ripping off the Gullahs. Chas looked surprised."

She nodded. "I saw that and I'm as much in the dark as he seems to be. Have you asked your brother what he meant?"

"No, not yet, but I will." I absently scratched The Colonel behind his ear as I considered what I knew and, more importantly, what I didn't. "You know, it stands to reason whatever is going on between Bradley and the Gullahs has something to do with Pennington Place. You're sure you know nothing about this?"

She shrugged. "Sorry, I can't help you. My brother, and my father for that matter, don't include me or Chas in their plans. We just get orders. Well, I do anyway. Chas always manages to wiggle out of work."

I could attest to the truth of her statements on that score. For the life of me I couldn't understand why she put up with them. Felicia laughed when I mentioned it.

"It's my fault. I've let them walk all over me." She snorted and a glint appeared in her eye. "But that's about to change."

My brows rose. "Well, good for you! Remember, they need you more than you need them." She smiled and ducked her head. "I mean it, Felicia. You're a great manager. Plenty of companies would love to have you on their team."

A flash of lightening illuminated the room. I nudged The Colonel to his feet and rose. "Well, I'd best be going. The storm will be on us before we know it, and I've more statements to take."

Felicia walked me to the front door. "Sorry I couldn't be of more help, but I'll see you at the house." Lightening flashed again, followed by a crack of thunder.

"Oooh, I'd best get a move on or we'll be getting wet. See you later, Felicia!"

The Colonel and I set off toward the main house as fast as my stiff leg allowed. Strong gusts were bending the trees and the sky was again leaden and ominous looking. Fat drops of rain began to fall, and I pushed myself into a trot while my mind ran over the few facts I'd gleaned from my talks with Quinton, Chas, Felicia, and Daphne.

Nothing but frustration had come from my attempts to converse with the elder Lyle, but Chas's drunken memories of a mysterious figure on the dock held promise; hopefully, Dewey had found something.

My time with Daphne had served to irritate me more than anything else. Despite her veiled attempts to intimidate me, I had all intentions of visiting Auntie Pearl, but I'd wait until after I'd spoken with Dewey. I had a feeling the old conjurer would feed me a line of mumbo jumbo and I wanted to be armed with concrete facts.

A couple of things stuck out from my chat with Felicia. I had no reason to doubt she'd been in the spa just as she'd said. However, she'd said Peter called around 10:00 p.m. That gave her and Peter loose alibis, but only if he'd made the call from his home.

Her response to my claiming the Pennington heir's reappearance was a motive also had me floundering. I was curious about why Chris had run away, and I was left with no real motive if what Felicia had claimed was true.

A text to my brother revealed he was hanging out in the pool house until the current band passed, so I mounted the steps and dropped onto the porch swing. Another round of storms settled in and I watched the fury as I considered my next move. Once I'd spoken to Dewey, I'd need to talk to the main house's guests: the Randalls, Dylan Carter, and Christopher Pennington.

Peter Kent was technically a member of staff. If Connie hadn't gotten to him yet, then I'd add him to my list. I'd also have to make a trip across the plantation to speak with Auntie Pearl.

Stifling a yawn, I leaned my head back and let the storm sing me to sleep. As my eyes drifted closed, I couldn't help but think that mother nature was creating a perfect backdrop for the mystery I'd been dropped into.

Chapter Thirteen

Dewey stomping across the porch brought me awake with a start. He laughed as I shook myself out of my stupor.

"Man, you were out like a light!" He chuckled. "Think it's wise to be lettin' yer guard down like that?"

I rubbed my eyes. "Under the circumstances, no." I sat up straighter and forced my mind to start working. "Did you find anything by the dock?"

He grinned and pointed across the porch. "Yep, found that hung up in the reeds."

I squinted but couldn't tell what it was from that distance. "Looks like an old sack. Bring it over here into the light."

Dewey got up to retrieve whatever he'd found. "Left it over here cuz it's damp and smells funny. Sure you want it?"

"Yes, how else am I gonna figure out what it is?" He dropped it at my feet and my nose wrinkled. "See whatcha mean about the smell. It reeks!" *It* was a lump of dark brown material, and the smell was pungent and a little bit sweet.

Gingerly, I spread the folds of the material until it was laying flat on the wooden floor. Splayed out, it was revealed to be a long robe with a hood. It seemed familiar but my brain was still foggy with sleep.

Dewey sniffed. "Reminds me of the stench in Heather's room." He flopped down beside me on the swing. "Why would someone toss that in the river? I mean, it's an ugly dress but..."

I cocked my head to one side and stared at it. "It is ugly ... reminds me of something—oh!" I glanced at Dewey. "It's a monk's robe, not a dress!"

"What? That's nuts. What would one o' them Sandpoint Abbey dudes be doin' over here? And why would they toss their dress into the river?"

"Monk's robe..." I corrected absently. "And I doubt it belongs to one of the Sandpoint Abbey men." Pushing aside the cowl, I looked for a tag. Finding nothing on the collar, I moved down the fabric and finally found a small white piece of material sewn into the seam near the bottom. "Ah, that makes sense! Look." I pointed to the label where the words Cosplay Chaos were written in bold print. "I'm betting someone at the wedding wore this as a costume."

Dewey's eyes widened. "Oh yeah, that makes more sense than one of them monks comin'—hey, where ya goin' it's pourin' down rain?"

"Need to talk to Jeff and Carrie."

I had one foot on the top step when Dewey hollered. "Well, they ain't at the cottage no more." He tipped his head toward the house. "Moved up here, didn't they."

Perfect! I wouldn't have to get drenched. "Great. Come on."

He groaned and started muttering about being comfortable but finally followed behind me as I went in search of the bride and groom. Connie caught up with me as I was crossing the hall.

"Hey, I finished talking to the staff." She grimaced. "Well, I talked to the maids. They did turndown service for all of the rooms at eight o'clock. Then they restocked the housekeeping cart and went home." She winced. "Sorry, but I couldn't find Peter and Elijah was on the phone, so I figure I'll take a break and then go see him."

"Thanks Connie. So the maids are accounted for. Don't worry about talking to Peter right now. I spoke with Felicia and she was on the phone with him around 10:30. He claimed to be at home and she could hear the TV in the background." I shrugged. "Unless something turns up to counter that claim, we'll assume he was telling the truth."

"Okay, then that just leaves Elijah."

Considering all that we'd collectively done and what still needed to be, I remembered the burned paper I'd found in Heather's fireplace. "Did you figure out what those burned papers were?"

She shook her head. "No, haven't had time. Figured I could do that once we're stuck inside for the storm."

"I'll talk to Elijah; get on the paper puzzle first. I found several clues in her room that need to be investigated—oh!"

"What? Is something wrong?"

"No, well yes. I completely forgot about Heather's pocketbook. I left it in our room. Can you go through it, see if there's anything that might tell us why she was murdered?"

"Sure, what are y'all doing?" She looked at the crumpled cloth in Dewey's arms.

"Ha, we hit paydirt, or rather Dewey did. He found a costume stuck in the marsh grass and we're going to talk to Jeff and

Carrie." I motioned for her to follow. "Leave the paper and purse for now."

She frowned. "A costume? Think it has something to do with the murder?"

"I do." I told her what Chas had reported seeing as we walked down the hall. "I'm wondering if we can find out who was wearing this costume at the wedding."

"What's that gonna tell us?"

I shrugged. "Not sure, Dewey. But someone wanted this costume to disappear. There has to be a reason."

The desk clerk thought the happy couple were in the library and a few minutes later she proved to be correct. The two were cuddled on a sofa, oblivious to the world until The Colonel jumped up and planted himself in Jeff's lap.

"Oh, I'm so sorry. Colonel, off!"

Jeff laughed and hugged my boy's neck. "He's all right, a little heavy though. You need to lay off the treats, my man."

We all laughed and then I got down to business. "Sorry to interrupt y'all but we need your help."

I told them what Chas had seen and then showed them what Dewey had found.

Jeff looked at his bride. "I don't remember seeing anyone dressed like a monk, do you honey?"

Carrie shook her head. "No, I saw plenty of Henry the VIIIs and lots of princesses, but I don't recall seeing anyone in a robe like that. Sorry we can't be of more help, Holly."

My shoulders slumped. I'd been so sure they could identify the wearer. Disappointed, we all fell silent until Connie cleared her throat. "Um, what about pictures. Y'alls photographer was taking candid shots at the reception. Maybe they caught this person?"

"Connie, that's a great idea!" I turned to Carrie. "Don't suppose you've gotten any pictures back yet?"

She shook her head. "No, they were going to email me proofs, but not until we got back from our honeymoon."

"Email? Then the photos were digital?"

"Sure, we get to look them over and decide what we want printed. Why?"

Not bothering to explain, I asked another question as I pulled out my phone. "You used Ever After photography studio, right?" At her nod, I typed the name into a search and soon had the phone number. "Is it okay if I ask them to email us the pics?"

Carrie nodded and I made the call. In a few minutes, I was once again feeling optimistic. "Connie, I gave them the resort's email address. Can you go wait for it in the office?"

"Sure, you want me to call you when they come in?" She walked to the door.

"Go ahead and look through them, first. If you find any that show someone dressed like a monk, call me. Oh, and don't forget about the other things we found."

"On it!" Connie rushed off to do my bidding. I thanked the bride and groom again and apologized for interrupting, then motioned for Dewey to follow me.

A glance in the dining room showed it was empty, though sounds of clanging metal were coming from the kitchen. I hoped that meant Elijah was working. I'd talk to him after I spoke to Dewey.

"You think Connie will find anything in them pictures?"

I shooed The Colonel away from a buffet table being set for lunch. The dining room was a dangerous place for my always ravenous pooch. "I hope so, Dewey."

"Well, I think it's a waste of time. What does it matter—"

"Never mind that." If my brother couldn't put two and two together, I wasn't wasting time doing the math for him. "I need you to tell me what's going on with Bradley and the Gullahs."

He scratched his head. "Don't see what that's got to do with a murder but"—he shrugged—"I didn't hear nothin' other than Elijah tearing Bradley and that wife of his a new one."

"Tearing a—" I huffed. "Dewey, what were they talking about?"

My brother shook his head. "I don't know! Was just passin' the office when I heard 'em shoutin'." I scowled and he held his hands out. "Hey, don't eat me! All I caught was somethin' about breaking his promise and he mentioned the golf course."

"A broken promise and a golf course? Who said that?"

"Was Elijah, but don't ask me what they was fussin' about—"

"Never mind." I rolled my eyes. "I'll ask the source."

Dewey nodded and moved to stop The Colonel from snagging a corn muffin off the buffet. "You done with me? Think this boy needs a good walk and maybe a snack."

I shooed them both out of the dining room, reminding my brother not to overfeed my little beast, and then considered what I'd learned. I needed to gather my thoughts before speaking to the chef.

Dewey's claim that Bradley was double crossing the Gullahs made sense, as did his assumption that it all centered around the Pennington Place golf course. There'd been a lot of opposition from both the Gullahs and the other residents of Belle Isle when Bradley had proposed clearing almost a hundred acres to put the Par 4 course in. I'd heard the dispute was over destruction of wildlife preserves and the environmental impact and runoff associated with course maintenance.

The Gullahs had abruptly stopped their protests, and without their voices added to the environmentalists, the commissioners approved the development. What Dewey was suggesting led me to believe they'd struck a deal with the Lyles. Only, what deal could the Gullahs have asked for?

Elijah Jones would be the man to ask. Unlike his sister, he'd always been friendly. He'd also grown up on the estate. Perhaps he knew something about the mystery surrounding Christopher Pennington, too.

Chapter Fourteen

Once Dewey and The Colonel left the dining room, I made my way into the kitchen and found Elijah busy at the stove.

"Hello! Lunch will be served soon. Help yourself to the relish tray, if you can't wait."

"Hey Elijah. Thanks, but I'm not hungry. Something sure smells good though. Is that gumbo?"

"Yes ma'am." He pulled a sheet pan of cornbread from the oven and set it on a cooling rack. "Got gumbo and cornbread for lunch and dinner goin' be Frogmore Stew."

"Mmm, can't wait!" My mouth watered. The local dish now more commonly known as Lowcountry boil was one of my favorite meals. I looked around and saw numerous dishes in various stages of completion. "Are we all set to ride out the storm?"

He looked over his shoulder. "Oh yeah, we goin' ta eat good, no bad-tempered Isabella goin' leave us starvin'." He motioned toward the center island. "Got sandwiches and some finger foods made and a big ol' pot of Gullah Red Rice for tomorrow. No need to be worryin' about food, Ms. Holly."

"Never doubted you, Elijah." I leaned against the stainless-steel island. "Can you spare a few minutes to answer some questions?"

He set the metal spoon down, lowered the flame under the pot of gumbo, and perched on a stool. "Sure, I have a few minutes before the I need to finish settin' up the buffet, what's on your mind?"

"Thanks. I'm taking statements for the police and need to ask where you were Saturday night around 11:00 p.m."

His smile never faltered. "Saturday night? Let's see. That fool Lyle sent all nonresident staff home before checkin' with me, so I was here cleanin' up the kitchen and preppin' for today's meals until ... oh around 10:30 I guess."

"And you went straight home after?"

"Sure did. I was burned to a cinder."

"I'll bet." I cocked my head to one side and watched his face as I asked, "Can anyone verify you were at home?"

His gaze dropped to the floor and he shifted on his stool. "My sister. She was sleepin' when I came in, though."

He was lying and a wave of disappointment washed over me. I'd always liked Elijah and had considered him honest to a fault. I kept my tone light. "Funny, Daphne says she was visiting with your aunt..."

He stiffened. "Nah, she was in t'a bed—" He glanced at me and must have realized I wasn't buying it because his shoulders drooped and he sighed. "Sorry, that was another night. Daphne was with Auntie Pearl. I heard her come in about midnight."

"Elijah, why were you going to lie?"

He snorted. "A Gullah not havin' an alibi when a white woman is killed? Add in that my aunt just made a public curse on this place? What would you do?"

He had a point, had it been anyone other than me investigating that is. I had always had good relations with the Gullah community. I'd thought there was mutual respect. "I understand. Can't say I'm not disappointed, but thanks for deciding to be truthful."

His expression showed remorse. "I'm sorry. You've always been straight with us. But Holly, me and my sister didn't kill that woman. We had no reason to. Heck, I was helpin' her!"

I frowned. "Helping Heather?" He nodded. "How were you doing that, Elijah?"

His gaze drifted off and his body language showed he wanted to ignore my question. "Elijah? Does your help involve the curse Auntie Pearl put on this place?"

That brought his head up. "What? Nah, that's all Daphne and Auntie's doin'. Don't hold with such foolishness. I got other plans."

"I see. What do those plans involve?"

He huffed. "Anyone ever tell ya you're as stubborn as your bulldog?"

I laughed. "No, but it's probably an accurate assessment." He grinned and the tension in the room faded. "Come on, Elijah, just tell me how you were helping Heather and I'll get out of your kitchen."

Shaking his head, Elijah conceded defeat. "Was goin' ta give my statement to the executors. You know, back up her claim that he's the real Chris Pennington."

Ah, now we were getting somewhere. "So you believe he's telling the truth."

"Course he is! Known him all my life. It's C.J."

"That's what Felicia says, too. But if it's so obvious, why are the rest of the Lyles fighting his claim?"

Elijah chuckled. "They got a couple of million reasons, don't ya think?"

I did. "You think one of them killed Heather to stop her from giving testimony?"

He shook his head. "I can't see it. I mean, they got a reason to want her out of the way, but it wouldn't solve much. Still got me and Felicia backing C.J., and Chas for that matter."

"True. But if the question of inheritance was a done deal..." I wrinkled my nose. "Any other idea why someone would want to kill her?"

He shook his head and slipped off the stool. "No ma'am, I surely don't." He stirred the simmering gumbo. "She was nice enough and real pretty. Can't think she'd get on someone's bad side, leastwise not enough to kill her."

"You were helping her. Did you ever talk about personal things? Boyfriends, her job? Was she involved in anything that might have created enemies?"

He grinned and waggled his eyebrows. "Other than tickin' off the Lyles you mean?"

I returned his smile. "Yes, other than that. Did you ever learn where she was living? What she did for a living?"

He shrugged. "We didn't talk much about anything like that, but she mentioned having to get back to Lynchburg soon."

"Lynchburg, Virginia?" He nodded. "Any idea where she worked?"

He shook his head. "Not the company, but we got to talkin' politics once and she laughed and said until you've been a consultant, you've know idea what goes on in government." He shrugged. "Figured that's what she did."

It was a reasonable conclusion. "So she lived in Virginia and did something in politics." I fiddled with an oven mitt while I considered what I'd learned. "That's a field where you could make some enemies..."

Elijah laughed. "That's an understatement."

I chuckled. "So it's possible that someone in her line of work was out to get her." Elijah nodded as I continued to think out loud. "Trouble with that theory is they'd have to be one of the people staying at the resort. We found no evidence someone from outside the plantation committed the crime."

Thinking about the murder and the clues I'd found in her room, I recalled the pale mark on her finger. "Elijah, did you happen to hear if Heather was married? Engaged perhaps?"

"Sorry, we never talked about nothin' like that. But the way she was sniffin' around C.J., I sure hope she wasn't."

Dewey had said much the same. I was at a dead end, again.

A timer went off and Elijah took a lump of dough out of a bowl and started kneading. "Was there anything else, Ms. Holly? Only, I gotta get this bread shaped and start on a trifle..."

"You go ahead, I uh, wanted to ask you one more thing."

"Shoot! I got no secrets." He picked up the dough and slapped it back onto the counter.

I doubted that was true, but he'd opened the door. "Care to tell me what you and Bradley were arguing about last night?"

His shoulders stiffened but otherwise he was business as usual. "Any sense in denying it?" He folded the dough into thirds and transferred it to a waiting loaf pan.

"Not really, you were heard."

Elijah sighed. "Dem walls be thin, I guess." He covered the pan with a shower cap and pulled another hunk of dough onto the board. "Boss man come in here tryin' to tell me how to run my kitchen. Said I needed to serve the regular menu, hurricane be damned." He snorted. "Gave him an earful, I can tell you. Imagine him tellin' me my business." He continued to mutter under his breath. "Not like I aint' lived here all my life..."

I let his claims go unchallenged for a beat. "I don't doubt you did tell him off. But what does food preparations have to do with broken promises?

He stilled and for a moment I thought he'd blow off my question, but after a long pause, Elijah huffed and turned to lean against the counter, arms crossed. "Dem walls got good ears."

I snorted. "In this case, yes they do. What did you mean, Elijah? Why is Bradley an Indian giver?"

He shook his head and sighed. "Cuz the pig is going back on our deal."

"Does this deal have anything to do with the golf course?"

He scowled. "If'n you know, why you still pesterin' me?"

"Because I don't know anything for a fact. I'm guessing."

"You sure good at it, Ms. Holly. Hit the nail square on the head." He turned and wiped crumbs from the counter before starting in on the second loaf of bread. "You 'member when they was petitionin' the county to let 'em put dat course in?"

"Yes, I remember the Gullahs and the environmentalists were against it, then the Gullahs dropped their objections. Why did they do that?"

He slapped the dough against the marble slab. "Cuz we were promised the Lyles would deed us ownership of Pennington

Village." He glanced at me. "You know how our families been livin' here for centuries? Handin' down the houses and such?"

"Yes, it's a remarkable feat. Keeping it in the family as y'all have. Not many of our kind left."

"Yes ma'am. Your family been on the land about as long as ours has. Only, y'all own dem houses. We Gullahs never got that privilege. It's always been ours so long as there's a relative livin' in 'em. Family dies out or decides to move, and they can't sell their property." He shook his head. "T'aint right. So, we made a deal with Bradley and Quinton. We'd support that course if they deeded the village to us, only now they're going back on their word."

"I'm so sorry, Elijah. That's wrong in so many ways. Can't you take them to court?"

He turned and shook his head. "Could, but it was a spit and handshake kinda agreement. I trusted them to honor their word, more fool me."

"So that's why Auntie Pearl has cursed Pennington?"

"Yeah, for all the good it'll do."

"You mentioned other plans. Those involve Chris Pennington?"

"Yep. Soon as C.J. is officially the owner of all this, he's gonna keep the bargain I made with those rats. And, lest ya think I ain't learned nothing from this, I got that in writing."

"Good for you." The mystery of the Gullah curse was solved. Connie could finally relax. Unfortunately, it didn't help me solve a murder.

"Thanks for being truthful, Elijah. I hope everything works out for you and the Gullahs." I walked toward the door when I remembered wanting to ask him about Chris running away.

"Hey Elijah?"

He glanced up and smiled. "Ain't you gone yet? Body can't get nothin' done..."

I grinned. "Just one more thing, I promise. Do you know why Chris ran away all those years ago?"

The look in his eyes said that he did but all he said was, "That's his story to tell, Ms. Holly."

I'd figured Elijah wouldn't voluntarily carry tales about his friend, but it'd been worth a shot. I was about to try cajoling him into spilling the beans when a shriek echoed through the house.

Elijah and I ran toward the sound and skidded to a stop as we arrived in the hall to find old Auntie Pearl and Bradley struggling over a glass jar clutched in her hand.

Chapter Fifteen

Before Elijah and I could reach the sparring pair, Auntie won the tug of war. Her final pull was strong enough to put Bradley off balance. His arms windmilled for a second and then he crashed into a table, sending a vase of flowers crashing to the heart pine floor.

Shocked that a woman as tiny and seemingly frail as Auntie Pearl was capable of toppling the younger man, I stared a moment too long, giving Bradley time to regain his balance and launch himself at the old woman.

Auntie was game and the proverbial fur began to fly. Bradley's hands went around her neck and the little woman smacked him upside the head with the jar, shattering it. The murky water and bits of debris soaked Bradley and puddled on the floor. Auntie Pearl started chanting in syncopation with her blows. Elijah jumped into the fray, trying to pull his aunt away, and I shook off my surprise and tried to restrain Bradley.

Chaos ensued. The Randalls and Connie, drawn by the noise, were screaming and attempting to help, but the combatants, fueled by fury, were besting our attempts to regain control. Attempting to subdue Bradley and his flailing arms, I wrapped mine around him from behind. He shrugged me off and I went down, falling on my bad leg.

Struggling to stand, I was about to intercede again when a crash of metal followed by a shout rang out. "That's enough!"

Everyone came to a standstill as Christopher strode down the stairs, a metal trash can in one hand and an umbrella in the other. He set his makeshift noisemaker on the bottom step and stepped between Auntie Pearl and Bradley.

"What's going on here?" Without waiting for an answer, he sneered at his stepbrother. "Beating up old women? A new low for you, Brad."

Bradley hissed. "This doesn't concern you!"

"On the contrary," Christopher smirked. "If it involves *my* resort, it's nobody's business *but* mine."

Bradley's face turned scarlet and he began to sputter. "Arrogant impostor! I'll see you locked up for attempted fraud! I'll sue you for every penny you don't have! I'll—"

"You'll do nothing but pack your bags." Dismissing him, Christopher nodded at Elijah and then took Auntie Pearl's hand. "Auntie, I understand you and your people have suffered a terrible wrong. Will you allow me to make amends?"

A soft smile spread across her face. She raised a gnarled hand and cupped Chris's cheek. "'Bout time you claim what's yers. Welcome home, Mr. Christopher. Ain't been the same since you left." She glared at Bradley. "No account trash been stinkin' up the place."

Christopher smiled. "Don't worry, the garbage is about to be set on the curb." He glanced at Elijah and then back at Pearl. "I'm told you were promised ownership of Pennington Village in exchange for your support of that monstrosity marring our landscape. I can't restore the fields, but I can and will honor the deal. I've been speaking with the estate lawyers, and they are working on dividing the village into parcels and creating deeds. You'll have ownership before Thanksgiving."

"You can't do that! You have no authority. We don't even know who you—"

"Oh, give it a rest Bradley," Chas strolled in from the bar, Felicia right behind him. "We all know he's Chris." He gave the man in question a hug. "As the lady said, welcome home, brother."

Curiously, Felicia kept her distance. "I'm glad you've decided to claim your inheritance, Christopher." She smiled softly but there was a hint of sadness in her eyes that puzzled me.

"I—we've missed you."

Christopher extended his arms as if to hug her too, but Felicia ducked away and scurried toward the back of the house. I was mulling over their exchange when Elijah clapped his hands, drawing everyone's attention.

"The prodigal has returned. This calls for a celebration. Gumbo and cornbread in the dining room. Y'all come get it while it's hot."

The Randalls, puzzled expressions on their faces, nervously followed Elijah while Chas jumped into conversation with Auntie Pearl and Christopher. After shooting a venomous look at Christopher, Bradley stalked out the front door.

Connie met my gaze and waggled her eyebrows. I stifled a laugh as Christopher spoke. "Now then, Auntie. You reckon it's time to take that curse off us?" Chris glanced at the mess littering the floor.

The wizened old woman chuckled and patted his cheek. "That weren't no curse, Mr. Chris." She glared at the door her nemesis had just scurried through. "Dat jar was de cure. I was comin' to make peace afore that witch Isabella gits here."

He laughed. "Good thing, too. We're gonna need all the mojo you can muster to protect us from this storm." He wound an arm around the old lady's waist. "Come on, let's get some of your nephew's gumbo before they scarf it all down."

The drama was over, leaving me without a strong motive for Heather's murder. Based on what Felicia and now Chas said, the Lyles has always known the man brought to Pennington Place by Heather was not an impostor. Killing her would have served no purpose because her testimony was not needed to secure the inheritance.

Sleepy and disheartened, I was ready to hang the whole case up and let the police handle it, when Connie touched my arm.

"I found something in those photos."

My brows went up. Just like that, my interest in the investigation was stoked. "Something that'll tell us why she was murdered?"

Connie shrugged and waved her hand toward the back of the house. "Come back to the accounting office and I'll show you."

Connie sat before the computer, and with a few clicks of the mouse, I was looking at blown up images of someone dressed in the monk's robe Dewey had found. Speaking of Dewey ... I glanced at my watch. He and The Colonel had been gone quite a while. I was about to ask Connie if she'd seen the pair when she clicked the screen and another image appeared.

My eyes widened. "That's the dessert table."

"Yep, think we found our killer. Watch this." She scrolled to the next image and used the cursor to point to the table holding the groom's cake. "See? The photographer snapped three pictures in a row, I think, because in the first one you see the monk out in front of the dessert table. The next one, he's closer, then this last one you see a bit of the robe as whoever this is exited through the patio door but look at the cake!"

The image showed the groom's cake, minus it's dagger cake topper. Connie was right. It was circumstantial by legal standards, but the assumption could be made that whoever was in the monk's costume took the dagger and, as I'd suspected, left via the side door.

It was good news, but not case breaking. Connie's excitement dimmed as I broke the news. "But at least we know who took the dagger!"

"Yes, it's a good start, but we can't identify the person wearing the cloak. We can't even tell if it's a man or a woman." I sighed and dropped into a seat. "The best way to find this person is to figure out why they wanted her dead."

Connie propped her chin in her hand. "Well, the idea that the Lyles wanted her dead so she couldn't testify for Christopher is bunk, right?"

"Yes and no. I've discovered the family has known from the start that he was the real heir but that doesn't necessarily mean they wouldn't want Heather silenced. When he arrived, Chris claimed amnesia—"

"Yes, why did he do that? It's obvious he knew who he was all along." She snorted. "Or will he say his memory just miraculously returned once he was in a familiar setting?"

After I finished laughing, I commented on her theory. "Gotta admit, that goes quite well with the soap opera theme." I shook my head. "In all seriousness though, I can't think of a reason, but whatever it was that kept him from coming forward, I'm pretty sure it has nothing to do with his cousin's murder. While the Lyles appear to have been planning on contesting his claim regardless of the truth, I don't think they killed Heather."

She frowned. "So we got nothin'."

It looked that way but now that we knew someone in costume had stolen the dagger that killed Heather, I wasn't ready to throw in the towel. "Well, we don't have a clear motive, but we do have evidence."

"True. Those scraps of paper you found in the fireplace being one. I can't tell you what the contents were, but I scanned one of the larger pieces and did an online search." She pushed the plastic bag containing the fragments toward me and pointed to a large piece burned around the edges. "This is the only piece that had anything discernible on it. Unfortunately, the only thing legible was part of the letter head. Pretty sure it's the state seal for the Commonwealth of Virginia."

Frowning, I turned the bag several different directions but still couldn't make out anything other than the letters *VIRG* and, as Connie said, part of a logo. "So the internet search identified it as a state document?" She nodded. "Wonder what was on the paper?"

"It could be most anything. A letter from some state agency or even a record of some kind."

Studying it a few more times, I gave up. "Good work, Connie. I'd have never been able to find that on the internet."

She grinned. "Well, with your computer skills on par with your cooking abilities..."

"Hey, I have a variety of talents, those just aren't among them."

She laughed and pulled out a sheet of paper and an ink pen. "So as far as evidence is concerned, what do we have?"

I sighed and tipped my head back, closing my eyes. "Let me think. The monk's robe and the fireplace paper..." I thought back to the examination of the victim's room. "There was that pale spot on her finger, though I'm not sure it's pertinent, and the voodoo doll dressed like a bride is in the same category."

"Okay, I got those down." She tapped her pen against the desk. "Hey, I forgot about her pocketbook!"

I opened my eyes. "I did too. Get on that right away, maybe there's something in there to explain that letter."

"Will do." She looked at her list. "It's not much to go on."

"Yeah, I was hoping for a smoking gun in those pictures. Did you look through all of the photos? There was nothing else?"

Connie wrinkled her nose. "Not really—oh! That reminds me, I wanted to show you this picture of the head table. We really outdid ourselves on this wedding." She opened another tab on the computer. "Check this out."

The photo was a wide shot of the banquet room. The centerpieces we'd designed sparkled in the candlelight and the costumed guests fooled the viewer into thinking they'd had photography in the Middle Ages. The floral arch we'd constructed to frame the bridal table caught my eye.

We'd thought about that feature for weeks. The wall of windows behind the couple provided an incredible view of the river, but it also detracted attention from the bride and groom. To remedy that, we'd designed an arch made out of grapevines.

On either side of the arch were broadswords, their hilts decorated with a floral spray, and in the center hung our pièce de résistance—two winged dragons holding interlocking silver hearts. It'd been our wedding gift to the couple and had been a show stopping decoration.

"I think you should ask Carrie for a copy of this and put it in a brochure. It'd be great advertising!"

I nodded and let Connie's marketing plan go in one ear and out the other as something behind the head table caught my eye. "Hey, can you zoom in on that shot?"

She frowned. "Sure, what are you looking for?"

"Not sure, but I want to see who's standing outside those windows. There're two people talking, and judging by the way one has their arm raised, it doesn't look friendly."

She clicked something on the screen and the image started to magnify. "I can kinda see what you mean, but it could be anyone..."

"True, but the red hair is what I noticed."

She leaned closer to the monitor and squinted. "Wow, you're right! I would have blown right by that. Heather had gorgeous red hair."

"I know," I murmured as I watched the image get bigger, and unfortunately, more distorted. "Very distinctive hair. That's definitely her, but who is she arguing with?"

"I can't ... pretty sure that's a man but it's too grainy at this resolution."

"Darn it. Any way that could be enhanced?"

She started to shake her head then smiled. "Here, let me try something."

Connie worked some kind of computer magic with pixels and something else that went right over my head. A few seconds later, the image was better. Not perfect, but good enough to see the features of the man talking to Heather.

Connie met my gaze, excitement shining in her eyes. "It worked. I can't believe that worked!"

I grinned. "Great job, my friend! Can you print that?" She handed it to me and I rose, heading for the door. "I'm off to find out what Dylan was arguing with Heather about."

Chapter Sixteen

With one thing on my mind, I made a beeline for the front desk. I'd just asked the desk clerk to ring Dylan's room when the Randalls walked over.

"Afternoon, Holly. Did your brother find you?"

My brow furrowed. "Um, no, was he supposed to?"

"Walt and I were taking a walk and ran up on him and your dog. He was urging The Colonel to hurry and finish his business because he needed to talk to you."

"Oh, well I'd best stay put then."

The clerk hung up the phone. "I'm sorry, Holly. There was no answer in his room."

I sighed. "Dang it, have you seen him lately?" The clerk shook her head. I smiled at the Randalls. "Y'all excuse me, I've got to find Dylan Carter."

"Oh, he was outside a minute ago. Walt and I waved, but we didn't stop to chat. He was smoking and I'm allergic."

"Wonderful! You just saved me an exhaustive search of the grounds. You said he was smoking?"

Maude nodded. "Yes, he was standing by the side of the house." She pointed toward the left. "I'm sure he'll be along in a minute."

Deciding she was probably right, I made small talk with the friendly couple. "Thanks again for helping with the storm shutters, Walt. You guys got it done in record time. Lucky for us you're so handy."

He chuckled. "Well, owned a chain of hardware stores and did many a DIY project so I ought to be!" He shook his head. "This younger generation though. Don't they have shop class anymore? That Dylan boy was all thumbs. In fact, the way he handled the tools, I was afraid he'd lose a thumb!"

"Oh Walt, it's nothing to do with age." Maude lectured her husband. "Not everyone can be mechanically minded. Why take my father for example. He was a boiler man in the Pacific during WWII and yet mother had to call a repairman for every little thing that broke. Why, when I recall—"

"Excuse me, y'all," I nodded toward the front door where Dylan had just entered. "I need to speak with him. It was nice talking with you, and if you see Dewey, tell him I'm in the library."

I rushed down the hall and caught Dylan as he was mounting the stairs. "Hey, got a minute?"

A puzzled look flitted across his face but then he smiled. "Sure, whatcha need? Please tell me I don't need to help move another stiff!"

He'd meant it as a joke, but I didn't find anything humorous about murder victims. However, I managed a lukewarm smile. "No, thank goodness. Just taking witness statements from all of the guests and you're next on my list." I tipped my head toward the library door. "Join me?"

He skipped down the steps and followed me into the book lined room where he flopped onto the sofa. "Ready when you are, Sheriff!"

Again with the levity. I began to wonder if he took anything seriously. "It was deputy, but I'm retired now." My correction didn't seem to faze him.

He grinned and gave me a mock salute. "Well, for the moment, you're the high sheriff of the plantation. What did you need from me?"

I leaned against the writing desk and watched his face carefully. He was relaxed, full of good humor, and his eyes showed nothing but mild interest. It was clear he expected my questions to be routine. I decided to oblige and then catch him off guard with what I'd seen in the photo.

"I'm asking everyone where they were around 11:00 p.m. last night."

His lips twisted into a mocking smile. "In bed, remember? That scream was enough to wake the dead and me!" He laughed. "Never jumped out of bed so fast. Lucky I remembered to grab a robe or everyone would have gotten a show!"

Another forced smile from me kept him relaxed, but something about his story was nagging at me. I was mentally reliving the moment when he cleared his throat.

"We done?" He dragged a hand through his hair. "Only, I've been outside and want to grab a shower before the storm comes around again. Don't want to get electrocuted!"

"Ha, definitely not a good idea." His movement caused the ring on his finger to catch the light. It was a gold band on the third finger of his left hand. "I didn't realize you were married. Your wife couldn't make the trip?"

He chuckled and fiddled with the band, drawing my attention to a dark brown spot of something caked on the underside of his wrist. "She probably could have, had I asked her!" My confusion must have shown on my face because he continued. "This was supposed to be a golf weekend with a buddy of mine, but he canceled when he saw the forecast." He snorted. "Chicken."

"Or maybe he didn't want to get stuck in the middle of a hurricane. Why didn't you cancel? Not the weather for golf."

He didn't appear bothered by my question, merely shrugging and flashing me another megawatt smile. "I was already here when the hurricane path changed. Figured I could get a couple of rounds in then drive back to Madison Heights." He laughed. "Didn't figure on the bridge being out, though!"

On that we could agree. "No one did. Madison Heights. Where's that?"

"Little town in Virginia. Nice place, bit quiet, but the wife likes it." He chuckled again. "And the way the housing industry is booming, I can't complain."

"That's nice." Busy formulating a way to steer the conversation toward what I'd seen in the photo, I kept up the small talk. "Did you say you're in real estate?"

He shook his head. "Nah, construction." A flash of lightening lit the room. "Look, I don't want to be rude, but I really do need a shower."

"Sure, just one more thing." My attention was focused on him like a laser beam. "You didn't know the victim, right?"

"Yes, I never saw her until you asked me to, well you know..." He cast his eyes down and gave a slight shudder. Coupled with his boyish good looks and charm, most people would think him the picture of respectful innocence. I wasn't buying it.

Something about Dylan felt contrived. He was too cheerful, too helpful, too ... much. Or maybe, I was basing my opinion on the photo I'd seen. Telling myself to be careful of rushing to judgment, I played my trump card.

"Mr. Carter, are you sure you didn't know Heather?"

He blinked. "What? Yeah, I told you I never saw the woman—"

"Then explain this photo." I dropped it on the coffee table and waited.

Dylan frowned. "What's this?" He maintained the innocent act, but I'd had enough.

"Mr. Carter, that is a picture of you and Heather standing outside the barn where the reception was held." I pointed.

"You're aggressively pointing your finger at her. Care to tell me what you were arguing about?"

"I don't..." He scratched his head. "Hold on, now I remember!" He chuckled and poured on the charm. "I didn't realize it was the same woman. She was fussing at me for smoking." He met my gaze, a pleading look in his eyes. "You gotta believe me! I'd forgotten all about it..."

On the surface, he appeared to be telling the truth but something about him didn't ring true. I was about to push him a little harder when Connie burst into the room.

"Holly, come quick!" She turned and rushed back out, explaining as she ran. "The Colonel's on the porch and he's got blood on him!"

Chapter Seventeen

Tongue lolling, sides heaving, The Colonel lay on the porch gasping for breath, but as soon as he saw me, he scrambled to his feet and raced to over to sit at my feet. He emitted one sharp bark and threw his paw up, hitting my leg.

His side was spotted with blood. Connie gasped and dropped to her knees, running her hands over him and muttering prayers for his health, but I knew he wasn't injured.

"He's fine, Connie. Come on..."

"What?" She got to her feet and followed me off the porch. "Holly, he might be hurt! I didn't get a good look—"

"No, the blood's not his. I think something's happened to Dewey." I commanded The Colonel to "find Dewey" and pushed myself to a fast trot as he struck out across the lawn.

Connie ran to keep up. "How do you know Dewey's hurt?"

"I don't." My pace combined with the thick humidity made it tough to breathe. "But The Colonel is trained to alert with one bark." I glanced at her and snorted. "It's the only command he consistently follows. I've learned not to ignore it."

"You're kidding."

I took no offense at her disbelief. The Colonel didn't give the appearance of being the sharpest tool in the shed and she'd been around him enough to know he was only as well behaved as he chose to be.

The Colonel turned toward the river, and without breaking stride, I pulled Connie to follow.

"Wait, is he leading us to Dewey?"

"Yep, my buddy is a regular Lassie when he wants to be."

Connie shook her head. "This is unbelievable, but why do you think it's Dewey that's in trouble?"

A few yards from the river's edge, The Colonel veered off onto the path that led to the golf course and Pennington Village. Before it gave way to the manicured areas of the course, the path wound through dense native forest. I was on high alert for varmints, both two and four legged, and it took me a minute to answer.

"Because, in The Colonel's hierarchy, I'm first, but Dewey is a close second. If The Colonel somehow got off his leash, he wouldn't run from my brother. Well..." I corrected myself. "He would, but he always comes back." I shook my head. "For him to run back to the house without Dewey..."

"Oh gosh, I see what you mean." Convinced my concerns were legitimate, Connie picked up speed. "Come on, Holly. That was a scary amount of blood!"

I agreed, but with my leg injury, I was going as fast as I could manage. Less hindered, Connie ran ahead. She rounded a bend and my hair stood on end as she screamed.

Gritting my teeth against the pain, I pushed myself into a run until Connie came into view. She was on her knees. Dewey was sprawled across the path, still as a stone. My heart stuttered.

"Is he?" I ran forward and dropped beside my brother, feeling for a pulse. Thready, but there. Oh, thank God! My shoulders sagged with relief and I mumbled a prayer of thanksgiving while looking him over.

"Oh, it's his head!" I looked up to see Connie's hands covered in blood.

Gently, I rolled Dewey's head to one side. His dark hair was matted with blood and the whole side was swollen. He groaned and mumbled something.

I leaned closer. "What is it Dewey? What happened?"

His eyes remained shut but he mumbled again. "Leopard..."

"What? A leopard? Dewey, there are no leopards in South Carolina." I shook him gently. "Stay with me, Dewey. Stay awake!"

His answer was another moan before he fell silent. I sat back and studied him. "Connie, he's probably concussed."

"Yes, that's a nasty wound. What caused it? A knife? A bullet?"

I shook my head. "Don't think so, there's no entry wound. I think he was hit, or something fell..." I glanced around and saw no fallen limbs, but a few feet away I did see a rock, with a suspicious dark spot. "There." I tipped my head toward the stone and Connie retrieved it.

"Oh my Lord, it's covered in blood! How—"

"Someone did this." Fat drops of rain began to fall and lightening cast eerie shadows on the trees. "Connie, we've got to get him back to the house and we can't carry him."

She glanced at my leg and nodded. "I'll go."

Having done his job, The Colonel planted himself beside my brother and refused to budge. Patting his head, I told him what a good boy he was and settled on Dewey's other side.

Hurry Connie, I whispered. Rain was falling harder now. If not for the dense canopy, we'd already be soaking wet. But that tree coverage was a mixed blessing. The wind increased and the trees were bending with every gust. We needed to get out of the woods before a busted limb finished us both off.

The Randalls had been on the porch with us and had alerted management rather than follow. Connie's run to the house was cut short when she ran into Chris and Elijah on the ATV. They efficiently bundled Dewey into the vehicle and had him tucked into an empty room in no time.

He was whiter than the sheets and still hadn't regained consciousness, but his pulse was steady and the bleeding had stopped. Connie and I bandaged his head and applied cold compresses. Now all we could do was wait.

Leaving Connie and the Randalls to watch over Dewey, I stepped into the hall and leaned against a wall. Seeing my brother near death had shaken me as not much else could. If we hadn't found him ... thank God for The Colonel.

My buddy had earned a boatload of treats, but he'd stuck to Dewey like glue since we'd found him. No matter what I did to entice him, he refused to get off the bed and growled if anyone other than Connie or me tried to get near Dewey. It'd taken all my powers of persuasion to convince him the Randalls were friends. He now allowed them to tend to my brother, but he watched them like a hawk.

The storm building outside had nothing on the one I found myself in the middle of. Right now, it was like being in the eye of a hurricane. Everyone was calm, but any minute I felt like it'd pass and we'd be in the thick of it.

I had to find the killer before Isabella hit. The attack on Dewey was proof we were dealing with a dangerous person willing to do anything to keep from being exposed.

With Dewey in capable hands, I considered my next move. I'd taken Heather's purse to Connie; she was going to look through it while she watched over my brother, and we'd borrowed the resort's laptop so she could continue researching the burned paper I'd found.

While not lucid, Dewey had regained consciousness long enough to mutter something about leopards. He'd come to again while we were tending to his head, but I still had no idea what leopards had to do with the matter at hand. Connie was sure he was delirious but I wasn't so sure.

If he'd been talking a bunch of random nonsense, I might have dismissed his rambling but twice he'd fought through the gray mist of unconsciousness long enough to say leopards. It had to mean something.

I straightened and gave myself a shake. This was getting me nowhere. Hurricane Isabella would be upon us by midnight, 1:00 a.m. at the latest. If I wanted to ride out the storm without worrying about being murdered, I had just under six hours to find a killer.

Trouble was, I didn't have any strong suspect. My theory Heather was killed to stop her from confirming the identity of the Pennington heir seemed to be unfounded. Lacking any better ideas, I went looking for Olivia. She, her husband, and Chris were the only people we hadn't interviewed.

Whoever had been wearing that hooded cloak took the dagger. Unless they had an accomplice, they were my killer. My last three suspects had all been absent from the reception. It was possible they dressed up and stole the dagger. Lacking a clear motive, I was shooting in the dark, but interviewing the remaining suspects was all I had.

Checking with the front desk, I was told Olivia was probably in the suite adjacent to the executive offices. While the Lyle family had moved into the art deco monstrosity when Miriam died and Bradley took over running the hotel, he and Olivia had created a private suite and an office out of the old master bedroom.

Wondering if I was on a wild goose chase, I wound my way through the rabbit warren of halls leading to the back of the house. The clerk had said *probably*, and odds were fifty-fifty Olivia had returned to the family home. The rain was slashing at the windows and thunder periodically shook the house so if she'd went there, interviewing her would have to wait; I'd no intention of getting drenched again, much less struck by lightning.

As I rounded a corner, I heard a screech, followed by harsh words from what sounded like two women. I picked up my pace and found my quarry giving Felicia hell.

Olivia's face was scarlet, and with the venom spewing from her tongue, I wouldn't have been surprised to see foam around her mouth. Neither woman noticed me so I hung back and listened.

"Olivia, I won't stand back and watch you—"

"You better keep your mouth shut!" Olivia's hand was wrapped around her sister-in-law's arm, her long red nails appeared to be digging into Felicia's flesh.

Felicia had tears running down her face and she was struggling to break free of Olivia's grasp. I was about to intervene when Olivia gave Felicia's arm a hard shake and took a step back. "If you know what's good for you, you'll mind your own business and stay out of my way!"

Olivia turned on her heel and entered the suite, slamming the door. I hurried to check on Felicia but she ran off before I could say a word.

Debating whether or not to go after Felicia or stick to my agenda, I wondered what their fight had been about. Felicia had said she wouldn't stand back and allow Olivia to do ... something. Did it have to do with the resort and Chris's inheritance or was it something else entirely?

I could go ask Felicia, but Olivia was already in my sights. I knocked on the door, and when I got no answer, I walked in.

"What are you doing in here?" Olivia scowled.

"I knocked."

"And I didn't answer. How dare you just barge in here!"

My response hadn't been at all apologetic and her response was expected, not that I cared. "I need to talk to you—"

"Come back later, I'm drawing a bath." She turned toward the bathroom.

"We'll talk now. What were you arguing with Felicia about just now?"

She wheeled around and glared. "I said I'm busy now, but to answer your question, I wasn't arguing with Felicia."

I quirked a brow. "Olivia, I heard you and saw you grab her arm. She was in tears when she ran off." I pinned her with my gaze. "I'll ask again, what was that all about?"

Jaw clenched and eyes narrowed, Olivia stared at me with hard eyes. For a second I thought she'd ignore me, but in the blink of an eye her expression morphed into a bland smile. She shrugged. "Not that it is any of your business, but Felicia was careless with some records for the spa and I was calling her on it." She lifted one shoulder and sniffed. "Not my fault she can't take criticism. Now, if you'll excuse me, my bath water is getting cold."

She turned and waltzed into the bedroom. I was hot on her heels. "Olivia, I need to know where you were last night around 11:00 p.m. When I called for the family to meet and discuss the situation with Heather, we had to wait almost twenty minutes before you arrived at the house."

"I'm done talking, Ms. Daye. Make an appointment."

She started toward the bathroom and I put out my hand. "No, that isn't how this works, Olivia. You'll answer my questions now, or would you rather wait until the police arrive? When I tell them you won't cooperate, I'm sure they won't mind hauling you in for questioning."

The look she gave me was filled with equal parts venom and contempt, but my tactic had worked. She huffed and moved to sit on the side of the bed, picking up an emery board and studiously applying it to her long, talon-like nails.

"I was here, sleeping. I had a migraine and retired around 7:30 p.m." Her tone was bored, but her body language screamed tension. My gut said she was lying, but how to prove it?

"Can anyone vouch for you?"

Olivia sniffed and looked down her nose at me. "My word has always been good enough, however, if you want to challenge me, ask the desk clerk. They called and woke me up when you asked to speak to the family."

"That was after the murder. Nothing to say you left your room in between those time."

She pursed her lips. "Oh for goodness' sake." She reached for a teal wrapped chocolate sitting on her nightstand. The length of her nails made unwrapping the candy difficult but eventually she managed. "I had no reason to want Heather dead." She popped the chocolate into her mouth and grimaced. "Ugg, if I've told those maids once I've told them a thousand times. Girard's are fragile and go stale quickly." She swallowed and took drink of water from a bottle beside the bed. "Serves me right for not eating them until today."

I frowned. "Those are from last night's turn down service?"

She huffed. "Of course, they'd hardly bring news ones today. It isn't even close to eight o'clock."

Something was niggling at the back of my mind but Olivia rose from the bed, distracting me.

"Now, if you're done wasting my time?" She directed a pointed stare at the bathroom door.

My eyes widened. Time! "Olivia, you said you went to bed at 7:30 p.m.?"

She rolled her eyes. "Yes, are you hard of hearing?"

I cocked an eyebrow. "No, I hear quite well. In fact, I remember every word you said. You claim to have gone to bed around 7:30 p.m., and yet you are eating the chocolates left by the maids when they do turn down service. You also said they don't do that until 8:00 p.m. Mind telling me how you got those chocolates? There is no way they'd enter a room where a guest is sleeping."

Her eyes widened. "Um, I was mistaken, I must have picked these up from the housekeeping cart."

Her gaze was unwavering and I had to hand it to her, she was brazen in her lies. But did that make her a killer? "That's bunk, Olivia, but go take your bath before the storm hits. I'll find out where you really were when Heather was murdered, and for your sake, I hope it *wasn't* in her room."

It was my turn to make an exit. Ignoring her stammered protests, I turned and marched out of her room, slamming the door behind me.

Chapter Eighteen

The confrontation with Olivia left me seeing red. Her open contempt for me as well as her indifference to Heather's death made my blood boil. My anger also short circuited my brain. Letting her get under my skin had made me forget about the wedding guest in the monk's robe.

Bradley and Olivia had attended Jeff and Carrie's ceremony but hadn't made an appearance at the reception. The only Lyle that I'd seen during the party was Quinton. I needed to add a question to my interviews, and I'd need to return to Olivia.

I dithered in the hall, debating asking Olivia while I was thinking about it, but she'd infuriated me and I wasn't up to another round right away. With mere hours to spare before Isabella arrived and we were all forced into close proximity, I couldn't afford to lose focus and that would happen if I lost my temper.

The latest storm band had faded to a light drizzle. A brisk walk around the grounds would clear my head. I could hear animated voices coming from the living room, and not wanting to be drawn into conversation, I ducked outside via the kitchen door.

The misty rain and thick humidity gave me pause, but I needed to think so I sucked it up and headed for the tree covered path that led toward the golf course. A harsh pace for a few minutes served its purpose, and feeling calmer, I started mulling over what little I knew concerning the murder of Heather.

Everyone I'd talked to, except for Olivia, had an alibi for the time of the murder. I still needed to speak with Bradley and Christopher, but neither were at the top of my list. Peter Kent, on the other hand, had a mental asterisk beside his name.

Connie had been unable to track him down for an interview, but Felicia had been talking to him around the time of the murder. He claimed to be at home watching television, and Felicia had heard background noises to suggest that part was true.

Trouble was, with a cellphone, he could have called from a variety of places, so long as it had a television. Off the top of my head, I could think of two other places at the resort that had televisions. The pool house and the clubhouse at the golf course—at least I assumed it would.

Every other course I'd ever visited had multiple sports playing in the bar. Added to my doubts about his location was Chas's assertion that Peter and Heather had been drinking together in the clubhouse.

Chas had hinted that they'd been *very friendly.* I inferred he'd meant the two were more than friends or perhaps friends with benefits and that jibed with Felicia's claim that Peter's lecherous ways were the reason she had not accepted his proposal.

In my desire to work off my anger, I'd chosen the path that led to the course. Might as well stop in and see if the golf pro was holed up there.

If something didn't turn up in the interviews with my three remaining suspects, I was at a dead end. Working without a clear motive had me stumped, but perhaps the answer to Heather's murder lay in the evidence we'd found.

The rain ended and a pleasant breeze was blowing in off the water. We were in the calm before the main event, and I hoped that peace might rub off on me.

Casting my mind back, I visualized my search of Heather's room. I'd photographed the sleeping area while Dewey worked on the other side of the room. He'd interrupted me when he moved to the door and found the strange odor.

When we'd determined the smell was coming from the door, I'd inspected the area, but only found a small pile of gray powder on the floor. The odor had been concentrated around the locking mechanism, and a sticky residue had left my gloves stained when I lifted the latch. I was convinced that smell tied into how the killer had exited the room and locked the door behind them.

However, for the life of me I couldn't figure out what that item was. The strange smell had also been on the monk's cloak that Dewey fished out of the marsh. It was a pungent, sickly sweet smell that was both offensive and tantalizing. Could it have been food? When I'd first smelled it, the odor made me think of the holidays, though if pressed I couldn't define it.

I pondered the mysterious smell for another second and then pushed it aside to focus on the other things we'd found. While bagging Heather's hands I'd noticed the pale mark that suggested she was in the habit of wearing a ring on the third finger of her left hand. Was it a clue? So far, it didn't appear to be relevant and yet something told me that it was.

Had she removed the ring or had the killer? Judging by the color of her skin, I felt the removal of the ring had been recent but that was all that I could say for certain.

What little we knew about Heather led me to believe she'd been single, but I couldn't confirm that. I'd seen her making a pass at Christopher, Dewey had seen her doing more than that with her cousin, and if I added in Chas's innuendo I could conclude that, married or not, Heather had liked to play the field.

I made a mental note to ask both Peter and Christopher then moved on to the papers in the fireplace. Connie's amazing internet skills had only told us the paper had been some kind of official letter from the Commonwealth of Virginia.

We had no way of knowing which agency had sent it, nor what the significance, if any, might be. I also didn't know whether the paper had been destroyed by the killer or by Heather.

Frustrated at how little was in my mental "know" list versus the overwhelming number of unanswered questions, I attempted to clear my head by focusing on the natural beauty surrounding me. That had been a mistake because I'd chosen to pay attention to my surroundings just as I reached the place where we'd found my brother.

My gaze went to the spot Dewey had fallen. The blood had been washed away by rain, but in my mind I could see him lying there, still as death. My mouth went dry. If not for The Colonel, our family might have been missing a member.

Staring at the ground where he'd lain, I began to pant as déjà vu reared its head. The night I'd been shot, I'd been bleeding out on a sandy dirt track in the middle of the forest. Drifting in and out of consciousness, I'd wondered if someone would find me in time or if I'd die and become fodder for predators.

My stomach churned thinking of my baby brother going through a similar circumstance, and hard on the heels of that thought, I worried about his recovery. We'd done the best we could to bandage his head and make him comfortable but other than a few seconds of incoherent mumbling, he'd never regained consciousness.

Connie had suggested I call Mama, but I'd resisted. What could she do but worry? But now I was second guessing myself. What if his injury had fractured his skull? What if the swelling was damaging his brain? My hands shook as I considered what might go wrong. None of us had any more than basic medical knowledge, and even if we did, we had nothing but a few rolls of gauze and an ice pack. He needed a doctor, a nurse, someone with healing skills—Auntie Pearl!

My eyes widened as I thought about the old Gullah root worker. How stupid had I been? Along with concocting hoodoo curses and protection spells, the root doctor was a skilled herbalist. I grabbed my phone and texted Connie.

Hitting send on my message to ask for Auntie Pearl's help, I paced and waited for a reply. I was bending down to pick up a piece of clear cellophane when my phone chimed. Cursing litterbugs, I tucked the trash in my pocket and opened up my text messages.

Good thinking! She came right away & says he needs a poultice 4 the swelling. Chris is driving her over to the village for supplies.

Phew. I blew out a breath I hadn't realized I was holding and replied.

Thank God! Is he any better? Has he come to?

Connie's reply was immediate.

No real change but he did open his eyes and whisper something about the leopards again. Do u think an animal attacked him instead of a person?

If I hadn't been so worried about Dewey, I'd have laughed. Shaking my head, I typed a reply.

There r no leopards here. IDK what he's rattling on about but it scares me. Is he running a fever?

Nope, he's fine except the bump on his head but Y is he talking about leopards?

I had no idea what was going on in my brother's head and told Connie it was probably the concussion talking. I continued walking toward the golf course, stopping when she sent a reply.

I guess? Weird though. Maybe he was watching a nature show on TV recently.

That made me laugh. Dewey was more likely to watch hours of reality TV than a documentary. Connie replied with a laughing emoji and then asked what I was doing. I typed that I was on my way to talk to Peter and we ended our conversation.

Feeling better about Dewey's prognosis now that Auntie was tending to him, I was able to focus on my mission of finding a killer.

A few minutes' walk and I was at the deserted golf course. The winding golf cart track would take me on a roundabout trail to the clubhouse, so I elected to cross the fairway and in short order I walked through the main doors.

Passed reception, I followed the signs to the bar without encountering a soul. I'd just about concluded the place was empty when I turned the corner and heard commentary on a golf tournament coming from a television.

I stuck my head through the doorway and saw Peter perched on a barstool, nursing a beer, and staring at the TV. He jerked around as I entered.

"We're closed until after the storm. Wait, you're that policewoman, right?"

Not bothering to correct him, I took the stool next to him and offered my hand. "Holly Daye. You're a hard man to find, Mr. Kent."

He grinned, showing perfectly even and brilliantly white teeth that could only be achieved with major dental work. "Glad to see my plan is working." He saluted me with his beer bottle and then drained it. "Join me?"

"No thanks. Why are you hiding down here? Everyone is supposed to stay in the main house to ride out the storm."

He cocked an eyebrow. "You answered your own question." He mock shuddered. "The girls in housekeeping and ol' Gator and Daphne will be here soon. We're having our own hurricane party. None of us want to be stuck in that house with the Lyles and a bunch of scared tourists."

I smirked because he had a point. "Not to mention a murderer is running loose..."

He snorted. "Yeah, that too. What's up with that?" He moved behind the bar and grabbed another bottle of beer. "I was talking to Daphne and she said Heather's been killed?" He shook his head. "That's messed up. Who would do that?"

I studied his expressions and body language. Nothing alerted me to think that he was anything other than mildly curious. Still, everyone was a suspect until proven otherwise. "That's what I aim to find out, Mr. Kent. Starting with everyone's alibi. Can you tell me where you were last night around 11:00 p.m?"

His eyes widened for an instant and then he chuckled. "Man, never thought I'd hear that in real life." He shook his head and took another pull on his beer. "Straight out of a TV show."

"Perhaps, but you didn't answer my question."

His brows rose. "You were serious?" The look on my face was sufficient answer because he gulped and dragged his hand through his sandy blond hair. "Um, I was at home? Let me think..."

Based on his nonchalance and the empty bottles lined up on the bar, I suspected he was more than a little buzzed, but he sobered quickly when he realized I wasn't playing.

"Saturday night I closed the pro shop."

"What are the hours the shop is open?"

"Uh, on Saturday we usually open at 9:00 a.m. and close at 7:00 p.m., but with the storm coming I didn't open until noon, and that was only because we had a few tee times booked. A diehard foursome played nine holes and finished a bit after 4:00 p.m." He shrugged. "I stuck around, did some inventory and the storm prep and left a little after 6:00 p.m."

That committed golfers were willing to dodge the storm bands to get one more game in didn't surprise me, though for some reason I'd thought the course had been closed all of Saturday. I frowned, trying to recall where I'd heard that, but Peter cleared his throat and broke my concentration. It'd come to me.

"Uh, we done? Only, I gotta throw some burgers on the grill before the girls get here..."

Directing my cop stare at him and hiding my smile as he squirmed, I considered his movements on Saturday. The wedding ceremony started at 11:00 a.m. and the reception followed directly after, but the bride and groom had taken pictures while guests held a cocktail hour, so the reception kicked off at 1:00 p.m. The cake cutting and missing dagger would have been discovered around 2:30 p.m., because the Gullahs started their curse ceremony shortly after 3:00 p.m. which effectively ended the reception.

It was easy to verify he'd had the pro shop open during the times he claimed which meant that Peter couldn't have stolen the dagger. Still, it paid to be thorough. "Just a few more questions, Mr. Kent." He sighed and slumped his shoulders, but I wasn't concerned with his feelings. "You closed the pro shop at 6:00 p.m.?" He nodded. "Where did you go after that?"

"Oh, uh, I begged some dinner from Elijah and then went home." He shrugged. "Boring, but every night can't be a party."

I nodded. "Felicia says you were talking to her around 10:30 p.m."

Peter nodded. "Yeah, yeah, I did call her about that time. She was still working."

"Yes. According to her, you were watching TV when you called. Can anyone verify that you were at home when you called?"

His eyes got huge and then he dropped his gaze to the bar and started fidgeting with the label on his beer. "My word isn't good enough?"

"This is a murder investigation, Mr. Kent, no one's word is good enough." He nodded but still wouldn't meet my gaze. "Mr. Kent? Can anyone confirm that you made that call to Felicia at your house?"

"Yeah…" He drew a deep breath and glanced at me, before returning to his study of the beer label. "But you gotta promise not to tell Felicia."

I rolled my eyes. "Mr. Kent, if it's pertinent to my investigation it will be a matter of public record." He hunched over his beer, a clear sign he was going to stop talking, so I hurried to reassure. "However, your relationship with Felicia is none of my concern and I have no intention of carrying tales. Was someone with you last night?"

"Yeah." He sighed. "Charise brought a six pack over. We watched the golf highlights on TV and ... you know."

My eyebrows rose but I refrained from comment. Privately, my estimation of Felicia's intelligence went up a few notches. Peter was not marriage material. "And Charise will confirm this? According to my assistant, Charise claimed to be at home with her roommate."

"She was, for a while. But Joanie has a cold and went to bed early." Peter shrugged. "Charise was lonely."

And you were happy to provide her companionship. I struggled to keep my tone neutral. "I see. You understand that I'll be checking with her..."

His head jerked up. "Go ahead! I'm telling you the truth." He frowned. "You can't seriously think I killed the woman. I didn't even know her!"

"Really?" I quirked an eyebrow and pinned him with my stare. "Because I have witnesses that say you and the victim were in this bar a few days ago looking very cozy..."

He paled and looked anywhere but at me. The tense silence stretched for a long minute before Peter sighed. "All right, so we hooked up a couple of times. What's the big deal? We're both single and consenting adults."

What was the big deal? Again, I silently congratulated Felicia on the correct assessment of her would-be fiancée's character. But I wasn't there to judge his morals or lack thereof. I was there to find a killer and something Peter had said was blinking like a neon sign.

"Mr. Kent, did you happen to notice Heather's jewelry when you were um, *hooking up*?"

The gaze he turned on me was equal parts puzzled and relieved. "Uh, jewelry? I don't pay much attention to that stuff..."

I nodded. "Understandable. But think back to when you were having drinks. Was she wearing any rings?"

He huffed and started to argue but a hard look from me brought him into line. He frowned and closed his eyes. "She had a watch on. I remember because I asked the time and she looked at it when most people nowadays use their phone."

He glanced at me. "That good enough?"

"Is that all you can remember? Think hard, please. Was she wearing any rings?"

He closed his eyes again. "Um, why is this important? I mean—"

"Mr. Kent, you said it was no big deal that you and Heather got together because you are both single. I'm trying to verify if that is true. Please, concentrate. Was she wearing any rings?"

He swallowed and fell silent for a few seconds before meeting my gaze. "Yeah, she had an emerald and diamond ring on her finger."

"Which hand? Which finger?"

He scoffed. "Oh, come on how am I"—he rolled his eyes and then closed them—"I know, I know, think..."

He was quiet so long I was beginning to think he'd fallen asleep, but just as I started to prod him, Peter blinked and shook his head.

"Okay, it was on her left hand. Why's this important?"

I shrugged and got to my feet. "I'm not sure that it is, Mr. Kent, but thank you all the same."

I strode to the door, ignoring his calls for me to explain. He'd answered my questions and confirmed his character. Anything else was surplus to requirements.

Chapter Nineteen

The long walk back to the main house was spent mulling over what I'd learned from Peter. Aside from our differences in morality, I'd confirmed that Heather was in the habit of wearing a ring on her left hand. Peter hadn't been able to tell me which finger the ring had been on, but I could make an educated guess.

What I couldn't do was definitively say what the significance of my discovery was. So she usually wore an emerald and diamond ring. Had it been a wedding ring? Engagement ring? I didn't know. Nor did I know if Heather had removed it or the killer had.

Could her murder be as simple as a robbery gone wrong? If not for the voodoo doll I'd lean in that direction, but instinct told me the murder of Heather was more complex.

I was sure Heather had known her killer. The theft of the dagger, the construction of a doll ... there was no doubt the murderer had planned to kill her and put thought into covering their tracks. That wasn't usually true for robberies.

Running through possibilities and scenarios occupied me for the remainder of the walk. My first priority upon arrival was to run upstairs and check on Dewey. He'd rolled to his side and seemed to be in a natural sleep, but appearances could be deceiving. Connie and Auntie Pearl were sitting by the fireplace but they motioned for me to step into the hall when I started asking questions.

"He's resting comfortably, Ms. Holly. The wound ain't deep and he come 'round long enough to tell me his name. He'll be okay I think."

My shoulders sagged. "Thank God, and you Auntie." I gave her a hug. "Is there anything we can do for him?"

She shook her head. "We just goin' let 'im sleep for now. Me and Ms. Connie takin' turns layin' the compress on his head every half hour, but rest is what that child needs most right now."

I nodded, though I still felt helpless and wished there was something I could do. "You said he woke up? He knew his name? That's good, right?"

"Yes ma'am, I'd be worried if'n he didn't. He's groggy and wasn't sure what day it was, but that's understandable. A'fore he fell back to sleep he was ramblin' on about leopards though." Auntie chuckled. "Scared me he'd done went out of his head, but Ms. Connie says he been sayin' that nonsense since y'all found him."

"Yes and I have no idea what he's trying to say."

She snorted. "Nor me, but so long's he don't run no fever or fall unconscious we'll just have to wait. I mixed up an herbal tea for when he wakes up good and proper. That'll help take the swellin' down some more and get his blood flowin'."

I grabbed her hand. "Auntie Pearl, I don't know how to thank you—"

"Go on with ya, now. You go find dat killer so's we can all be at peace. I'm goin' back to tend to your brother. Dat dog and I finally made friends after I gave him a big soup bone."

She cackled and returned to the bedroom. Connie grinned. "You should have seen it, Holly. The Colonel wasn't having anybody but me approach the bed, but Auntie started singing to him and then she pulled out this huge bone ... she's a regular dog whisperer."

"I've never known The Colonel to be so protective. He's attached to all of us and he's saved my life a few times now, but it's always been by accident." I chuckled. "I didn't know he had it in him."

Connie laughed. "It's those sad eyes and droopy jowls. We underestimate him."

I laughed and then Connie got down to business. "So, I got a chance to look through Heather's purse."

My eyes widened. It had slipped my mind. "What was in there? Anything good?"

She wrinkled her nose. "Yes and no. The good news is I found her cell phone, bad news is it needed charged and now I can't get into it." At my puzzled look she explained. "She uses a fingerprint security system and..." She shuddered. "I wasn't up for going to the barn and—"

"Understood. Give it to me, I've still got to talk to Bradley and Christopher, but I'll run down and unlock the phone."

She pulled the phone from her pocket. "Did you find Peter?"

I slipped Heather's phone into my pocket only to hear a crunching noise. "Yes, I talked to him. What is in my—oh!" I handed Connie the piece of trash I'd found on the path. "Throw this out, will you?"

"Sure, but what is it and why are you carrying it around?"

I laughed. "Garbage. Found it while walking to the golf course. I hate a litterbug."

"Me too! Makes me so mad when I see trash on the side of the road. People have no respect for our habitats or wildlife." She looked at the plastic I'd given her. "This looks like a wrapper of some sort."

Clear cellophane with a band of gold on one side, it did look like a decorative wrapper. "Candy maybe?" I shook my head. "Regardless, it won't be clogging up some poor animal's innards now."

She nodded and crumpled the piece in her hand. "So did Peter tell you anything helpful?"

"Yes and no."

Connie stuck her tongue out at me. "That's my line!"

I grinned. "Yes, but applicable here. He backed up what Felicia told me. He was at home watching TV when he called her."

Connie frowned. "You sure he isn't lying?"

"Yeah, he had a visitor he was reluctant to name. Finally got it out of him on condition I didn't tell Felicia."

Connie's brows shot upward. "Oooh, like that is it?"

I snorted. "Exactly like that and more, but Felicia isn't engaged to him and is fully aware of his character flaws so I'm staying out of it." I looked around to be sure we weren't overheard. "Get this. He also was *friendly* with Heather, just as Chas said."

Her eyes lit with excitement. "Oh! You think he killed her?"

I shook my head. "Sorry, but no, I don't. But he remembers Heather wearing a ring. Emeralds and diamonds and it was on her left hand."

Connie whistled softly. "So she *was* married! You think jealousy is behind all of this?"

"Honestly? I don't know. It's as plausible as any other theory but we can't say for sure that ring on her finger was a wedding ring or even an engagement symbol."

"But why else would she wear it on her left hand?"

I shrugged. "Many women wear rings on both hands. It doesn't necessarily follow that they are in a relationship."

Her expression turned glum. "So we're back to square one."

I'd been excited by the news about the ring, but while relaying the information to Connie, I'd realized the knowledge I'd gleaned from Peter wasn't a smoking gun. But I wasn't going to fall down into the dumps with Connie. Someone had to stay upbeat, if only to pull the others out. "Not necessarily. We have another piece of the puzzle."

A crack of thunder rattled the windows, making us both jump. Connie clutched her chest. "Gosh, that was close!" She sighed and shook her head. "You said the ring is another puzzle piece." I nodded. "Well, how many more do we have to find? The storm is going to be on us in a few hours and we've no idea who killed Heather!"

I squeezed her hand. "We're getting closer, Connie. I can feel it. Sit tight and I'll run and unlock the cell phone. You can look through it while I talk to Bradley and Chris." She nodded, but the defeated expression remained. "All we can do is keep moving forward, Connie."

I started toward the stairs then turned and added, "And pray. Have a little faith and everything will work out, you'll see."

Despite my pep talk for Connie, I was feeling far from confident in our ability to unmask the killer before Isabella arrived. I'd meant it when I claimed we were making progress, but whether the disparate things we'd uncovered would lead us to solving the mystery in time was anyone's guess.

Storm clouds were building again, and as the eye of Isabella got closer, the violence of her storm bands would increase. Bolts of lightning ripped across the sky and the wind had whipped the river into a froth that rivaled the ocean. The trees were bending under the gusts, making the old live oaks creak and groan.

Forgoing the protection of the trees out of fear from falling limbs, I was drenched by the time I entered the barn. I'd just opened the cooler door when the lights flickered.

"Oh, heck no." With no desire to be in the dark with a corpse, I stomped on my squeamishness and made quick work of unlocking her phone. A few swipes of the screen and I'd removed the security lock. I was about to look through her emails when the power flickered again and sent me scurrying back to the main house.

Dropping the phone off to Connie, I suggested she start with text and email messages and left her to get on with it while I tracked down my final suspects. It was time to gather what I hoped were the last pieces of the puzzle.

Chapter Twenty

A check with the front desk and I was headed back toward the executive suite, only this time my quarry was in the adjacent office. I gave a perfunctory knock and walked in to find Bradley slouched in a leather chair, feet propped on the mahogany desk. Despite the rightful heir finally asserting himself, Bradley still acted like he owned the place.

"Time we talked."

He scowled, "What do you want now? Haven't you caused enough trouble?"

I snorted and sat in the chair opposite of his desk. "Pouting over the rightful heir claiming what is his? You know, he seems to be a pretty decent guy. Maybe if you found your manners and came off your high horse, he'd let you continue working here."

He sneered. "Work for him? Never. Who do you think turned that pokey B&B Miriam started into a five-star resort? Me, that's who! And if you think I'm going to stand by while that no-good trust fund brat takes what's mine—"

"Enough Bradley." I'd had enough drama from him to last a lifetime. "I've bigger concerns than the state of your bank account or your ego. I need to find Heather's killer and time is running out. Or do you like the idea of being holed up here with a murderer on the loose?"

He rolled his eyes. "Think you're a regular Joe Friday, eh?" He snorted. "You've been watching too many movies, Daye."

The man was so pompous. The imp that dwelled in my head wanted to be let loose desperately, and in other circumstances I'd have flayed him with my tongue, but I needed to be the better person, for now.

"Just tell me where you were around 11:00 p.m. last night and I'll get out of your hair."

He scoffed. "I don't have to answer—"

"We've been through this. Sheriff Felton has put me in charge, and as I told your wife, you'll answer to me or be taken in for questioning by the police. Your choice."

His face tightened with frustration, but he knew he had no other option. With a resigned sigh, he replied, "Fine, but I really don't see where this is going. You were a glorified secretary with a gun, not a detective. Really think *you* can find the murderer?"

"Since I've done it several times in recent months, yes I think I stand a very good chance. Now, what were you doing at the time of the murder?"

He smirked. "I was right here." He nodded toward a flat screen hanging on the wall opposite his desk. "Watching the weather channel."

"Your suite is right next door, why watch in here?"

He huffed. "Not that it's any of your business, but Olivia was in bed with a migraine. I was being a considerate husband."

Based on what I'd seen of their relationship, that'd be the first time he'd shown such concern. "Why should I believe you? You had several million reasons to want Heather gone."

Bradley's face flushed and his feet hit the floor as he took exception to my statement. "Hardly." His voice dripped with scorn. "She was a gold-digging tramp, and no court was going to take her seriously. You think this is over because of what happened in the hall?" He snorted. "Lady, we've just begun to fight and all his assurances to that old witch were just words." He slammed his fist on the desk, knocking over a pencil holder. "Damn Miriam! This was all supposed to be mine! How dare she leave all of this to that pitiful excuse for a son!"

I quirked a brow. "Bradley, why would she leave it to you? Christopher is her son and an actual Pennington. What right do you have to any of this?"

"Right?" He laughed. "That's rich. I may not have been her child by blood, but I'm the one that stuck around. I'm the one that took over when she got sick. I'm the one that—"

"I get the point. But any way you slice it, Christopher is the rightful owner of Pennington."

"Please. Amnesia?" His lip curled. "You believe that line of bull he's feeding everyone?"

"What I think is irrelevant. Three people, two of them your siblings, confirm he *is* Christopher Pennington. As I stated before, it'd behoove you to try and make amends before he tosses you out on your ear."

He snorted. "Chas is a drunk, Elijah has a village's worth of reasons to lie, and Felicia?" He snorted. "She'll say anything to hurt me."

"What?" His perception of Felicia was so far from reality, I had to ask how he'd arrived at his conclusions. "Why would Felicia lie about that?"

He propped an elbow on his desk and started scanning the papers strewn across it. Without bothering to look up, he replied. "To get back at me of course. She's always been jealous of my success. Now, if that's all."

"No, it isn't. Why didn't you attend the wedding reception? I saw you and Olivia at the ceremony, but only your father went on to the reception."

Still absorbed in work, or pretending to be, Bradley snorted. "I had better, more important things to do."

"Like what?"

He huffed and scribbled something in the margins of a document. "A myriad of things is required of me every day, Ms. Daye. However, on Saturday, I was checking that we had the necessary supplies to ensure my guests are comfortable despite a hurricane blowing in." He finally looked at me. "This is easily confirmed. I spent a considerable amount of time with both Elijah and the housekeeping staff. Now, I have a hotel to run." He bent his head and began crossing out paragraphs while muttering, "God knows, no one else in my family does anything."

I shook my head at his willful obtuseness. The man was convinced he single-handedly ran the resort and that he had a right to Pennington Place, despite having no blood ties to it. I bit my lip and considered.

Once I'd learned the truth about Chris Pennington, the motive for the Lyles went out the window. That was still true for Quinton and the others, but Bradley? His anger seemed to be personal and whether it was jealousy or spite that drove him, both were powerful motives.

"Bradley?"

He looked up and frowned. "What now? Can't you see I'm busy?"

Gritting my teeth to keep from taking him down several pegs, I forced myself to stay calm and unemotional. "Why did Chris runaway?"

A wary look flickered across his face so fast, if I'd have blinked, I'd have missed it. He shrugged. "How should I know."

Oh, but his body language said that he did. "Did something happen between you two? A fight maybe? Or ... what, did he steal your girlfriend?"

I'd been chumming the waters not expecting to get a hit but at the mention of a girlfriend, he stiffened and a nerve ticked in his cheek. "That's it, isn't it? Something happened between you and Chris over a girl."

His eyes narrowed and his knuckles turned white as he clenched an ink pen. I held my breath, waiting for the explosion I sensed was building, but after a long, hate-filled stare, he drew a deep breath and shook his head. "You're being ridiculous and wasting my time." He turned his attention back to the paperwork on his desk. "See yourself out, Ms. Daye."

I rose, but not because he'd dismissed me. I'd gotten far more from Bradley than he realized and now it was time to pry the truth from Christopher. Whether it had any bearing on Heather's murder remained to be seen, but something told me I was digging in the right place.

Crossing to the door, I paused. "One more thing, Bradley."

He glared at me. "I've said all I intend—"

"Just explain why you called Heather a gold digger and I'll leave you alone." For now anyway, I silently added.

Since I'd changed the subject, he was happy to oblige me. He leaned back in his chair and laughed. "Because she was! That's the only reason she tried to foist that impostor on us."

My brow furrowed. "That makes no sense. What would she have to gain from finding the heir to Pennington?"

He snorted. "Two hundred and fifty thousand is what the witch had to gain. Miriam included a finder's fee in her will." He shook his head and returned to his work, muttering, "Some detective you are..."

I left Bradley's office finding myself in agreement with him for once. I was a shoddy detective for not knowing about that reward. Question was, had anyone else known?

Chapter Twenty-One

I sabella's full fury was currently wreaking havoc near Tybee Island, but her outer bands were putting on quite a show. Through the slats of the storm shutters I could see the trees bending and the driving rain beat a harsh tattoo against the roof. It wouldn't be long until she arrived on our shores.

A check of my weather app showed winds were gusting over 40 mph. Add in the heavy downpour and it was doubtful anyone had ventured far from the house. I made a check of the ground floor and, not finding Chris in any of the rooms, headed upstairs.

Knocking on his door several times in as many minutes, I stood around twiddling my thumbs until my final knock produced results. Chris swung the door wide and stood, wrapped in a robe, toweling his hair.

"Hey, I was in the shower when I heard you knock. You been waiting long?

"Not really." Drops of water were visible on his neck and his hair was wet giving credence to his claim. I was reminded of the night Heather died when the opposite had been true. "Can I come in?"

"Sure, let me get dressed." He gathered clothes and headed to the bathroom. While I waited, I glanced around his room. Piles of books were stacked on the nightstand as well as the small table in front of the fireplace. A laptop was laying on the bed, and the remnants of lunch sat on a tray nearby. It was clear he'd been using his room for more than sleeping.

I was flipping through a book on wildlife management when Chris came back. He swept aside more books and dropped onto the sofa. "So, what brings you to my humble abode?"

Chuckling, I set the book aside and joined him near the fireplace. "Humble? Pennington Place is anything but!"

He grinned. "True." His gaze roamed around the room. "You know, I grew up in this house and never really appreciated its beauty until I left. Ever really look at this house? The workman-ship is incredible. Especially as it was all done by hand."

"Mmm, I know what you mean. My family owns two historic homes. The Oaks is in Sanctuary Bay and Myrtlewood is on Saint Marianna Island. It's hard to understand the awe visitors have for these old places when you've lived in them all of your life."

He snorted. "Familiarity breeds contempt?"

"Eh, more like familiarity breeds complacency, at least for me. It wasn't until my father died and the burden of our homes fell to me that I truly appreciated the work involved in maintaining them." I sighed. "And it's not just the labor involved but the responsibility. Every day I feel the pressure to keep the taxes paid and repairs done so they can be passed on to future generations."

Chris nodded. "I'm beginning to feel the same way. We're not owners so much as caretakers."

"Exactly." I looked at the stacks of books. "Been reading up on plantation management?"

He smirked. "And a lot of other things." He rose and walked to the window. "What it takes to run this place is overwhelming. I'm beginning to wonder if..."

He'd left the thought unsaid but I could follow his line of thinking. "You're having second thoughts about coming back?"

A quirked eyebrow was his only response.

"Why did you come back?" I winced at my lack of subtlety. Never known for an abundance of tact, my lack of sleep had only exacerbated that trait.

Chris didn't seem to mind or was too polite to point out my social faux pas. His smile was rueful when he turned from the window. "Ah, a question I've asked myself repeatedly since Heather stormed back into my life. The truth is, Ms. Daye, I have no other reason than it was time."

I frowned. His tone was nostalgic and at odds with someone of his age but considering the unusual life he seemed to have led since running away...

"You obviously love Pennington." I tipped my head toward the piles of books. "And feel a responsibility to it. So what made you leave in the first place?"

His lips twisted into a mockery of a smile. "Ah, the question uppermost in every citizen of Sanctuary Bay's mind. You don't recall the incident at the high school?"

My brow furrowed. Chris was twenty-five years my junior. He'd run away at sixteen. I'd been in my early forties at the time and my life had revolved around work and my family. My son had already graduated, and I had little interest in the happenings surrounding the school system. I vaguely recalled a dustup though. "There was a break-in around that time. A school bus was stolen, minor vandalism of the school..."

He snorted. "That's it. But the bus wasn't stolen so much as taken out for a joy ride and dinged up. It happened homecoming weekend."

I cocked my head to one side. "Let me guess, that was you?"

The corner of his mouth lifted. "Allegations were made, yes."

"By your tone, I'm guessing you weren't involved?"

He shrugged. "I was there for some of it. But I didn't enter the school and did not take the bus."

He was hinting at something but either I was particularly slow on the uptake or it'd been a long weekend. Either way, I was tired of the runaround. A gust rattled the storm shutters and drew my gaze to the window. Even with the shutters I could see the ominous clouds swirling; the clock was ticking.

"Chris, what does a minor act of vandalism have to do with your running away from home and not coming back for a decade?"

"Quite a lot, actually." His voice lost its nostalgic tone as he began to pace. "Mother had just announced her intention to turn this house into a B&B, her world revolved around the renovations and Quinton." He met my gaze and smirked. "She was besotted with him and I'll freely admit I hated it. She passed off my anger at her marriage as jealousy and loyalty to my father, but that wasn't the case."

I was skeptical and it must have shown on my face because he smirked and added. "Well, not all of it at any rate." He huffed. "She refused to see the truth about Quinton, always took his side and, by extension, his kids." He met my gaze. "Particularly Bradley."

My eyes widened as the truth began to dawn. "Bradley was the one that did the damage at the high school."

Chris nodded. "Got it in one, Ms. Daye." His eyes took on a faraway look. "He was just like his father, still is really. Arrogant, entitled, petty, and jealous."

"What happened that night?"

Chris's smile was self-deprecating. "Someone had thrown a kegger. I don't recall who, but it's irrelevant. We were all there: me, Bradley, most of the football team."

"Felicia?"

He shook his head. "No, she begged me not to go."

My brow furrowed. "Why?"

He shrugged. "Probably because she knew her brother better than I did." He stared out the window, lost in his past. "Typical, I didn't listen." He snorted. "More fool me, I thought what'd happened a few days before was no big deal." He glanced at me. "I was naïve and didn't fully appreciate how much Bradley despised me. Won't make that mistake again, I promise you."

I nodded. "He's jealous of you."

Chris tipped his head. "Yep, jealous and resentful ... of what I don't really know, but either way, I went along with him to this kegger. Everyone was drinking heavily and cutting up, you know how teenaged boys are."

Having raised one, I certainly did. I had no trouble imagining how a bunch of hormonally fueled jocks, loaded with beer, could end up trashing a school.

"Whose idea was it to go to the school?"

His brows rose. "Who do you think?"

"Bradley."

"He was the ringleader, yes. The party was in a field behind the high school. We could see the stadium lights from the party. Someone got the idea we should go over to the football field for a game and that was it. Someone grabbed a football, and we all stumbled our way across the field. Only, Bradley had other ideas."

"He wanted to break into the school?" Chris nodded. "Why?"

He drew a deep breath. "Oh, he spun a tale of playing a prank on the principal, but I knew what he really wanted to do, which is why I refused to participate."

"What was Bradley's real agenda?"

"Stealing the answers to the math midterm. He was failing, you see, and the punishment for failing grades was losing car privileges."

"You said you didn't go in. Did you go home?"

He shook his head and sighed. "God, I wish I had ... no, Ms. Daye, my sixteen-and-a-half-year-old self wasn't quite that bright or forward thinking. I returned to the party and passed out."

"So you had no idea what the rest of them did?"

"Nope and it wasn't all of them. Only Bradley and his side-kicks went into the school, the majority went and played ball like they'd planned. Bradley and his crew broke into the school and when they couldn't find what he was after, they trashed the place."

"Where does the stolen bus come in?"

He chuckled. "Well, I wasn't there but best I understand it, they were drunk and needed a place to crash. The bus was there, the doors were easily pried open..."

"Okay, they slept in the bus. How did that turn into a joyride and crash?"

Chris smirked. "They said it got cold; it was November, re-member, and they were gonna try and make it home when someone noticed the keys had been left in the bus. They started it up and one thing led to another as it often does with drunk yahoos."

Engrossed in his story, it took me a minute to realize there was a hole in his plot. "Um, if you were passed out back at the kegger, how did you get accused of those crimes?"

His brows went up and his tone was mocking. "Oh, that's the best part. You see, the guys that went to play football left before I went back to the party spot, and after they finished playing, they all went home. No one knew I was sleeping it off by the dwindling bonfire." He shook his head. "I was so dumb. The next morning, I woke up to find Bradley sitting nearby. We drove home to find the cops here and the house in an uproar."

"How had the police traced it back to you?"

"They didn't, not me specifically anyway. Someone had seen the bus being driven around, recognized Brad and called the cops. But they crashed it into a street sign and ran off before the cops arrived." He met my gaze. "See, I had no idea what had happened after I passed out. When I woke up and saw Brad, I figured he'd been there all night and he didn't disabuse me of that notion. But he knew why the cops were here and ... he's quick on his feet, I'll give him that."

"What happened?"

"What do you think? The cops had a witness to put Brad in the bus with two other boys that they couldn't identify so, when they asked who'd been with him, he said it was me. Said it was all my idea, actually."

"And it was your word against his."

"Pretty much. The cops were friendly with my mother and said if they'd make restitution and have us do community service there'd be no charges. She jumped on that and they left it in her hands, but once they were gone she put the hammer down, well it was Quinton's idea but she was firmly behind him."

"What did he want to do?"

Chris looked at me and the loathing was clear on his face. "Bastard started ranting about how my bad influence had turned his saint of a son into a delinquent and that I was to go to military school…"

"And your mom went along with it?"

"Sure, she was under his thumb so bad … it was disgusting. Seeing her believe that louse and his jerk of a kid when I kept protesting my innocence … it was the last straw. I stormed out, and the rest is history."

Wow, I had no words. As a mother I couldn't imagine not sticking up for my son. If Junior had done something like that I would have punished him yes, but if he'd said he wasn't a part of it, I'd believe him. That Miriam Pennington hadn't supported her son ... Chris's tale answered a lot of questions. In his shoes, I couldn't say that I wouldn't have stayed away either.

I told him as much and chuckled. "Thanks, I think most mothers would be like you. But Miriam..." He shook his head. "She was always weak minded. I didn't see it at the time, but looking back I can see why she fell under Quinton's spell. My father had indulged her, my grandfather before him. She was used to adoration from men, thought it was her due, I think. And she had no discernment, she was easy prey for a flattering gold digger."

Anger on his behalf made me disagree. "No Chris, there's no excuse for what she did. A mother's first and highest priority is her children, always."

He smirked. "That's not been my experience, but I don't disagree it should be that way." He sighed and sat down on the couch. "But it's all water under the bridge now. Heather found me, convinced me to come back and here I am. However, whether I'll stay is still to be determined."

My eyes widened. "What? But you told Bradley—"

"Oh, I'm not letting him have Pennington." He snorted. "It'd be a cold day in hell before I let that happen. In fact, it's the only reason I came back. When Heather told me about my mother's will and how Quinton and Bradley were destroying Pennington ... no, I couldn't let it continue."

His reasons for running away and not coming back cleared up a lot of questions, but I still had a few. "Chris, you said that Heather found you. From what I gather, your mother paid a lot of money to private investigators over the years and no one she hired ever found a trace of you. How did Heather manage it?"

He laughed. "Because my cousin knew where I was." He shook his head. "Correction, she knew where to start looking and she knew me well enough to guess the rest."

"I don't understand. You claimed to have had amnesia ... was that a lie?"

"Oh no, I was in a coma for several weeks and woke up with no idea who I was, but it did come back eventually."

I nodded. His story was sounding less and less like a cheap soap opera. "You said Heather knew were you'd been?"

He nodded. "Yep. She was a few years older than me but we'd been close. So, when I ran away, it was natural to head to Atlanta. She was a freshman in college, and she put me up for a couple of nights, tried to talk me into going home ... I refused and couldn't stay in a girl's sorority house." He laughed. "That was an interesting few days! Heather and a friend hid me in their room, brought me food ... but obviously it wasn't a long-term arrangement."

So he'd run to Heather. That didn't explain how he ended up in Bimini though.

Chris chuckled. "Long story, but basically some friends of Heather's were driving to Florida for the Thanksgiving break and let me tag along. They dropped me off in South Beach." His smile was rueful. "So young and dumb. I really thought I could get a job, find a place to live, make a life..."

"What happened?"

He smirked. "What happens to a lot of runaways. I wasn't even seventeen. Couldn't get legitimate work, panhandled, slept in parks and on the beach. Started selling drugs, then using drugs ... got mugged one night and ended up in the hospital. Spent almost two months recovering from that beating. When the hospital realized I had nowhere to go, no ID ... they set me up with social services, but I got scared they'd send me to foster care. You hear a lot of horror stories being homeless."

"I can imagine. So, how did you end up in Bimini of all places?"

"Luck," he grinned. "I didn't know who I was or where I came from, but the sea is in my blood. I ducked out of the hospital before social services could get me, wandered the streets, ended up sleeping rough by the marina. One day this old guy starts bringing me coffee and a donut, offering me odd jobs around the place ... we became friends of a sort. He heard my story, what little I knew of it, and it ended up with him getting a friend to hire me. It was a small commercial fishing boat. Weeks at sea? Suited me fine. But the captain was getting old and talking about retirement. My dream job was going to end and I'd be back to square one, if a little flusher in the pocket. So, one day when we pulled into port in the Bahamas, I jumped ship and ended up running a deep-sea fishing boat off Bimini."

"Wow, from the kindness of strangers. You're right, you were very lucky."

"Yeah, I'd been on Bimini for about six months when my memories started coming back. They were bits and pieces at first, but eventually I remembered my name and where I'd lived." He scratched his head. "Funny thing. I kept getting flashbacks of the day I ran away long before I figured out the rest. Odd how the mind works, huh?"

He was talking to someone who'd been through a trauma that resulted in PTSD; he had no way of knowing but I related all too well.

While I'd been enthralled with his tale, the room had darkened appreciatively. A glance at the clock showed it was only around seven o'clock. The darkness had to be Isabella. As if to announce her presence a brilliant flash of lightning lit the room followed quickly by a crack of thunder and an earth-shattering crash.

Chris and I jumped up and ran to the window. Peering through the slats of the shutters, we saw a massive pine a couple yards from the house laying on the ground, smoke curling from the debris.

Wide-eyed, I turned to Chris. "We should get downstairs." He nodded, grabbed an armful of books and went ahead of me.

I slipped into Dewey's room and found Auntie peering out the window.

"How is he?" I whispered.

She motioned me into the hall.

"Dat boy can sleep through anything! Me and de Colonel 'bout come out of our skin when dat tree fell but he didn't budge."

"That's good, right?"

She nodded. "Yes. He's sleepin' the sleep of a chile and dat the best thing for him." She chuckled. "Though I keep lookin' o'er my shoulder for dem leopards he's mumblin' about."

"He's still going on about that?" I smiled but I was puzzled. It was like Dewey's brain was a record needle stuck in a groove. Was he trying to tell us something? I thought about it for a minute, but for the life of me I could not figure out what leopards had to do with the price of tea in China.

I glanced at the window at the end of the hall. The winds were sustained now, and I was sure if I checked the radar I'd find Isabella was on our doorstep. "Should we move him downstairs? That wind is fierce."

She shook her head. "Nah, if'n it get much worse we can think about it but he's comfortable and I ain't scared of dat witch Isabella."

I bit my lip. The safest place was the lowest in the house, but the shutters were up. They'd stop any debris from crashing through the windows, and no trees were in danger of falling on the house. It was probably safe enough. I'd worry either way, but perhaps it was better to keep Dewey away from the others. He was vulnerable and I still hadn't figured out who the killer was.

I nodded. "Okay, you holler if you need me. I'll be right downstairs."

Auntie Pearl nodded and went back into the room while I headed to the ground floor. I'd finally gotten the full story of the prodigal son, but I was no closer to solving Heather's murder.

It was time to get my investigation back on track. I had a few more questions for Chris but my gut said he hadn't killed his cousin. Hopefully, Connie had found something because we were out of time.

Chapter Twenty-Two

C onnie, the Randalls, and Dylan were in the living room, and I'd seen Quinton and Chas in the dining room. Felicia had been walking toward the kitchen carrying a tray of dirty dishes.

Dylan and Walt were playing cards while Maude watched. She was a bundle of nerves and jumped at every sound. Having no wish to cause her more alarm, I motioned for Connie to follow and went into the library. Fortuitously, Chris was already there, engrossed in a book.

"Hey, can we join you?"

He smiled and set the book aside. "Of course, Bradley and Olivia are holed up in the executive suite, but that's okay, I prefer this room. At one time, it was my father's office."

I smiled and Connie and I took the chairs in front of the fireplace. "It's a beautiful room. Very British."

Chris looked around the paneled room lined with bookshelves and laughed. "You're right. Makes sense. The Penningtons hail from Devon I believe." He cocked his head to one side. "Did you need privacy? I'm more than happy to—"

"No, no you're fine. I actually need to talk with you a bit more if you don't mind."

He reclined against the back of the leather couch. "Shoot. I've no secrets." He grinned. "Anymore."

Connie looked puzzled but I mouthed *later* and turned back to Chris. "I've asked everyone else this so please don't be offended." His eyes grew round but he nodded.

"Okay, first where were you when Heather was killed? I heard the scream around 11:00 p.m. so I'm estimating that as her time of death."

A wary look flitted across his face but his voice was matter of fact when he answered. "I was in my room. I'd just gotten out of the shower, remember?"

"Yeah, that's what you said, but do you usually take a shower without washing your hair?" I routinely did that, but I'd never known a man to.

He licked his lips and looked at the fireplace. "Um, not sure where you're going with this. I was in my room—"

"Not disputing that. I saw you come out, but you weren't taking a shower, were you. Can anyone vouch for you being in there a few minutes before we all gathered in the hall?"

He swallowed hard and bit his lip. "You're very observant, Ms. Daye. I wasn't in the shower when I heard the scream, but I was in my room."

"Doing what?"

He stared for a long minute and then shrugged. "If you must know, I was busy trying to get Olivia to leave."

My eyes widened and Connie gasped. I had not seen that coming, though upon reflection, I should have. "Olivia was in your room when Heather screamed."

He snorted. "Not by my invitation, I assure you."

On that, I had no doubt. I'd seen him brushing her amorous advances off. I mentioned what I'd seen the afternoon of the reception and Chris laughed. "Yeah, she is a determined lady. She and Heather were two of a kind."

Connie leaned forward and cleared her throat. "What does that mean?"

He smirked. "Just that Heather and Olivia were both vying to become mistress of Pennington Place. Two women fighting over me. Every guy's dream, right?"

His tone was filled with loathing. "But not yours."

"Oh, heck no! Barracudas, the both of them."

Connie frowned. "You didn't like your cousin?"

Chris laughed. "Like her? Sure I did, but that didn't mean I wasn't aware of how she was." He shook his head. "Behind Heather is a trail of broken and scarred men a mile long. Been wild since our teens. She dated so many guys. For Heather it was always about money, fame, power. She had to have the captain of the football team or the guy with the richest family in town. I loved my cousin, but I had her number."

"And Olivia? You said she was just like Heather."

He nodded. "Yes. I don't know if she was as loose with her favors as Heather, but when it comes to prestige and money, she's the same."

"Is that why she was coming on to you?"

He shrugged. "That's the vibe I got. Once she realized I wasn't a fake, she started flirting and it only got worse. She came to my room Saturday night," he snorted. "Should have seen her.

Decked out in this see through gown, a bottle of champagne ...
she's a—well, you know."

Connie frowned. "She's married to your stepbrother!"

I laughed at her outrage. "Connie, Olivia sees her time as lady
of the manor ending and figured she'd offer herself to the new
lord."

"That's what I figured, Ms. Daye, and she wouldn't take no
for an answer, even when she found out about me and Fel—er,
that I am kinda in a relationship. Didn't matter to her one bit."

My eyes narrowed. He'd been about to say Felicia, I was almost
positive. If I were correct, then so many things I'd seen and heard
made sense. "You stopped yourself, but you're involved with
Felicia, aren't you."

He bit his lip and looked at the floor for a moment and then
nodded. "We're close, always have been really. It's early though
and we don't want anyone to know..."

"We won't say a word. But can I say that you couldn't do much
better than Felicia? She's a good person."

The smile that filled his face was full of love and affection. "I
know. I've always known. She's the best of the bunch."

I smiled because I'd thought the same thing. Something was
nagging at me. I frowned. I recalled Bradley's reaction when
I'd suggested his hatred of Chris had something to do with a

girl. From that memory, I recalled Chris telling me about the incident at the high school and how he shouldn't have went after what had happened days before...

"Chris? Did you and Bradley fight over your relationship with his sister?"

His eyes widened and he drew a deep breath. "You're *very* good, Ms. Daye..." I tipped my head in acknowledgment of his compliment and he snorted and stared at the far wall. "To answer your question, yes." His gaze returned to mine. "Bradley tried to frame me for his stunt because he'd caught me and Felicia ... well you see where I'm going with this?"

I did, and my mouth dropped open in shock. A glance at Connie showed she was feeling the same way. "Are you telling me that Bradley did all of that because you were involved with his sister?" I shook my head. "From what I've seen, he treats her like dirt. Is that a result of what happened?"

Chris shook his head. "No, not really. Bradley never acted like a protective and loving older brother."

I was confused. "If he never liked Felicia, why would he care if you two were seeing each other?"

Chris shrugged. "No idea, but Felicia and I both think his anger over our relationship was what made him accuse me. It's why she didn't want me to go to that party with him." He snorted. "She knew her brother better than I did and suspected he'd try and get revenge."

I shook my head. What a sordid and tragic tale. It seemed ridiculous that anyone would go to such lengths just because their sister was involved with someone they didn't like, but knowing Bradley Lyle...

Pathetic. The man was pathetic and not worth expending mental energy on. I had more important things to think about. I cast my mind back over all the information I'd gleaned from interviewing everyone at Pennington.

Despite not wanting to think about anything involving Bradley, my chat with him popped to the front of my mental list as I recalled something he'd said. "Chris, Bradley called Heather a gold digger. He claimed it was because she wanted the finder's fee, but could it also have been because she was after you?"

His brows rose. "He called her that?" He chuckled. "Well if anyone ought to know, it's him. He married one after all."

I laughed along with him but Connie frowned. "So, let me get this straight. Olivia and Heather were trying to seduce you. To what, get you to marry them?"

He shrugged. "That, or just make them a mistress. I don't know, but either way I wasn't interested." He snorted. "Not that I could get that through to them. Felicia tried talking to Olivia—"

"And got assaulted for her trouble."

"What? Olivia hit Felicia?"

His blue eyes had turned dark and a fury as strong as Isabella's was rising on his face. I cursed my thoughtless comment and quickly shook my head. "No, nothing so drastic. I saw Olivia and Felicia in the hall outside of the suite. Olivia grabbed her arm and dug her nails in a bit." My attempt to calm Chris wasn't successful. His jaw clenched and he looked ready to leap from the couch and pummel Olivia.

"Felicia's fine, Chris. She ran off in tears, but I just saw her going into the kitchen and she appears to have recovered."

He started to rise anyway. "I need to check on her."

I put out my hand. "In a minute please, I'm sorry but I really need to find Heather's killer and you're my last hope. Tell me more about her. You said she was after you and you're sure it wasn't because she was in love with you?"

He stayed seated but didn't relax and I knew I would only hold his attention for a few more minutes. Stupid of me to have mentioned Felicia had been hurt. I was losing my touch.

Chris laughed at my question. "Heather and love are two words that aren't in the same zip code, unless it's self-love." He snorted and shook his head. "No Ms. Daye, Heather did not love me in the way you're thinking. Heck, the money was the whole reason she set out to find me!"

"You mean it wasn't by accident?" A puzzled look crossed his face. "The rumor going around is that she was vacationing in the Bahamas and ran into you."

A bark of laughter erupted from him. "Man, that's hilarious! It was no accident. The only reason she put any effort into finding me was to claim the finder's fee. Heather is, or was, in debt up to her eyeballs. Her car was about to be repo'd, her house is mortgaged to the hilt, and she spends an obscene amount of money on clothes and jewelry; all on a credit card. Getting 250k just for finding me? She couldn't resist."

His statements painted a vivid picture of Heather, and with that type of personality as well as the debt she was in, a zillion motives now appeared. But how had she known about the finder's fee? If it'd been common knowledge, my sharp-eared Mama would have known.

Chris smirked when I posed the question. "Nice to know that all of my families' business isn't in the public domain. As to Heather knowing—that's simple. Her mom isn't well and hardly leaves the house. My mother left her sister some money and"—he shrugged—"some family heirlooms, I think. But regardless, Aunt Lois was unable to attend the reading of the will so Heather came in her place."

I nodded. "So she learned about the finder's fee and set out to find you. If she was so desperate for money, I wonder what she'd have done if her search was unsuccessful?"

It'd been a rhetorical question, but to my surprise, Chris had a ready answer.

"Hah, she was going to hire someone to impersonate me." He rolled his eyes and shook his head. "As if that would have worked. It was a dumb plan, but then we're talking about Heather, so..."

Connie frowned. "But if she'd found someone that resembled you and fed them your background..."

Chris laughed. "Nope, still wouldn't have gotten her the money. It's been kept a secret, but when Mother put that clause into her will, her attorneys made her give a DNA sample." He shrugged. "I provided mine last week and the results came in a few days later. No one else could have gotten their hands on this estate."

"Clever of them. I'd wondered how the executors would prove the rightful heir without DNA. With your mom being cremated, I assumed they'd file an exhumation order for your father's remains."

He nodded. "That would have happened, had the lawyers not thought ahead." He snorted. "Never thought I'd be grateful for smart attorneys!"

We all laughed and then Connie asked Chris why he'd run away. Since I'd heard all of it, I tuned them out and considered what I'd learned.

Heather had been a woman of loose morals. Heavily in debt and determined to get her hands on easy money by any means necessary. Once she'd found Chris, she'd seen the opportunity to not only pay off her debts but be set for life if she could snare him for good. Was that what got her killed? Olivia was also looking to score big. Had the two fought to the literal death?

Not that I wouldn't put it past Olivia, but she had an alibi. I was out of ideas until I recalled Heather's backup plan if she hadn't found her cousin. To foist an impostor on the executors, she would have had to have had an accomplice and what had Chris said?

Heather had left a trail of broken-hearted men in her wake. What if she'd done that one too many times?

The pale line on her ring finger flashed in my mind. "Chris?" He'd been walking to the door, no doubt to check on Felicia. "Was Heather married? Engaged maybe?"

His brow furrowed. "Gosh, not that I'm aware of, why?"

I told him about the mark on her finger and that Peter confirmed she'd been wearing an emerald and diamond ring in the weeks prior to her death. I also told him about the voodoo doll dressed like a bride.

His eyes widened and he let loose a low whistle. "Wow, this is some sick mess." He stared at the fireplace for a second, lost in thought. "I didn't know about any relationship, but where men and Heather are concerned, anything is possible. I can confirm she was wearing a ring. Big, gaudy thing."

Connie leaned forward and frowned. "But Holly, I thought you said whoever killed her was staying at the resort."

"I did—which leaves me slim pickin's for suspects."

Connie sat back; a glum look on her face. I was about to ask her about the contents of Heather's purse when the lights flickered.

While we'd been talking, the wind had increased, causing a constant rattle of the shutters to accompany its howl. I was opening the weather app on my phone when the lights flickered again, and then with a click, everything went dark.

Connie gasped and a screech rang out from the other room. "Oh God, what was that? Do you think the killer—"

"Relax, Connie, I'm betting that was Maude. She's terrified of the storm."

My friend snorted. "She's not the only one."

I flicked the on my phone's flashlight in time to see Chris opening the door. "I'd better see if everyone's okay and do a check on the house. So far the shutters are holding, but..."

He left Connie and me sitting in the library with only the dim glow from my phone. In the shadowy light I could see her nibbling at her thumb nail while her gaze roamed around the room.

"Relax, Connie. The generator will kick in if the power stays out more than a min—" A soft click and the lights came on, along with the hum of the air conditioner. "There, you see. Everything is fine."

She scowled and moved to the chair next to mine. "I don't know how you can be so calm! That's a Cat 1 out there and we have a murderous nut in here!"

She wasn't wrong, but laughter threatened to erupt so I bit my lip and managed to keep my voice level. "I can't do anything about Isabella, but maybe, if we put our heads together, we can identify Heather's killer."

Connie's eyes were wide. "That wind is roaring and I'll bet the river is like a boiling pot!" She glanced at the window. "How far do you think the water will come?"

I blew out my breath and considered my reply. I hadn't been exaggerating when I told Maude we'd had storm surges up to twelve feet during another Cat 1. But that storm's eye had come closer than Isabella was expected to. Subtracting a few feet based on the storm's location, we'd still see surge levels around nine to ten feet and with that much water, a few feet wasn't going to make much difference.

The parking lot and half of Goodwin Park had been three feet under with the other Cat 1. I hadn't been on Belle Isle that go 'round and wasn't that familiar with the island's flood zones, but even though Pennington Place sat on what could be called a hill in the Lowcountry, we'd probably see water up to the barn. The main house was a few hundred yards farther than that from the river, making it doubtful we'd have flooding affect us.

I decided to temper my estimation for Connie's sake. "The river will probably reach the barn, but I don't see it coming much farther."

She nodded and looked less tense. Congratulating myself on the judicious use of editing, I didn't mention my real concern. No need to remind her that snakes and gators were going to be driven out when their habitats flooded.

A knock at the door, followed by Chris poking his head in the room, broke the silence. "Hey, just wanted to let y'all know the shutters are holding, no water seeping in, and Auntie Pearl gave me some herbs to make a calming tea for Maude."

I grinned. "Might want to bring a cup for Connie, too!"

My friend huffed as Chris laughed. "I can do that, but Elijah has laid out a banquet fit for a king. Better get it while it lasts!"

"We'll be along in a minute. No way I'm missing out on that man's food."

Chris laughed and we were alone once more. I glanced at Connie. My friend was still looking as if she was sitting on a bed of nails. She needed a distraction, and I needed to solve the case. "Connie, let's go over what we know about Heather and the murder." She looked at me like I'd lost my mind and I laughed. "Come on, it'll keep your mind off the storm."

Her skeptical look spoke volumes, but after a beat, she nodded. "Okay, but let's grab a bite, first. Maybe that will settle my nerves."

Happy to oblige if it kept her calm, I followed Connie to the dining room. As we crossed the hall, I couldn't resist teasing her. "Sounds good, but with the state of your nerves, we'd better add in a whole pot of Auntie Pearl's tea!"

Chapter Twenty-Three

Once we'd stocked our lair with pimento cheese sandwiches and iced tea, Connie and I settled down to ferret out a killer. She swallowed a bite of sandwich and then went to the desk for a pen and paper. "Okay, we were talking about Heather's relationship status before the lights went out. Do you really think that's the key?"

"Don't know." I shrugged. "But we have evidence that fits that theory. She was in the habit of wearing a ring. Why did she remove it? Or did the killer take it from her?"

Connie shook her head. "How would we know?"

"There's no way that I can think of." We were both silent until I said, "Okay, enough with the ring, let's think of who might have been in a relationship with her."

Connie's brows went up. "If we're sticking to the idea it's someone on the property ... you said it was slim pickin's."

"Yes, slim, but there are some." I nodded toward the paper she'd brought over. "Write these names down. Walt Randall, Peter Kent, Dylan Carter..." I paused until she'd caught up.

"Okay, are you listing every man here?"

There was nothing to say Heather hadn't been in a relationship with a woman, but based upon her history I thought it was safe to assume she'd stick with men; she'd apparently perfected the art of manipulating them.

"Yes, for now. Add Christopher Pennington, Elijah Jones, Gator..."

"And if we want to be fair, Dewey, right?"

Connie was right if I was going to be unbiased. "Yes. Add his name and Jeff's for that matter." She scribbled and then looked up. "Now the Lyles: Bradley, Quinton, and Chas."

I waited until she'd finished. "Okay, I don't think I missed anyone." When she nodded her head, I moved on to part two of the exercise. "So, now we get to eliminate these men."

Connie grinned. "I'll start. Dewey and Jeff. Jeff because he only has eyes for Carrie, and Dewey because he only arrived at Pennington Saturday."

"Oh, take the easy ones why don't you!" She laughed and I rolled my eyes. "All right, that's Jeff and Dewey off the list … two can play this game so, I'll take Christopher and Walt."

Connie wrinkled her nose at me but crossed off the names. "That leaves us with Elijah, Gator, Peter, the Lyles, and Dylan." She tapped her pen on the table. "I can't see Quinton or Bradley getting mixed up with Heather. They were both furious that she'd brought Chris here."

I agreed. "Yes, and with Elijah growing up with Chris and being good friends, I'd think he was well aware of Heather's reputation."

Connie nodded. "True, but sometimes men don't use their brains when it comes to women, and Heather was gorgeous."

"Very true, but Elijah has an alibi and no motive. In fact, he claimed to be helping her, though he really meant helping Chris. His testimony would lead credence to the legitimacy of Chris's claim." I remembered what Chris had said about Miriam's DNA and said, "I should add that Elijah didn't *know* about the DNA on file so he'd have *thought* he was helping."

She nodded. "Yes, either way, he didn't have a reason to want her dead. So..." She stared at the paper. "That leaves us with Gator, Peter, Dylan, and Chas. Which do you think is most likely?"

Drawing a deep breath, I ran through what I'd learned from each man, plus what I'd thought of their behavior and characters. "Definitely not Gator. He's scared of his own shadow *and* he's not what I'd call a player. He also has nothing someone like Heather would want." Connie nodded and crossed the old man's name off the list. "Now, Chas is a wannabe playboy."

Connie tipped her head to the side and frowned. "I'm confused. Are you saying that's a reason for or against him being the killer?"

Her question made me consider and I did my best by thinking out loud. "I'm not sure, Connie. He's following in his father's footsteps as far as being an alcoholic and slacker but..." I recalled his alertness when he'd heard Dewey accuse Bradley of cheating the Gullahs, and when I'd attempted to shame him into cooperating it had not only worked in that regard, but the residual effect had been him prodding his father into sobering up and helping with the storm preparations.

I relayed all of those observations to Connie. "So, if you take the few hints of character trying to break through the fog of alcohol he seems to live in, and add in that he was the one that saw someone throwing what we now know was the monk's robe used to conceal the identity of whomever stole the dagger..."

"I see where you're going." She started to draw a line through Chas's name but stopped and met my gaze. "He could have done it though. According to you, he was in the pool house but there's no one to verify that, and if he is the killer, he was the one that tossed that costume into the river. How about putting him last with a half line through his name?"

She wasn't wrong about Chas's ability to be the killer, but I had to laugh at her notetaking methods. "That's fine. Let's move on."

Connie made whatever notations she'd deemed appropriate. "Well, you said Dylan is married, right?"

"Yes, that's what he said."

"Okay, then Peter must have killed her."

I didn't particularly like Peter. He was as amoral and grasping as Heather, but that wasn't a reason to accuse him of murder. On the other hand, Dylan was friendly, helpful, married. "Connie? I hate to say this, but I don't see either one being the killer."

She scowled and dropped her ink pen. "Well, someone had to have killed her!"

"I'm aware of that, Connie, but why would either have done it? What would they have to gain?"

Her expression turned mulish. "Does there have to be a motive?"

My brow furrowed. "Um, Connie. Very few murderers do so without some motivation. I mean, apart from a homicidal maniac and frankly, I haven't seen any of those running around Pennington. Have you?"

Her lower lip jutted out and I thought I should apologize. My tone had been heavy on the sarcasm. Before I could get the words out, she huffed and went to the desk, returning with a clean sheet of paper. "Okay," Connie said as she plopped back onto the sofa. "We've narrowed it down to two men. Assuming for a moment that Heather wasn't involved with a woman, let's see if any of the evidence we've collected ties to these guys."

It was a good suggestion and I should have thought of it. I stifled a yawn and nodded toward the new sheet of paper. "Start with what we found in Heather's room." I waited until Connie had prepared her paper. She drew a *T* down the page and wrote "Suspects" at the top of one column, and "Evidence" on the other.

"Got it. We'll list all of the stuff we found and then maybe draw lines to whichever person we think it's pertinent to?"

I grinned. "You're the list maker, I'll leave that to you. Put down burned papers. What do we know about them?"

Connie scribbled and then said. "They were burned—by the killer or Heather we can't say." I nodded and she continued. "My research suggests it was some kind of official document from the state of Virginia, but again I can't say what was in the letter."

Virginia. Heather had lived in Lynchburg. "Dylan is from Virginia..." I was musing, but Connie wrote the information down and drew a line to Dylan.

"Did you find out what part? It's a big state."

"Yes, some place that began with an *M*." I sighed as my brain refused to pull up the name. "Sorry, I'm so tired, my brain is on strike."

Connie grinned. "No problem. I pulled the registration papers. They're in our room. Want me to run and get them?"

"In a minute, let's keep going before I run out of energy."

She laughed and looked at her list. "Burned paper with Commonwealth of Virginia letterhead and Heather was from Lynchburg. We aren't sure where Dylan's from exactly, but we know it's also in Virginia." She cocked an eyebrow. "The missing ring? Should that be next?"

I shrugged. "Might as well. Though we don't know anything that connects it to either of the men. I will say that Peter had to think pretty hard before he recalled she was wearing one and it didn't seem like he was acting."

"Well, that's disappointing. How about her purse?"

The mention of Heather's pocketbook made me snap to attention. "I'd forgotten about that. Did you find anything in there? And what about her phone?"

"Nothing but the usual stuff in her bag, but the phone had an email from a lawyer." She rolled her eyes. "I thought I'd told you but, with the storm and then Dewey ... sorry."

"Don't worry about it, we are all running on fumes. You said the message was from a lawyer?"

"Yep, the message is not much help. Just a 'Ms. Franklin, we've started proceedings, please give us a call at your earliest convenience...'"

"No help then."

"Maybe, maybe not. I looked up the firm. It's a family law practice. Think that might lead us somewhere?"

My ex-husband was an attorney, and over the years I'd learned more than I ever wanted to know about legal practices. "Well, family law handles divorce, custody issues, guardianship, domestic abuse, adoption, parental rights..."

Connie's eyes lit up. "Divorce? So she was married!"

"We can't say for sure. She was also adopted remember. Maybe Heather was looking into her adoption. Trying to find her birth parents or something. Chris mentioned Heather's mother wasn't well. Could be Heather was planning to get guardianship or something like that."

"Oooh, I give up! I really thought we had it!"

I smiled. "We might have, Connie. Don't give up. It's another piece—"

"I know! Another piece of the puzzle. But gosh, how many pieces are in this darn thing?"

That made me laugh. "With the way our luck is running, I wouldn't be surprised to discover this puzzle has over a thousand and is 3D!"

Connie gave me a mock glare and shook her finger at me. "Hush! Don't even put that out into the ether!" Ignoring my laughter, she looked over her notes. "Papers, ring, and phone message. What else?"

Good question. I forced myself to concentrate. "Don't ask me what it is, but there's the odd smell Dewey noticed by the door in Heather's room. It was also on the monk's robe."

She wrote the information down and looked at me. "Speaking of the robe, do we know anything about it?"

"Not really. Chas saw someone toss it in the river, and from the wedding photos we are assuming the killer used the costume to blend in and steal the dagger." I shrugged. "Not much else to go on, except as I said, it smells just like the lock on Heather's door."

Connie frowned. "About that. Could it be as simple as some kind of polish? I could check the housekeeping cart..."

"Thanks, but I don't think it's a cleaning product. If I hadn't found it on the robe, I might have leaned in that direction? But it's concentrated around the brass plate of the lock and when I went to unlock the door, the latch was sticky and left a brown residue on my gloves—oh!" Connie gave me a puzzled frown. "I just remembered while Dewey and I were searching for the source of the smell, I found a little pile of gray dirt. I'm not sure what it was really, because dirt wouldn't turn into a powder and disappear when touched."

"But what does all of this mean?"

"I think the killer put something in the latch mechanism that allowed it to lock behind him. It's the only answer for how a murder was committed in a locked room."

Connie nodded, but her expression showed disappointment. "This is a waste of time, isn't it? I mean, we were trying to find the killer before the storm hit so we wouldn't be locked up in here with them but…" Her gaze moved to the window and her point was made.

Isabella was right outside. We had failed at our mission.

I was unwilling to give up, but we were both tired. Perhaps a break would clear the cobwebs. I got to my feet. "Come on, let's join the others and relax for a while. I need to check on Dewey, too."

Getting no argument from Connie, we left the library. She went into the living room and started talking to Maude, but I wanted to see how Dewey, Auntie Pearl, and The Colonel were fairing.

I was halfway up the steps when I realized The Colonel hadn't eaten since breakfast. Changing course, I went into the kitchen and prepared a bowl of chicken and sweet potato for my little hero then made a tray for Auntie and optimistically, added some soup for Dewey.

Opening the door to Dewey's room, my gaze went to the bed. Dewey's eyes were closed, but his lips were moving. Remembering that he'd been mumbling about leopards, I grinned and scolded myself for not including his imaginary friends in the feast.

Chapter Twenty-Four

C hatting with Auntie had been like a walk down memory lane. The old woman entertained me with humorous tales about some of Sanctuary Bay's most illustrious citizens. I particularly loved hearing stories about my daddy and his friends. Auntie knew all of their escapades and I was both shocked and amazed to discover my father had been a wild teen.

Dewey never woke up, though he'd remained consistent with his leopard hallucinations. The Colonel decided to follow me downstairs, and though I was happy to have my buddy by my side again, I suspected he needed to use the facilities. I was working out the safest way to let him answer the call of nature in the middle of a hurricane when I entered the living room, and everyone started fussing at me.

"Holly! Thank goodness, maybe you can talk some sense into him!"

"You tell him, Ms. Daye, idiot won't listen to—"

"Please stop him from—"

My gaze flew around the room as I tried to make sense out of the melee I'd walked in on. It was an impossible task, and I reached my tolerance for the confusion and put two fingers in my mouth, emitting a sharp whistle.

Everyone stared at me, but at least they'd stopped talking. I smirked. Worked every time. Now, what had the commotion been about?

A quick glance around the room failed to enlighten me, though seeing Chris and Felicia seated on the love seat looking cozy did make me smile. Predictably, Quinton was slumped in an armchair by the fireplace, an empty high ball glass on the table beside him, while Olivia and Bradley were on opposite sides of the room looking daggers at each other and at Chris and Felicia. I dismissed them; hate, envy, and jealousy were negative emotions and people that succumbed to them weren't worth my time.

Chas and Elijah were sitting across from each other. They looked to have been playing a board game. Chas seemed to be sober, a fact I attributed to Elijah since he was a staunch teetotaler from way back. I could think of few better role models for Chas and I hoped their association continued after the storm passed.

Connie and the Randalls were spread out on the sofas opposite the fireplace. Judging by the look on Walt's face, he'd been caught napping, and a stack of books and magazines suggested how Connie and Maude had been occupying themselves.

Dylan was standing by the French doors that led to the covered porch, but I didn't see the bride and groom.

"Where are Jeff and Carrie?"

Connie grinned. "We told them to get a room."

I smirked. "Glad someone is making good use of their time stuck up in here. Now, what the heck was all that racket about?"

Connie tipped her head toward Dylan. "Please tell him it isn't safe to go outside right now! He wants—"

"Come on, I just want to grab a smoke!"

Bradley started in about the resort's policy, which ginned up the arguing again but I'd had enough. "Quiet!"

Everyone stared in shock. I turned to Bradley. "I think you can make an exception to the rules for today."

The sound of crinkling plastic drew my gaze. Dylan was pulling cellophane off a pack of cigarettes. He let the plastic fall to the floor and Bradley hollered. "He's not smoking in here!"

I rolled my eyes, "Of course not." I looked at Dylan. "Mr. Carter?" I pointed to the floor. "That's not helping your cause."

He shrugged and picked the litter up, crumbling it before shoving it into his pocket.

Shaking my head at his lack of respect, I pointed to my right. "If you're determined to go out, and I strongly advise against it, stay on the west side of the porch, up against the house. If you manage to remain on your feet, you'll get wet, but the porch is deep enough that you should be safe from much of the flying debris."

The same couldn't be said for me and The Colonel unless I managed to coax him into going on the porch and cleaned up later.

I was snapping The Colonel's leash to his harness when Dylan crowed. "You're a star, Ms. Daye!" I straightened in time to see him open the French doors. The wind tore it from his hand, slamming it against the wall hard enough to make a dent.

"Fool!" Bradley cried. "Close the door! Felicia, grab some towels before the water ruins the floors!"

Dylan was unfazed. He ducked his chin and stepped onto the porch. As he struggled to pull the door closed, I heard him yell. "I'm off to the leper colony, wish me luck folks!"

As the door slammed shut, Maude snorted. "Leper colony indeed. Such a filthy habit!"

Silently agreeing with Maude and shaking my head at Dylan's inappropriate levity and foolhardy behavior just to satisfy an addiction, I looked down at The Colonel. He'd been pacing and as we approached the door, he started his little dance; a sure indicator that he had to go.

"Oh buddy, I wish I'd trained you to use a puppy pad." I glanced over my shoulder. "Chris? Come brace this door as I slip out, please."

He rushed over and stood in front of it. "Ms. Daye, this is a bad idea."

I snorted. "Don't I know it. But he's got to go." I motioned for him to let me out. I slipped through the crack and had to pull The Colonel through. No fool, my boy was having second thoughts, but we were out so it was now or never. The wind buffeted me and I struggled to keep my balance. "Come on boy, just a little farther…"

I'd underestimated the strength of the storm. Stepping less than two feet from the house I was pelted with rain. It felt like thousands of needles hitting my skin. The Colonel backed up and planted his feet but after much cursing and coaxing, I got him to move away from the door a few feet.

As I'd advised Dylan, I guided The Colonel toward the relative protection of the west end of the porch, sticking as close to the house as possible. I'd kept my head bent but a cough made me look up. Dylan was about ten feet ahead of me. He'd squatted into a tight ball and was using his hand to shield his cigarette from the blowing rain.

Insane what people did to feed their habit. Once we'd walked back and forth a few times and The Colonel realized we were not going back in until he did what I kept urging him to do, he started sniffing and finally ventured closer to the edge of the porch and hiked his leg.

It seemed to take him forever to drain his bladder, no doubt because he'd held it for hours. The wind was making it hard to stand, and I marveled that my bulldog was able to balance on three legs when I'd about lost mine several times.

I raised my head and stared out at the landscape. I'd been through numerous storms in my lifetime but in all of those years, I'd never been outside. As dangerous as it was, I was in awe of the storm's power.

Belle Isle was taking a beating from Hurricane Isabella. The wind was sustained now, and at a guess I'd put it somewhere close to the 70 mph that had been predicted. Sheltered by the house and the porch, I was barely able to walk and could only imagine how much worse it was on the east side where the storm was coming from.

The rain was like a solid curtain of water, making everything hazy. I could see limbs down, some of them as thick as my thighs. There were also shingles littering the ground and blowing across the lawn. There'd be right many repairs needed at Pennington once Isabella moved on.

The Colonel finished his business and pulled me toward the doors. I reached them at the same time as Dylan. He motioned for me to go first and slipped in right behind me. Someone had placed towels on the floor and more were stacked on a nearby table for us to dry off.

I reached for two and handed one to Dylan.

"Thanks, that wind is fierce. Imagine being out there without any protection!"

I bent to dry The Colonel off. "I have no desire to even think about it. Did you see that downed limb?"

"Yeah, incredible. This storm is a monster and it's only a Cat 1!"

I snorted. Only? Dylan was hyped on adrenaline and talking a mile a minute, clearly enthralled with the raw power of the storm. Nature was impressive, but all I could think about was the damage no doubt occurring all over my beloved islands, and I prayed our family homes wouldn't be torn apart too badly.

I finished with The Colonel and stood up, reaching around Dylan to grab another towel. As I did, I caught a whiff of something that made my nose twitch.

Dylan was still chattering and the others had started asking questions about what we'd seen while outside, but I tuned them out and took another sniff, then another.

Pungent, a bit sweet, it was the same odd smell we'd found on the door in Heather's room and on the monk's robe. A few more sniffs as I dried off and it finally hit me. The smell that had reminded me of the holidays was clove, or maybe cinnamon. But where was it coming from?

Dylan tossed his dirty towel on the floor and walked toward the drinks cart. I bent to pick it up and caught the strange scent again. My eyes narrowed and I looked over at Dylan. It was him. The smell had to be coming from him!

What to do? If I was right, and the odor was on his clothes ... from the corner of my eye, I saw him pour a drink and settle in a chair by the other set of French doors. He was looking at his phone and was several feet from the others. I felt it was safe to leave him for the moment.

As casually as I could manage, I sidled over to the couch and asked Connie to keep an eye on The Colonel while I ran up to our room. It took me a few minutes to locate the stack of printed registration records Connie had compiled. With Dylan's in hand, I trotted back downstairs and headed for the library.

I was almost certain the smell had been on his clothes. Cologne? I shook my head at the idea. Cologne wouldn't have transferred to the door ... think Holly!

I sat on the couch and tipped my head back, closing my eyes to aide my concentration. If I was going to accuse a man of murder, I needed to have my facts straight. The smell alone wasn't conclusive.

I frowned and considered the scent. What had he been doing—oh my gosh, it was his cigarettes! I recalled seeing him smoke just after he'd helped us move Heather's body. The box the cigarettes were in was odd; brown with something written in a language I hadn't recognized.

And what had he said just before he'd risked the dangers of Isabella just for a smoke? Leper colony. His joke ran through my mind and solved one puzzle. I snorted and shook my head.

That's what Dewey must have been trying to tell me with all of his muttering about leopards. Not leopards, but *lepers*!

Curious, I pulled out my phone. We'd already lost internet service but I still had a cell signal, albeit a weak one. It took forever and a day for a search engine to load and longer still for the results of my search to appear, but as I'd suspected, there was a type of cigarette imported from India that was flavored with clove and other spices.

Funnily enough my search connected another dot. The cigarettes were banned in the US, but the Bahamas were one of the few places near our shores that still sold them. Had Dylan accompanied Heather on her search for Chris? Or had she brought him a carton?

Knowing that the odd smell had come from Dylan's cigarette, so many pieces of the puzzle clicked into place.

Knowing he'd done it didn't explain why, but he'd told me he had driven down to Belle Isle from Virginia, and Heather had lived in Lynchburg ... Madison Heights, the registration said. Was that close to Lynchburg by chance?

I tried an internet search but my luck had run out or maybe just my patience. I left the search engine spinning and rose to examine the bookshelves lining the walls of Chris's quintessentially British library.

The books he had scattered all over his room confirmed it was a well-stocked library, with many reference volumes. Surely, I could find an atlas—ah! I pulled the book down and found a map of the Commonwealth of Virginia and in short order, confirmed my hunch.

Madison Heights was a suburb of Lynchburg, Virginia. Two strikes against Dylan. I didn't need a third, but I did wish that I was armed. He'd been congenial, at times almost too nice and friendly, but something told me he wasn't going to surrender peacefully.

However, as my daddy always said, if wishes were horses, peasants would ride. Convinced I'd found Heather's killer, I made my way back to the living room mulling over the best place to contain Mr. Carter until the police arrived. There were enough strong men present to assist me in arresting him, should my hunch prove correct and he became difficult.

Everyone was as I'd left them, except for Olivia, who had left the room, and The Colonel; He'd decided Connie's lap was the best place to take a nap. Shaking my head at the eighty-pound bully that thought he was a lap dog, *and I was being generous with that estimate*, I leaned against the doorframe and considered the best way to unmask the killer in our midst.

I'd watched my share of mystery shows where the detective gathered all of the suspects together and teased them with how one or another might be the killer before finally revealing the actual culprit. It made for riveting television, but a Cat 1 hurricane was enough stimulation of the nerves for one evening, thank you very much.

My beliefs leaned toward the theory it was better to rip a Band-Aid off quickly and I was a fan of being consistent and true to oneself. I straightened and cleared my throat, drawing everyone's attention.

Great Holly, now what? "Um..." I cleared my throat again and searched for a gentle opening to an unpleasant conversation, but coming up empty, I fell back on being blunt. "Mr. Carter?" He looked up from his phone and quirked a brow as I approached.

"By the authority granted to me from the Noble County Sheriff, I'm placing you under arrest for the murder of Heather Franklin."

Chapter Twenty-Five

S everal people gasped and Bradley jumped to his feet and started sputtering something about not harassing his guest, but I kept my focus on Dylan. With eyes narrowed and a twisted smile on his lips, Dylan leaned back in his chair and crossed his legs.

He quirked on eyebrow and chuckled. "Is this a joke?"

Several times I'd thought his flippancy inappropriate so I shouldn't have been surprised now. My gaze never wavered as I maintained a professional demeanor. "No sir, on your feet, please."

Dylan scoffed. "Oh come on…" Earning no quarter from me, he turned his charm on the others. "Mr. Randall, Walt. You know me, we were laughing it up while we put the storm shutters on. Do you think I could kill someone?"

Dylan's blue eyes were wide and without guile. Coupled with his wavy dark hair and dimple, he was the boy next door and he knew it. His smile was cajoling as he stared at Walt.

Walt's gaze flitted from me to Dylan and back again. "Well now, that's true, the boy was helpful and he seems like a decent man. Are you sure about this, Ms. Daye?" He glanced at Bradley and the others. "Doesn't seem right to let someone accuse a person of such a heinous crime without proof."

As Walt wavered, Dylan pounced. "Exactly!" He amped up the charm and looked everyone in the eye as he tried to get them on his side. "Ms. Daye is nice and all, but who is she to accuse anyone, much less me? She's a decorator! Are we going to let her railroad us into prison?"

Maude dropped her gaze to the floor. Bradley had his chest puffed out and looked about ready to try and wrestle control from me. Connie was looking at Dylan through narrowed eyes, but then, she was my friend and she'd seen the evidence, even if she hadn't put it all together yet.

Chris and Felicia were watching everyone and had no readable emotion on their faces, while Quinton merely looked puzzled and only semi-aware of his surroundings. Elijah looked skeptical but that doubt seemed to be directed at me *and* Dylan. Chas had a curve to his mouth that suggested he was waiting for popcorn to be served.

Maude wrung her hands. "Ms. Daye, this seems very unfair. Dylan is right. You're not the law and this is still a free country."

This had to stop. Given enough time, Dylan could use his boyish looks and glib tongue to lead a mutiny. I stared at Maude until she squirmed and stopped talking, then I made eye contact with everyone in the room.

"Despite what has been said by Mr. Carter, I am operating under the full weight of the law. Dylan Carter is under arrest and will be detained until such time as the Noble County Sheriff's Department can respond." I was about to request the assistance of Chris and Elijah when Walt again started to stammer about a free country and proof. Bradley and Maude added to his racket and the situation was heading to a point where I would lose control.

"Enough!" I held Walt's gaze since he'd been the first to succumb to Dylan's manipulations. "You're right, Mr. Randall. This *is* a free country, and we are all innocent until proven guilty.

That should be done in a court of law, but if you insist, we'll do it now."

"Now hold on a minute, I never said—"

"Yes, in fact you did. Quite clearly." I turned to Dylan. "Mr. Carter, I say you are under arrest, but you've managed to cast doubt and I need these people to help me detain you, therefore…" He started to object but I held up my hand. "*Therefore*, I'll present my case and let them be the judge."

He snorted. "What are you, Perry Mason?"

I smirked and quirked one eyebrow. "Oh no Mr. Carter, Perry Mason was a *defense* attorney … I'm your prosecutor."

I looked at the group assembled in the living room. "These people will hear the evidence and—"

"Now wait a minute!" Dylan's eyes were wide and he'd lost his smarmy smile. "Who is gonna be *my* defense?" He recovered his aplomb and flashed his pearly whites at the group. "I'm entitled to a defense, right? It's the Constitutional right of every American!"

I grinned and mine was every bit as cocky as his. "Mr. Carter, you misunderstand basic jurisprudence. What I propose is not a trial and these fine people are not your jury." His brow furrowed and I dropped the hammer. "They will act as the *grand jury* and determine if I've enough evidence to remand you for trial. Now sit down!"

Dylan continued to mutter but one look at the grand jury was enough to make him take a seat; it was obvious that, while a few had doubts as to his guilt, they were all ready to hear my evidence.

Ignoring him, I nodded at the others. "I'm going to present the evidence that I and my colleagues have gathered. You are not being asked to determine his guilt or innocence. All you need do is listen and determine if there is enough suspicion of guilt to help me detain him until the police can access this island and take him into custody. Are you all willing?"

Chris, Chas, Felicia, and Elijah readily agreed. Bradley started to argue that it wasn't appropriate but, to my surprise, it was Walt that told him to shut up and listen or get lost.

"Go ahead, Ms. Daye." He met the gazes of everyone else in the room. "We'll all listen and if your evidence is convincing, take whatever action is necessary."

I smiled and started to present my case. "Thank you everyone. If we look at the murder of Heather Franklin as a puzzle, there were many pieces collected. The first were found while my brother and I searched her room and prepared for removal of her body."

I held up my phone. "According to proper forensic procedure, everything found in her room has been photographed and or bagged and labeled. You're free to examine these items at the conclusion of my presentation if you remain unconvinced."

There was some murmuring among the group and I waited until everyone had quieted and was looking at me.

"Now then, the first piece of the puzzle was discovered by my brother. Dewey noticed an odd smell in one area of Ms. Franklin's room. Upon further investigation, we determined the smell was coming from the door that leads to the hallway. Specifically, the smell was unusually strong on the locking mechanism, which as you all know, is an old-fashioned latch that falls into a slot attached to the door jamb."

Bradley smirked. "A smell? We're supposed to pronounce this man guilty over a smell?" He snorted and rolled his eyes. "You've lost the plot, Daye."

"Not just any smell, Bradley. The sharp, slightly sweet smell of cloves." He started to argue but I ignored him. "This smell is also heavy on a monk's robe costume that we found in the marsh after a witness saw someone throw it in the river Saturday evening. Via pictures from the wedding reception, we know that the person that was wearing the costume stole the dagger that killed Heather."

Frowns appeared on the faces of several and Chas raised his hand. "I'm the one that saw someone throw it in the river. Do you know what caused the smell, Ms. Daye?"

I smiled. "I do indeed, Chas." I looked at Dylan. "The smell is the smoke from a clove cigarette. All of you witnessed how enthusiastic Mr. Carter is about smoking and his brand of choice is a clove cigarette made in India. It's also banned in the US but curiously enough, is still for sale in the Bahamas, where Heather vacationed and found Chris."

Wide eyes and nods followed my pronouncement. "It's my belief that Mr. Carter used a clove cigarette to make his escape from Ms. Franklin's room, leaving the door locked behind him."

Maude frowned. "I don't understand. How could a cigarette lock a door?"

"Simple. He placed a lit cigarette beneath the latch and pulled the door closed. When the cigarette burned away, the latch fell into place. I'm not sure why Mr. Carter felt that ruse was necessary, since regardless of the room being locked from the inside, I'd say it's very rare that someone commits suicide by thrusting a dagger into their chest. By the way, we also found a scattering of ashes on the floor by the door, adding weight to my theory."

Everyone started talking, discussing the smell, Dylan's smoking, and my theory. I allowed it for a few minutes before calling everyone to order.

"I heard one of you say a cigarette isn't enough to prove guilt. While I think it's pretty compelling, there's more. We also found a pale line around the third finger of Ms. Franklin's left hand. It was clear she was in the habit of wearing a ring. I've confirmed with Peter, the resort's golf pro, and with her cousin, Chris, that Ms. Franklin was wearing an emerald and diamond ring as recently as four days ago, yet we cannot find anything matching that description among her belongings."

I tipped my head toward Connie. "Then there's the burned pieces of paper we found in the fireplace. I asked Connie to examine the fragments and she found part of a letter head used by the Commonwealth of Virginia."

Walt started to ask a question but I raised my hand. "Hold on a sec, Walt. There's a bit more to these set of puzzle pieces."

He nodded agreement and I continued. "I confess what I'm about to tell you is speculation, but we aren't convicting this man, I simply want your help in holding him for the police. Ms. Franklin told people that she lived in Lynchburg, Virginia. Mr. Carter is from Madison Heights, Virginia. It's a small suburb of Lynchburg. It's my belief that Heather Franklin and Dylan

Carter were married and that they conspired to find Christopher and get the fee being offered by the executors of the Pennington estate. That fee is a quarter of a million dollars."

Elijah whistled. "Man, even with inflation, that ain't chicken feed!"

I grinned. "You're right, Elijah. It's a substantial sum, and I think it's a large part of the reason Heather was murdered."

Chris frowned. "I'm not following, Holly."

"Sorry, I should have mentioned another piece first. We also found Heather's cell phone. On it was an email from a lawyer. It merely said that, at her request, they had started proceedings." I shrugged. "Based on what you've told me about Heather's having a long string of broken-hearted men in her past, as well as how she was heavily in debt, I think she was planning to divorce Mr. Carter and keep the finder's fee for herself."

Walt's eyes grew round. "He's married. I don't know if it was to the dead woman, but he wears a wedding band and he also told me he was."

I nodded. "Yes Walt, he told me the same. Now, I want to point out something about Mr. Carter." I let my gaze roam over the crowd and then settled back onto Walt. "He lies. He has told several people that he works in the construction field, but as you pointed out, Walt, he doesn't seem to know one end of a screwdriver from another."

"That's true." He laughed. "Why, he was so ham fisted while we were putting up the shutters, I was afraid he'd hurt himself."

"Exactly. It's not proof of guilt, but it is proof that he will say whatever furthers his agenda."

I had a few more pieces to reveal, the cellophane found where Dewey was struck I believed came from a pack of cigarettes, and his jeans had been showing beneath his robe when he said he'd been in bed, but I didn't think they'd be needed.

A chair crashed to the floor just as Chris, Chas, and Elijah got to their feet. We turned to find a wide-eyed Dylan trying to make his escape.

"Come back here, Carter!" Chris rushed around the sofa, while Elijah and Chas wove around the fireplace seating arrangement. Carter was outflanked and my posse was closing in when Olivia stepped into the living room via the front foyer and cut them off.

"Olivia, get out—"

Bradley's warning came too late. His wife screamed as Dylan came up behind her and wrapped his arm around her neck.

"Stay back!" His eyes were wild and slightly unfocused, and I was reminded that an animal is most dangerous when cornered.

"Dylan, let her go. You don't need to—"

He ignored me and grabbed a lead crystal vase off a table. "Come any closer and I'll bash her skull in!"

I gulped and motioned for the men to back off. "He'll do it. He's the one that hit my brother."

Dylan smirked. "Idiot started talking to me while I was smoking. He sniffed and asked what the smell was, and I knew it was only a matter of time before he figured it out." He laughed. "It was so hard to keep from laughing as you guys kept talking about the weird smell!"

"You're a monster and a fool but put the vase down. Just come quietly and have your day in court—"

"Shut up." He dragged Olivia toward the French doors. "I'm not sitting around waiting for a bunch of hick cops to railroad me into prison!"

My eyes widened as Dylan turned the knob and the door flew open with such force it was almost ripped from its hinges. Olivia was screaming and fighting for all she was worth.

Everyone started shouting for Dylan to let her go, while I focused on the sound of the wind. It was roaring like a freight train, and I could see dried leaves spiraling upward.

Before I could reach him, Dylan threw the vase at me, thrust Olivia away hard enough to send her to the floor and ran out into the yard.

Chris and the others rushed to help Olivia as I followed after Dylan. Heart pounding, I kept my back against the house and clawed my way along the porch, looking for some sign of him.

The rain was coming down in sheets and the noise was deafening. A shadow caught my eye. Dylan was bent against the wind and struggling to stay on his feet, but he was headed toward the garage where the ATVs were stored.

"Dylan," I screamed. "Come back! I think there's a torna-do—"

A sharp crack stopped Dylan in his tracks. He turned in time to see a huge pine snap like a twig and careen toward him. I looked away as Dylan disappeared beneath a mass of limbs and pine needles.

Chapter Twenty-Six

As I'd predicted, the parking area for Goodwin Park and the downtown shopping district had flooded. Three weeks after Hurricane Isabella swept through the Lowcountry, you could still see bits of marsh grass and other detritus brought in from the river scattered around the park.

While waiting for Jessica to meet for our lunch date at Mario's, I decided to walk The Colonel. He was sniffing around the palm trees so I settled on a swing and surveyed the river. The copious amounts of rain deposited by Isabella had left it running higher than normal for late summer, but overall, Sanctuary Bay had come through the Cat 1 unscathed.

The same couldn't be said of Cotton's marina. A boat improperly anchored in the river had broken loose and been driven ashore, taking out three of the docks. The debris had been hauled away but it would be months before the marina would be restored to working order.

My family's town home, thanks to Whopper's preparations, had come through the storm with flying colors, and apart from the gardens being decimated by wind and rain, we hadn't needed to make any repairs.

Myrtlewood, our plantation on Saint Marianna Island, was not as fortunate. The old home would need a new roof and a tree had destroyed one of the outbuildings; thankfully we hadn't stored anything more than rusty garden tools in that one.

A stiff breeze tempered the heat of the day but there was a noticeable absence of rustling palm fronds. The storm had topped most of the palms that lined the river walk. It was a sorry sight, but in time, they'd renew themselves. When all was said and done, our region had gotten off lightly compared to others that were in the destructive storm's path.

A DNR boat flew past, bringing to mind the arrival of help to Pennington. It'd been several hours before we'd felt safe enough to venture outside to recover Dylan Carter's body. The storm surge had pushed the river up passed the barn, but we'd waded through it and placed him in the cooler. The irony of him joining his wife did not escape me and I couldn't help but wonder what torments awaited him in the afterlife.

Two days passed before it was possible to access the island and Detective Brannon and his crew arrived. As soon as they'd given their statement, Walt and Maude Randall couldn't leave fast enough. Despite them initially questioning my pronouncement of Dylan's guilt, they'd listened to the evidence and come to the right conclusion in the end. I couldn't fault anyone for standing by the founding principles of our nation.

Connie and I had helped them with their bags and walked them to their car. My friend had wished them a safe trip home and told them to come back next year, and I'd had to laugh. Walt was adamant that all of their future anniversaries would be celebrated with dinner at a nice restaurant close to home.

Brannon had taken statements from everyone, then listened to Connie and me present our findings, taken the evidence we'd collected, and let the coroner's office do their thing. With the suspect dead, there was nothing more required than filling out the paperwork.

Surprisingly, Joe congratulated me on solving the case and even complimented Connie, Dewey, and me for solving such a puzzling mystery. He'd also unbent a little when I'd found the culprit who poisoned Father Michael during the shrimp eating contest back in May, making me wonder if our relationship was taking a turn for the better.

Not that I was gunning for his job! Recalling Brannon's remarks about how many times I'd gotten caught up in local murder investigations, I snorted. While I didn't agree with his sarcastic comment that I had some kind of deal with the Grim Reaper, I had to admit death seemed to be following me like a dark cloud.

Considering my own brush with death, it wasn't a welcomed observation. My mind flashed back to the night I lay bleeding from a gunshot wound on a sandy road in Roland Dupree's hunting camp while Shawn Dupree's lifeless body lay a few feet away.

A shiver ran up my spine and I recalled the old superstition about walking over graves. Giving myself a mental shake, I passed off my foreboding as being a result of Jessica wanting to have lunch so she could tell me what she'd found relating to the photos retrieved from Roland's hunting camp trail cameras.

I'd given her my contact at the DMV's office, and under pretense of researching a news article, Jessica had been searching for the truck seen entering the camp a little before Shawn Dupree and I had arrived. There was nothing to worry about, I told myself. Anything Jess had discovered could only further our search for the truth about the shootings.

Glancing at my watch, I called for The Colonel and set off for Mario's. I ignored the little voice in my head that pointed out finding the truth was what was making me nervous in the first place.

Jessica was seated under an umbrella-covered table. Only a few diners had requested outdoor seating, yet Jessica had chosen a table closest to the river and conveniently several tables apart from others. I swallowed past a lump in my throat and wove my way across the patio.

"Holly!" Jessica half stood and gave me a quick hug. She patted The Colonel's head and, ignoring my frown of disapproval, handed him a bread stick. "Don't fuss Holly, he's a hero and deserves a treat."

Rolling my eyes, I sat across from her and opened the menu. "Needs a treat and The Colonel are things that do not go together." I looked at her across the top of the menu. "You realize I've had to buy him a larger harness?"

Jessica laughed. "He's big boned, aren't you boy?" Devoted to consuming his people food, The Colonel merely grunted. Jess chuckled and gave him another caress before opening her menu. "You can't deny the boy came through for Dewey. What sounds good?"

"Everything, but I'm going with a sausage and mushroom pizza. And yes, The Colonel saved the day and Dewey, thank God."

Jessica opted for a three-meat panini and we placed our orders. "How is Dewey?"

"Milking his bash on the head for all it's worth!" Jessica laughed. "Even though he is over the worst of his injuries, Mama has been waiting on him hand and foot."

Jess smiled. "Well, under the circumstances, I don't blame her. He's lucky to be alive."

On that I agreed. Once it had been possible for emergency services to access the island, Dewey had been taken to the hospital. No skull fractures, but he'd had a concussion and been kept for several days. His memories of the attack were sketchy, but he had been able to confirm my suspicions about the leopards.

He'd been walking The Colonel when he came upon Dylan, smoking near the HVAC unit or, as he'd dubbed it, the leper colony. They'd chatted and Dewey had noticed the odd smell.

Dylan had claimed not to have smelled it, but minutes after Dewey set off on the trail that led to the golf course, he'd heard someone running toward him. He'd been struck as he turned to look.

If not for my brother having turned his head and deflecting the blow, the doctors said he would have likely received a life-changing, if not fatal, injury. Hearing that had chased away any guilt I felt over Dylan's death.

Our food arrived and we tucked in, talking about the storm damage and local drama. I finished telling her Christopher Pennington's story and we exhausted our speculations on what was in the Lyle family's future.

Jessica tilted her head to one side. "So, Bradley pinned the high school vandalism on his stepbrother because he'd found out Chris and Felicia were in a relationship." She shook her head. "Why would he care?"

"Don't know. Chris was a good student, athletic, and had a good reputation as well as a bright future. Based on how Bradley treats Felicia now, it's a stretch to believe he acted out of misplaced concern for her." I snorted. "My assessment of his character suggests he was just as mean, spiteful, and jealous as he is now."

Jessica snorted. "I've run across him at various functions. He's a blowhard and not taken seriously by anyone in the business community. For the sake of the Pennington fortune, it's a good thing Chris returned."

I agreed and Jessica changed the subject. Donning her reporter's hat, she asked for clarity on some issues with the mystery we'd solved.

"So, I understand the clove smell and Dewey's babbling about leopards helped you connect the dots, but what was all that about the mark on the victim's finger? How did that tie into her murder?"

I went into detail starting with how I'd noticed the pale line on her finger to getting confirmation from Peter Kent and Chris Pennington that she was in the habit of wearing a ring. I shrugged. "The ring wasn't a direct clue, but it helped paint the picture for what I eventually thought was the killer's motive."

Jessica nodded. "And it was the killer that removed it from her hand? Not Heather?"

"Yes, I searched his body before we stored it in the cooler and found a very flashy emerald and diamond ring in his pocket."

Jessica sipped her tea. "So he removed it. But why?"

"Not sure, but if I had to guess, he was trying to hide the fact that she was married. Peter Kent is either lying or an idiot because that ring is obviously an engagement ring and wedding band; they were fused together by the bands."

She smirked. "Peter Kent is the playboy golf pro?" I nodded and she grinned. "Well, he probably lied, not wanting you to know he had no problem fooling around with a married woman."

"It's possible, but so is the other option."

We both laughed, then Jessica asked about the voodoo doll. "I get wanting to hide the marriage, but then why make a doll dressed like a bride?"

Connie had asked the same question. "My best guess has always been that the voodoo doll was a last-minute prop. He saw the Gullah perform the curse and figured it would throw investigators off the scent. It might have worked, had Joe Brannon been able to get to Pennington."

Jessica's lips curved. "You never bought into the curse."

I rolled my eyes. "Of course not. I think Auntie Pearl and other root doctors are skilled herbalists but putting curses on people?" I shook my head. "No."

She snorted. "Bet you're fun at Halloween."

A quirked brow was my response, making my friend laugh.

"I'm writing a follow-up article about the murder. Anything else you've learned as to Dylan's motive?"

I shrugged. "Not new, but we did get confirmation to my theory. Once we had phone service, I called that law office. The one that emailed about starting proceedings for Heather?" Jessica nodded. "It was as I'd suspected. She had filed for divorce."

"Ah, so she was cutting him loose and he wasn't going to get any of that finder's fee."

That was one possibility. By filing before she'd earned the reward, it would have been tougher to claim it was community property, but something told me money had not been the whole motive for Dylan.

"What makes you say that?"

My lips twisted as I thought about my answer. "Well, the ring that I found was ostentatious, but it also looked to be old. Maybe a family heirloom? But really, I'm thinking he killed her because she was dumping him. Chris said Heather had a habit of stringing men along, using them, then breaking their hearts."

Jessica bobbed her head. "Ah, so good old-fashioned jealousy."

"Most likely, but thanks to Isabella and a dead tree we'll never know."

We both fell silent for a minute and then Jessica cleared her throat and pulled some papers from her bag. The letterhead showed they were DMV printouts, and mouth dry, I stared at them like they were a snake about to strike.

Jessica's gaze roamed over my face. "You ready to talk about this?"

I swallowed hard and shook my head. "No, but that isn't going to stop me. What have you found?"

She gave me another long look. "You sure?" At my nod, she continued. "Okay, well as I was stuck indoors, I used the time before I lost my internet connection to go through those ninety possible matches to the truck. Most were simple to reject in one way or another, but I still have fifty that I haven't been able to reach by phone or eliminate through social media contact." She tipped her head toward the table. "These thirty, in my opinion, are the strongest suspects."

My eyes widened. Thirty? My friend wasn't a top investigative journalist for nothing. I licked my lips. "What should we do about these?"

Her brows rose. "I think we should talk to each one in person. Do you want me to do them all or..."

"Are you still convinced something is hinky with that fatal bridge accident?"

She nodded. "Yep, more so after I spoke with the insurance adjuster."

"Why is that?"

She lifted one shoulder. "Because he's ordered a forensics examination of the truck involved in the accident. The county's fleet are only two years old; he thinks it is unlikely to have been a failed hydraulic line. That puts him at odds with the county mechanics."

"Interesting..." She snorted, making me grin. "Sounds like you'll be busy with this story. Roland and I can interview these truck owners; my next job is just a small engagement party."

Jessica laughed. "Oh boy, haven't you had enough of weddings?"

"Yep, but can't avoid this one. It's Brooks Junior and Alexa."

Jessica smiled. "Oh they've finally set a date?"

"Yes and of course they've asked Connie and me to do the wedding." My smile was rueful as I recalled my son and his fiancée's assurances that theirs would be a traditional Southern wedding, no daggers in sight. "I accepted on one condition. They make it a long engagement and not hold it at Pennington Place!"

Jessica burst out laughing. "I can see why you made that request." She pushed her chair out and stood. "This has been fun but I've got to run. Press conference announcing preliminary findings in the bridge crash is in twenty minutes."

I stood. "Yeah, I need to go, too. I'm meeting with Connie. Apparently she's found us, or rather me, another big job." Jessica arched her brows. "Not a wedding, thank goodness. This is that mega church out by the highway. They are holding a fall festival. I had planned on taking a few weeks off but this job won't be until November so I couldn't say no."

Jessica grinned. "That far out you can still take your mini vacation and being in November, you won't have to worry about a hurricane!"

I laughed. "True, though hurricane season doesn't officially end until November 30th."

We walked down the steps and headed toward the parking lot. "Well, don't go borrowing trouble. It's rare we get late season storms."

I refrained from pointing out that Matthew had hit in October and done massive damage. Jessica was right. Cooler temperatures and no serious threat of storms ... the fall festival would be fun. I loved that time of year, and my mind was already thinking of decorating ideas.

We made it to Jessica's car and she hit the unlock button on her key fob. The horn beeped, pulling me from my decorating daydreams. "This is my stop." Her brow furrowed and she bit her lip. "Holly, be careful when you go knocking on some of those doors."

"Why?"

Jessica scrunched her nose. "I don't know. A couple are prominent people and one of the potential truck owners was a mechanic for the public works department."

I frowned. I could understand treading carefully with bigwigs, but a mechanic... "And? Why is that significant?"

Her gaze was troubled. "Because he was reported missing about two months after the shooting. That fact triggered my radar, so I did some digging. There is no active investigation, despite the suspicious nature of his disappearance."

"Suspicious how?"

"According to the initial report, his mother said the last time she saw her son he burst in the back door looking frantic. She tried to talk to him, but he was flying around throwing clothes into a bag. The last thing he said to her was 'don't tell anyone you've seen me.'"

My eyes widened. "That's um ... suspicious."

Jessica nodded. "To say the least." She hesitated for a second and added, "Holly, the assistant director of the public works department has never surfaced and I get nothing but stonewalling when I attempt to question the sheriff. And Earl Graham, the

Director of Public Works has been avoiding my calls for months ... my reporter's nose smells a story and now there's a possible tie in with the truck seen at Roland's hunting camp." She tipped her head toward the papers in my hand. "I'd put talking to Wade Hammond's mother at the top of the list."

With a nod, she drove off, leaving me frowning at the papers she'd given me. I clicked my tongue, drew The Colonel away from a discarded candy wrapper, and headed for the Scout.

Jessica's background on Wade Hammond had set my internal alarm clanging and my mind was whirling with questions. What were the odds two employees of a county department would disappear without a trace in under two years. And what, if anything, was the connection to the shooting that had left me with a permanent limp and Shawn Dupree dead?

The End

Did you enjoy riding out the hurricane with Holly and her friends? Why not leave a review and help others discover the denizens of Sanctuary Bay?

What's up with that pickup truck and the missing public works guy? Think Holly can decorate for a fall festival without stumbling into trouble? Keep reading for a sneak peak of Scarecrows and Scandals!

Available on Amazon and bookstores; ask your favorite store to order you a copy!

Scarecrows and Scandals

Rachel Lynne

I guard fields of grain but it'd be easier if I had a brain. Turn left and find me to set yourself free ...

Guard fields of grain, needs a brain ... I frowned and stared at the walls of corn surrounding me. The clue was obviously a scarecrow and according to the rhyme I'd find one when I turned left but I'd been walking through Jed Prine's corn maze for at least five minutes and there wasn't a scarecrow in sight.

Jed, who owned the farm adjacent to our family's plantation on Saint Marianna Island, had turned 25 acres of his farm into a corn maze. When Grace Harbor Community Church had hired me to organize a Fall festival, I'd convinced them to hold it at Jed's place and, by way of a *thank you for bringing me business, Holly*, Jed had decided I should be the guinea pig, er first person to try out the maze.

He'd purchased some kind of mystery package that included clues to guide a visitor through the labyrinth. After solving three murders in Sanctuary Bay, I'd gained a reputation for being good with puzzles but my alleged skills were nonexistent at the moment; I'd found the answer to the riddle, but locating the actual scarecrow eluded me and my temper was hanging by a thread.

The sun was setting, casting long shadows over the field. A cold front moving in brought chilly gusts that rustled the stalks and added to my sense of isolation. I wasn't one to let my imagination run wild but being lost and alone in a rapidly darkening corn maze was starting to get to me.

I wished I'd brought The Colonel with me; my English bulldog was no bloodhound, but with food as a motivation I had no doubt he'd have found his way out. But, thinking I'd only be gone a few minutes, I'd left The Colonel snoozing in the sunroom at Myrtlewood, our family's plantation.

Sighing, I pulled the front of my cardigan together, hunched my shoulders against the cold, and continued stomping along yet another monotonous row of corn. Darkness was creeping in and I didn't even have my cellphone. If we were going to let people traverse the maze in the evening, we'd definitely have to provide flashlights, or maybe suggest they bring their own ...

Making a mental note to add alternative lighting to my To Do list, I forced myself to quit grumbling and focus on the matter at hand. According to the riddle, I was to turn left but how many blasted left turns was I supposed to make?

So far I'd seen nothing but corn stalks and a few farming tools that posed a safety hazard. Adding another reminder to my mental list, I glanced up and noticed a turkey buzzard was making a slow circle over my head. Great. Probably waiting to pick my bones after I gave up escaping my self-imposed prison and sat down to await my fate.

Another gust left me shivering and marked the end of my patience. Making one last left turn without running into a scarecrow, I drew a deep breath and hollered. "Jed! Get me outta this thing!"

A rustling in the stalks somewhere off to my right made me stop. That hadn't been the wind. "Someone there?"

More rustling, and not a breath of wind. I narrowed my eyes. "I know you're out there ..."

No reply, not a whisper of sound aside from my breathing ... mouth dry I took a few more steps down the path that seemed to lead to nowhere. I turned another corner and faced a dead end. "Oh, for cryin' out loud- "

A muffled laugh interrupted my grumbling. "Jed? Is that you?" Hands on my hips, I debated stomping through the rows of corn, maze be damned. "Come over here and show me the way out before I trudge through your field and wreck the maze!"

Whoever was in the maze didn't bother to reply but I'd have sworn I heard them snicker. "On your head then!" I turned and stalked back the way I'd come. "I'm warning you, if I don't find the way out pretty darned quick, I'll take drastic action!"

Busy hollering threats toward the prankster in the maze, I paid little attention to where I was going and took another wrong turn. Faced with a wall of corn on three sides, I started to see red. Of all the ..., muttering under my breath I spun on my heel and gasped.

Standing feet from me was a scarecrow, its macabre grin at odds with its lifeless eyes. That had not been there a minute ago. I licked my lips and studied the silent guardian. Pinned to its chest was a piece of paper.

Happy as I was to finally find the next clue, the sudden appearance of my savior sent a chill up my spine that had nothing to do with the weather. Someone had to have put it in my path ...

Forcing my heart rate back to a normal rhythm, I peered into the rows of grain. "It's no use, I don't believe in mumbo jumbo.

Get over here and show me the way out of this maze, I've got a festival to finish!"

My demands went unfulfilled for several minutes before I heard the corn stalks rustle behind me. Despite what I'd said, being lost in the maze with darkness closing in and someone hiding amidst the stalks had started to creep me out. Tensing and prepared to fight, I whirled around and then rolled my eyes.

"Travis Prine!" I shook my head. "Boy, you scared the wits out of me!"

A bashful grin spread across his face as he ducked his head. "Sorry, Ms. Holly. Uncle Jed told me to mess with you."

Pursing my lips, I huffed and pointed at Jed's nephew. "Lead me out of this thing!"

He grinned. "Yes ma'am, there's an exit just around this corner."

Trooping along behind him, a litany of scolds ran through my mind. What had Jed been thinking? It was one thing to play a prank on an old friend, but to then send Travis into the maze and encourage him to act like a stalker?

In different circumstances, with a different person, the joke would have fallen flat and could have even led to violence. The mother and former cop in me wanted to lecture Travis but I didn't have the heart. Since his release from prison a month ago, he'd been morose and withdrawn; a shell of the teen I'd known.

If teasing me brought him a moment of relief from the demons that seemed to haunt him, I'd gladly play along. But his uncle and I would have words. Jed had to know the community was in an uproar over his nephew's release.

From the moment word of the higher court's decision reached Sanctuary Bay, the town had been burning up phone lines. The murder of Sally Hemsworth six years ago had shocked our small town and memories were long.

Despite what the courts said, most people believed Travis had murdered Sally and, while at the moment, people were content to bicker and complain amongst themselves, it'd only take a spark to fan their collective anger into a four-alarm blaze.

True to his word, the exit I'd been searching for was a short walk. In minutes, Travis and I were out of the maze and heading back toward the barn. I'd chosen that area for the other elements of the fall festival and, through the haze of twilight, I could just make out Jed amid a small group clustered around the pumpkin patch. They all turned and watched as we approached.

Travis turned to me, his eyes filled with a mix of gratitude and sadness. "Thanks for playing along, Ms. Holly," he said softly.

"I'm sorry if I scared you." He ducked his head and mumbled. "Shouldn't have went along with Uncle Jed's joke..."

I sighed. "You don't have to apologize, Travis., it was just a joke." I hesitated a moment debating whether to express my concerns to him or continue with my plan to discuss it with his uncle. Part of me wanted to shield Travis but there was a little voice in my head shouting that he was an adult and needed to be treated as such.

The little voice screeched the loudest. "Travis ...," I put my hand on his arm, drawing him to a stop. "The practical joke was no big deal." His brow was furrowed and he looked glum. "Really, it was funny! But Travis ..., if it had been anyone else ..."

He dragged a hand through his closely cropped hair and nodded. "I understand. Folks around here ..." He sighed and the defeated expression in his eyes broke my heart. "Everyone thinks I killed Sally and they're mad I was released. I know I gotta keep my head down and prove myself." He shrugged. "That's one of the things they tell us at Life After. That us ex-cons gotta be extra good to be accepted. It's hard though. Everywhere I go, I feel like people are starin' at me, judgin' me." He tipped his head toward the group waiting for us. "Like them. I know they're thinkin' I'm up to no good and I don't belong here ... I just want to move on, but it seems like nobody will let me."

I placed a hand on his shoulder and squeezed gently. "It'll take time, Travis. People are scared, and they need someone to blame. They can't believe someone else committed the murder because, if they do, it means we have a killer hiding among us."

Eyes downcast, he nodded. I nudged his arm. "Hey, look at me." I waited until he complied and then smiled. "People will see that they were wrong and until then, just keep on building your life. But I want you to know that there are people who want to help, who want to see you succeed. Don't let the negativity get to you."

He smiled weakly. "Thanks, Ms. Holly. I'll try. I just hope one day they'll see that I'm innocent."

Sally Hemsworth, only daughter of a captain stationed at the nearby marine base had been popular in Sanctuary Bay. Head cheerleader, student council treasurer, volunteer at the senior center ... I vividly remembered reactions to Travis' arrest.

Like father like son was a common refrain, while others simply sniffed and said they'd always known the kid was a bit off. Regardless of how it'd been phrased, there had been few innocent until proven guilty remarks and the town had breathed a collective sigh of relief when he'd been convicted.

A higher court overturning that verdict had only entrenched people's opinions and, barring the arrest of someone else, I didn't see that ever changing. Since I lacked anything positive to say I changed the subject and continued toward the barn. "That's the church festival committee probably wanting to go over some last-minute details." I glanced at him. "I hadn't planned on being over here that long and I left The Colonel at Myrtlewood. Do you think you could run over and feed him his dinner? Let him out afterwards?"

His relief at not having to join them was obvious. "Sure! I love your dog."

"Good, he loves you too."

Travis' smile faded as we joined the others. Jane Moore stepped forward and wrapped her hand around my arm, completely ignoring Travis as she started gushing about what I'd set up for the festival.

"Holly, we are just amazed at what you've done, aren't we?" She glanced a Tom Simmons and Martha Raines the other members of the committee.

Tom nodded. "Absolutely. you've truly turned a sow's ear into a silk purse!"

I winced at the insult and flashed Jed an apologetic smile. "I'm glad y'all are happy, but the farm is filled with so much natural beauty I can't really take all of the credit."

Pastor Cole Horton gave me an ironic smile as he offered his hand. "Ms. Daye, I agree, Mr. Prine's farm is a tranquil spot, but your decorations have captured the harvest season to perfection. We couldn't be more pleased."

"Thank you, Pastor. It was a group effort." I smiled at Travis. "This young man has put in long hours helping me set everything up."

There was an awkward pause and I was kicking myself for drawing attention to Travis when Lilly Adams, bless her heart, changed the subject. Though, unless it was a trick of the light, the committee didn't appear to want her presence any more than they did Travis'.

"Everything looks great, Holly! We were hoping for a tour and I think Pastor Cole wanted to add some things?"

The Pastor cleared his throat, ignoring the frowns forming on his committee's faces. "Uh, yes. Nothing major and it shouldn't be too much trouble- "

"I thought the committee was handling this festival." Tom's narrowed gaze flickered to Lilly and his lips tightened. "We've allocated just about all of the budget ..."

"Not a problem, Tom." Pastor Cole smiled, attempting to soothe his deacon before feathers were ruffled. He glanced at me. "We'll just need a table, maybe another tent if you have one."

All eyes turned toward me and I bit my lip. Adding a tent was no problem, but judging by the looks on the faces of the committee members, the request was a sore spot. However, at the end of the day, the pastor of Grace Harbor Community Church had hired me and I always deferred to my client.

"It's not a problem. Did you have a specific location in mind?"

"Wonderful." Cole looked around the barnyard area. "Lilly and I want a booth to run a raffle to benefit her mission work at Life After."

A sharply indrawn breath made the pastor pause. "Anything wrong, Tom?"

The look on his face showed he clearly had a problem. Silence fell and everyone's smiles became forced as the deacon and the pastor locked gazes. I was about to diffuse the situation with a random comment when Tom drew a deep breath and shook his head.

"Whatever you think best, pastor."

Jane's eyebrows rose and she and Martha exchanged speaking glances but Pastor Cole ignored them. "Ms. Daye, we'd probably get the best results if we situate the tent closer to the entrance ..."

I smiled, though I hadn't missed Tom's shoulders stiffen. I also hadn't missed the warning look he directed toward Jane. "Of course! I'll get Travis on that first thing in the morning."

"Perfect!" Cole clapped his hands. "If that's all, we'd best begin our tour before we can't see our hands in front of our faces." Everyone chuckled, though the committee members still looked perturbed. Pastor Cole made a sweeping motion with his arm. "Shall we begin?"

While talking, I'd been conscious of the passing time and the fact that my bulldog was unsupervised and hungry, was never a good combination. I nodded to the pastor and then turned to Travis. "I'm going to be a while longer and The Colonel is probably sizing up my furniture as a replacement meal. Are you still able to go over and feed him?"

From the corner of my eye I saw Jane's mouth drop open and Tom wore a disapproving frown. Reining in my desire to roll my eyes or worse, give them a lecture on the nature of forgiveness, I focused on Travis.

He kept his head down and answered in monosyllables, making me want to shake the church members. The poor kid was obviously ill at ease and their attitudes were to blame. Best to remove Travis from the situation. "The door is unlocked Travis and the food is in the pantry. It's the door just to the left of the stove. He gets one scoop. Don't let him tell you otherwise! The Colonel is a glutton."

Travis' body language still showed his discomfort but my teasing tone had managed to make him grin. "Sure thing, Ms. Holly. I'll take him out for a walk after if that's okay?"

"Perfect. Make him run off all of that food."

Travis nodded and started walking toward Myrtlewood as I addressed the committee. "Ready for the tour?"

Remnants of their sour expressions were still visible but I ignored it and continued. "Your volunteers will help guests park in the field over there," I pointed behind me. "And they'll direct everyone to this area where we'll have tables set up for your church pamphlets and whatever else you want to hand out. I'd suggest your members give them a welcome packet of information that also includes the corn maze mystery card. That way they'll be more likely to- "

"Excuse me."

We all looked at Lilly and she smiled. "I helped set everything up so, if y'all don't need me I thought I'd help Travis with Holly's dog ..."

Pastor Cole smiled. "That's fine, Lilly. We'll see you tomorrow at the grand opening!"

330

A sharp sniff made me glance at Tom as Lilly grinned and raced off across the field. His eyes were narrowed and there was a slight curl to his upper lip. Jane clucked her tongue and shook her head and I followed her gaze to see Lilly had caught up with Travis and the pair were now walking arm in arm.

My gaze returned to the committee members. All three were still staring at Lilly and Travis and their expressions ranged from disapproval to outright anger. I swallowed hard and pasted a smile on my face as I continued the tour but my unease over the situation with Travis was growing and, no matter how much I liked the young man, I couldn't help but wish he'd never returned to Sanctuary Bay.

Order your copy of Scarecrows and Scandals! Available on Amazon and bookstores. Ask your favorite store to order you a copy!

Welcome to Sanctuary Bay

H ey neighbor, new to the area? Let me bring you up to speed, because Holly and her friends have had several adventures!

Back when Holly was still a Noble Count Sheriff's Deputy, she tracked a ring of thieves and met The Colonel. Find out how Holly's little buddy got his name by reading the prequel novella, **Hounds and Heists**!

Visit www.rachellynneauthor.com to read this snippet of Holly's past for **FREE** as an eBook or find it in paperback on Amazon.

Holly has moved on from her law enforcement days and started *CoaStyle,* but decorating for events has certainly not led to a slow and safe lifestyle!

Following her debut as a decorator in **Masquerades and Murder**, Holly went on to create a Christmas market for the town in **Carolers and Corpses** and then tracked a killer to Sandpoint Abbey after a priest died during the Blessing of the Fleet.

You'd think our reluctant sleuth could catch a break by decorating for a wedding in **Plantations and Allegations** but, as The Colonel says, the *Lady that Pays the Bills* finds trouble wherever she goes.

Lucky for Holly her bulldog is always on the case!

After surviving the events surrounding the *wedding of the year*, Holly took a much needed vacation and then celebrated the cooler weather by organizing a fall festival.

But, with a corn maze full of **Scarecrows and Scandals** she's sure to find herself in the thick of things!

There will be 12 books in the Holly Daye Mystery Series as our decorator friend fills her calendar with clients every month and slowly unravels the secret behind the shooting that ended her law enforcement career.

Stay tuned, it promises to be a wild ride!

The Holly Daye Mystery Series
Hounds and Heists

Masquerades and Murder

Carolers and Corpses

Priests and Poison

Plantations and Allegations

Scarecrows and Scandals

The Cosmic Café Mystery Series
Fey Goes to Jail

Ring of Lies

Holly Jolly Jabbed

Broken Chords

Hey y'all!

Since you've finished my book, it'd be redundant to tell you that I'm a writer. But I'm also a mom, a grandma, a housewife, and a former grocery worker; all titles I proudly hold!

I wrote my first book, Ring of Lies in 2011, got the idea for Broken Chords and wrote a few chapters and then promptly let life get in the way. I did volunteer work while I homeschooled my daughter and helped my husband start a business but, when she decided to attend high school, I decided to find work outside the home.

I was managing a department in a grocery store, (which I loved doing) and I'd find myself writing stories while I put away stock; there is something about muscle memory work that lets the subconscious play. I started carrying a sharpie in my pocket along with my box cutter and, when I'd get an idea, a snippet of conversation between characters, or a creative way to axe someone I'd scribble it on a piece of cardboard!

As much as I loved my job, I realized I had some pretty good ideas on those scraps of empty boxes and that is when I quit and started writing full time. To date, I have 8 books published with many more to come: there's no stopping me now!

All of my books take place in and around the Lowcountry of South Carolina and Georgia because that is where I call home and I am in awe of this region's natural beauty and its history.

Join my newsletter, The Cozy Crew Club, by going to www.rachellynneauthor.com. You'll hear more than you probably ever wanted to know about the Lowcountry and its unique culture.

On my website you'll also find links to my Facebook and Instagram pages. Follow me and you'll see my crazy menagerie of animals, the day trips my husband I take, recipes, chapter readings, and more!

Hope to meet you soon!

Rachel

Made in the USA
Columbia, SC
02 November 2024

45544776R00189